THE SOCIETY OF S

Susan Hubbard is the author of two acclaimed short-story collections, *Walking on Ice* and *Blue Money*, for which she received the Janet Heidinger Kafka Prize. She teaches at the University of Central Florida and lives in Orlando and Cape Canaveral.

THE SOCIETY OF S

Susan Hubbard

**WALKER
BOOKS**

First published 2008 by Walker Books Ltd
87 Vauxhall Walk, London SE11 5HJ

2 4 6 8 10 9 7 5 3 1

Copyright © 2007 Blue Garage Co
Cover design: Honi Werner

The right of Susan Hubbard to be identified as author
of this work has been asserted by her in accordance with
the Copyright, Designs and Patents Act 1988

This book has been typeset in Fairfield

Printed and bound in Great Britain by Clays Ltd, St Ives plc

British Library Cataloguing in Publication Data:
a catalogue record for this book
is available from the British Library

ISBN 978-1-4063-1497-7

www.walker.co.uk

To

R

Just as God is the supremely good creator of good natures, so he is the most just ruler of evil wills, so that even though evil wills make an evil use of good natures, God makes a good use of evil wills.

— ST. AUGUSTINE, THE CITY OF GOD, XI, 17

For that which was not—for that which had no form— for that which had no thought—for that which had no sentience— for that which was soulless, yet of which matter formed no portion—for all this nothingness, yet for all this immortality, the grave was still a home, and the corrosive hours, co-mates.

— EDGAR ALLAN POE, THE COLLOQUY
OF MONOS AND UNA

Yet a little while is the light with you. Walk while ye have the light, lest darkness come upon you: for he that walketh in darkness knows not whither he goeth. While ye have light, believe in the light, that ye may be the children of light.

— JOHN 12:35

— Preface —

On a cool spring night in Savannah, my mother is walking. Her clogs make sounds like horses' hooves against the cobblestone street. She passes among banks of azaleas in full bloom and live oak trees shrouded in Spanish moss, and she enters a green square bordered by a café.

My father is seated on a stool at a wrought-iron table. Two chessboards spread across the table, and my father has castled on one when he looks up, sees my mother, and drops a pawn, which falls against the tabletop and rolls onto the sidewalk.

My mother dips to pick up the chess piece and hands it back to him. She looks from him to the two other men sitting at the table. Their faces are expressionless. They're tall and thin, all three, but my father has dark green eyes that somehow seem familiar.

My father stretches out a hand and cups her chin. He looks into her pale blue eyes. "I know you," he says.

With his other hand he traces the shape of her face, passing twice over the widow's peak. Her hair is long and thick, russet brown, with small wisps that he tries to smooth away from her forehead.

The other men at the table fold their arms, waiting. My father has been playing both of them simultaneously.

My mother stares at my father's face—dark hair falling away from his forehead, straight dark eyebrows over those green eyes, lips thin but shaped in a cupid's bow. Her smile is shy, frightened.

He drops his hands, slides off the stool. They walk away together. The men at the table sigh, and clear the chessboards. Now they'll have to play each other.

"I'm going to see Professor Morton," my mother says.

"Where's his office?"

My mother waves her hand in the direction of the art college. He puts his hand on her shoulder, lightly, letting her lead.

"What's this? A bug in your hair?" he says suddenly, pulling at what seems to be an insect.

"A barrette." She takes the copper dragonfly from her hair and hands it to him. "It's a dragonfly. Not a bug."

He shakes his head, then smiles. He says, "Hold still," and carefully slides a lock of her hair through the dragonfly, then pins it behind her left ear.

They turn away from the college. They're holding hands now, walking down a steep cobblestone street. It's growing dark and chilly, yet they pause to sit on a cement wall.

My mother says, "This afternoon I sat at my window, watching the trees grow dark as the sun went down. I thought, *I'm growing older. I have only so many days left to watch the trees darken. Someone could count them.*"

He kisses her. It's a brief kiss, a rough touching of lips. The second kiss lasts longer.

She shivers.

He bends to cover her face—forehead, cheeks, nose, chin— with small, quick brushes of his eyelashes. "Butterfly kisses," he says, "to keep you warm."

My mother looks away, amazed at herself. In a matter of minutes she has let so much happen, without hesitation or protest. And she isn't stopping it now. She wonders how old he thinks she is. She's sure she's older—he looks about twenty-five, and she has recently turned thirty. She wonders when she should tell him that she's married to Professor Morton.

They stand up and walk on, down concrete steps leading toward the river. At the bottom of the steps is a closed cast-iron gate.

"I hate moments like this," my mother says. Her shoes can't climb gates.

My father climbs over the gate and opens it. "It wasn't locked," he says.

As she passes through, she has a sense of inevitability. She is moving toward something entirely new, yet predetermined. Without any effort at all, she feels years of unhappiness being erased.

They walk along the strand beside the river. Ahead they

see the lights of the tourist shops, and as they reach them, he says, "Wait." She watches him go inside a shop that sells Irish imports, then loses sight of him through the door's wavy glass. He comes out carrying a soft wool shawl. He wraps it around her, and for the first time in years, she feels beautiful.

Will we marry? she wonders. But she doesn't need to ask it. They walk on, a couple already.

My father tells me this story, twice. I have questions. But I save them until he's finished for the second time.

"How did you know what she was thinking?" is my first question.

"Later she told me her thoughts," he says.

"What happened to Professor Morton?" I ask next. "Didn't he try to stop her from leaving him?"

I'm thirteen, but my father says I'm going on thirty. I have long dark hair and blue eyes. Except for the eyes, I take after my father.

"Professor Morton tried to keep your mother," my father says. "He tried threats. He tried force. He'd done it before, when she talked about leaving him. But this time she was in love, and she wasn't afraid. She packed up her things and moved out."

"Did she move in with you?"

"Not at first. No, she took an apartment downtown near Colonial Cemetery, an apartment that some people still say is haunted."

I look hard at him, but I'm not going to be distracted by the haunted apartment.

"Who won the chess game?" I ask.

His eyes open wider. "That's a very good question, Ariella," he says. "I wish I knew the answer."

My father usually knows the answer to everything.

"Could you tell she was older than you?" I ask.

He shrugs. "I didn't think about it. Age has never mattered much to me." He stands up, goes to the living room window, draws the heavy velvet curtains. "Time for you to sleep," he says.

I have a hundred more questions. But I nod, I don't object. Tonight he's told me more than ever before about my mother, whom I've never seen, and even more about himself.

Except for one thing—the truth he doesn't want to tell, the truth I'll spend years trying to understand. The truth about who we really are.

Part I

IN MY FATHER'S HOUSE

— One —

I stood alone outside our house in deep blue twilight. I must have been four or five, and I didn't usually wander outside alone.

The bracketed windows of the upper house were gold rectangles framed by green vines, the lower hooded windows yellow eyes. I was gazing at the house when suddenly I fell backward onto soft grass. In the same instant, flames shot from the basement. I don't remember hearing any explosion—one second, the night was filled with blue and yellow light; the next, red fire lunged at the sky. Someone swooped me up and carried me away from the house.

That's my earliest memory. I remember the way the air smelled that night—smoke mixed with the scent of lilacs—and the roughness of a wool coat against my cheek, and a sensation of floating as we moved away. But I don't know who carried me, or where we went.

Later, when I asked about the fire, Dennis, my father's

research assistant, told me I must have been dreaming. My father simply turned away—but not before I saw his face, eyes remote and guarded, lips set in an expression of resignation I had come to know too well.

One day when I felt bored, as I often did as a child, my father said that I should keep a journal. Even a dull life could make worthwhile reading, he said, provided the writer paid sufficient attention to detail. In his desk he found a thick notebook bound in blue, and he pulled a copy of Thoreau's *Walden* from a shelf. These he handed me.

And so I began to write. But all the details in the world couldn't make my first twelve years worth reading about. Children thrive on monotonous routine, I'm told, but I had more monotony than most. And so I'll try to tell what is necessary in order for you to understand what will follow.

I lived with my father, Raphael Montero, where I'd been born, in a Victorian house in Saratoga Springs, New York. If you ever want to hide from the world, live in a small city, where everyone seems anonymous.

My father's house had many rooms, but we lived in few of them. No one used the cupola at the top of the house (although much later I did spend several hours gazing through its oculus window, trying to imagine a world beyond the town). At the base of the tower, a long corridor ran past the doors of six vacant bedrooms. A broad front staircase led downward, interrupted by a landing with a recess beneath a stained-glass window; a carpet inside was strewn with large Moroccan cushions, against which I often lay to read and stare up at the glowing red and blue and yellow geometric panes of glass. Stained glass was much more interesting than the actual sky, which in Saratoga Springs appeared ashy most of the year, turning in summer to harsh cerulean.

Mornings began when Mrs. McGarritt arrived. She was a small, slight woman with thinning reddish hair; her narrow face had etched into it worry lines and smile lines in nearly equal measure. She almost always had a smile for me, during those days.

After getting her own flock off to school, Mrs. McGarritt came to our house and stayed until quarter of three, when her several children came home again. She cooked and cleaned and did the laundry. First she made my breakfast: oatmeal, usually, served with cream, or butter and brown sugar. Mrs. McGarritt wasn't much of a cook—she managed to undercook and scorch food at the same time, and she never added salt. But she had a good heart. And somewhere, I sensed, I had a mother who understood food.

I knew a great deal about my mother that no one had ever told me. You might think I'd made it all up, to compensate for having never met her. But I felt certain that my intuitions were sound, based on facts to which I simply wasn't privy.

Mrs McGarritt said that she'd heard that my mother became ill after my birth and went into the hospital. Dennis, my father's assistant, said she'd "been taken from us for reasons no one understands." My father said nothing. They all agreed on one thing only: my mother disappeared after my birth and had not been seen by us since.

* * *

One morning after breakfast, I sat in the library, studying, and I smelled something sweet mixed with the usual scent of starch. Mrs. McGarritt had a fetish for using heavy starch when she ironed my clothes (and she ironed everything I wore, except underwear). She liked the old-fashioned kind that you boil on the stove.

I took a break and went into the kitchen, a hexagon-shaped room painted apple-green. The oak table was covered with flour and bowls and spoons, and Mrs. McGarritt stood next to it, peering into an oven. She seemed dwarfed by the enormous old stove—a Garland, with six gas burners (the ever-present pot of starch boiling on one), two ovens, a broiler, and a griddle.

A cookbook with yellowed pages sat on the table near me, opened to a recipe for honey cake. Someone had drawn three stars in blue ink next to the recipe and had written the words: "Best when made from our lavender honey in July."

"What do the stars mean?" I asked.

Mrs. McGarritt let the oven door fall shut and turned around. "Ari, you always make me jump," she said. "I didn't even hear you come in." She wiped her clean hands on her floury apron. "The stars? I guess it was your mother's way of rating a recipe. Four stars are tops, I think."

"That's my mother's handwriting?" It slanted to the right, with even loops and curlicues.

"It's her old cookbook." Mrs. McGarritt began to gather up spoons and measuring cups and bowls. She put them in the sink. "And it will be yours. I should have given it to you,

I suppose. It's always been on that shelf "—she gestured toward a wall shelf near the stove—"ever since I came to work here."

The recipe called for one-half cup each of flour and honey, three eggs, and assorted spices. "'Our lavender honey,'" I read again. "What does that mean, Mrs. McG?"

Mrs. McGarritt had turned on the tap, and when she turned it off I repeated my question.

"Oh, that's honey made from bees that drink from the lavender flowers," she said, without turning from the sink. "You know that big patch of lavender by the fence outside?"

I knew it. The same flowers were on the wallpaper of the room upstairs that had once been shared by my parents. "How is honey made?" I asked.

Mrs. McGarritt began to make too much noise splashing the dishes in soapy water, and I knew she didn't have an answer. "You should ask your father, Ari," she said finally.

When I went back to the library, I pulled out the small spiral notebook I always carried and added the word *honey* to the list of questions I'd already made for the afternoon's lessons.

Every day at one p.m. my father came upstairs from the basement. He spent mornings working in his lab; his bio-medical research company is called Seradrone.

He taught me in the library from one until five, with two breaks in between: one for yoga and meditation, one for snacks. Sometimes, if weather permitted, I'd walk in the garden and pet Marmalade, the neighbor's orange tabby cat, who liked to sun herself near the lavender plants. I'd come back inside to join my father in the living room, where he read his journals (some scientific, some literary; he had a peculiar fondness for 19th-century literary scholarship, particularly work concerning Nathaniel Hawthorne and Edgar Allan Poe). I could read anything I liked from the library, but I mostly chose fairy tales.

At five we moved into the living room. He sat in the deep-green leather chair, and I sat in a dark red velvet-covered slipper chair that fitted me perfectly. Sometimes he asked me to open an envelope; he had trouble opening things, he said. Behind us stood a fireplace that had never been used, as far as I knew. A glass fire screen with butterflies embedded in it stood on the hearth. I sipped rice milk, and he drank a red cocktail that he said was "Picardo." He wouldn't let me taste it, saying, "You're too young." It seemed I was always too young, in those days.

Here I want to describe my father: a tall man, six foot four, with broad shoulders and a narrow waist, muscular arms, beautiful feet (I only realized later how beautiful, when I saw how ugly most people's feet are). Straight black brows and level dark green eyes, pale skin, a long straight nose, a thin mouth whose upper lip curves in a bow and lower lip turns down at its corners. His hair is satin black and springs back from his forehead. Even when I was small, I knew instinctively that my father was an extraordinarily good-looking man. He moved like a dancer, light and lithe. You never heard him come and go, but you sensed his presence the moment he entered a room. I felt that if I'd been blindfolded and deafened I'd know if he were there; the air around him took on a palpable shimmer.

"How is honey made?" I asked him that afternoon.

His eyes widened. He said, "It begins with bees."

And he traced the process, from nectar to comb to collection. "The workers are sterile females," he said. "The males are largely useless. Their only function is to mate with the queen. They live for a few months, and then they die." His mouth moved stiffly around the word "die," as if it were from an unfamiliar language. Then he described the way bees dance when they return to the hive: he used his hands to loop and waggle, and his voice made it all sound too beautiful to be real.

When he got to the part about beekeepers, he went to a bookshelf and came back with a volume of the encyclopedia. He showed me an illustration of a man wearing a large-brimmed hat, a veil masking his face, holding a device with a nozzle to smoke out the hives.

Now I had an image of my mother: a woman wearing thick gloves, draped in a long veil. But I didn't mention that to my father, or ask him about "our lavender honey." He never answered questions about my mother. Usually he changed the subject. Once he said such questions made him sad.

I wondered what lavender honey might taste like. The only honey I'd eaten came from clover, according to the label on the jar, and it conjured the green flavor of summer meadows. Lavender, I thought, would have a stronger, sharper taste, floral with perhaps a hint of smoke in it. It would taste violet blue—the color of a twilight sky.

* * *

In my father's world, time had no meaning. I don't think he looked once at the grandfather clock in the library. Yet he kept a regular schedule—largely, I suspect, for my sake. Every evening at six he sat with me while I had the supper that Mrs. McG (I'm tired of writing out her name, and that's what I called her, anyway) always left in the warming oven: macaroni and cheese, or tofu casserole, or vegetarian chili. It all tasted undercooked at the bottom and burnt at the top, bland and wholesome. After I'd finished, my father ran my bath.

Once I'd turned seven, he left me alone to bathe. He asked me if, as a big girl, I still wanted him to read to me before I fell asleep, and of course I said yes. His voice had texture like velvet. When I was six he'd read me Plutarch and Plato, but Dennis must have said something to him, because after that he read *Black Beauty* and *Heidi* and *The Princess and the Goblin*.

I'd asked my father why he didn't dine with me, and he said he preferred to eat downstairs at a later hour. There was a second kitchen (I called it the night kitchen) in the basement, along with two enormous furnaces, a laboratory where my father worked with Dennis, and three bedrooms originally intended for servants. I rarely visited the basement; it wasn't explicitly forbidden me, but sometimes the upstairs kitchen door to the basement was locked, and even if it wasn't, I knew I wasn't wanted there. In any case, I didn't like the smells: chemicals from the laboratory, gamey cooking from the night kitchen, mixed with the odor of hot metal from the furnaces. Yes, I preferred the smell of starch. My father's cook and all-purpose assistant, the loathsome Mary Ellis Root, ruled the basement domain, and she always looked at me with eyes that radiated hostility.

"How did you like it?" Mrs. McG hovered over the breakfast table, twisting a towel in her hands. Her face was shiny and her glasses needed cleaning, but her spotless red and green plaid housedress, belted at the waist, had been ironed, and its skirt fell in crisp folds.

She was asking about the honey cake. "Very good," I said—almost truthfully. The cake, a slice of which I'd eaten for dessert the previous evening, had a wonderful dense richness; if it had been baked a bit less, and if the pan had been greased more liberally, it might truly have been delicious.

"If I'd made it at home, I'd have used lard," she said. "But your father is such a strict vegetarian."

A moment later Mary Ellis Root slammed open the door that led to the basement and stormed in.

"What did you tell the courier service?" she said to Mrs. McG. Her voice sounded hoarse and low.

Mrs. McG and I stared blankly at her. It was unlike her to set foot upstairs, and never this early. Her black hair bristled with static, and her eyes blazed, yet she never made eye contact with either of us. On her chin three long dark hairs grew from a bumpy mole; they quivered when she spoke. Sometimes I imagined yanking them out, but the thought of touching her made me nauseous. She wore an enormous black, greasy-looking dress that smelled of metal and strained to contain her, and she paced the room like a bee-tle—impervious to anything but its insect agenda—pausing only to slam her fat fist on the table.

"Well, are you going to answer me? It's almost ten and no one has come."

The silver courier van stopped at our house two or three times a week, bringing supplies for my father's research and taking away flat white cartons labeled SERADRONE. On the van's doors and sides were the company name and logo: GREEN CROSS.

Mrs. McG said, "I don't know what you're talking about." Nonetheless, her left eyebrow and right hand twitched.

Mary Ellis Root made a low-pitched sound, a kind of growl, and slammed her way back to the basement, trailed by a lingering odor of metal.

"I never talk to the Green Cross man," Mrs. McG said.

The deliveries always came to the back door that opened into the basement. Mrs. McG's face said that her day had been ruined in the space of a minute.

I left my chair. I took my mother's cookbook down from its shelf and leafed through it. "Look," I said, to distract her. "She put four stars next to this one."

It was a recipe for cheese bread made with honey. Mrs. McG peered over my shoulder at the recipe, her face doubt-ful. I leaned back slightly to feel the warmth of her body, without touching her. I felt that this was as close to a moth-er as I was likely to come.

Being home-schooled had some advantages, I suppose. I

didn't have to worry about what to wear to school or how to make friends. Periodically I had to take a state-mandated examination, and every time I answered all the questions correctly. My father had stuffed my brain with knowledge of history and mathematics and literature; I could read Latin and some Greek and French and Spanish, and my English vocabulary was so advanced that I sometimes had to define for Mrs. McG the words I used. Occasionally Dennis taught me science; he'd been a medical student at one time, he said, but switched to biology, which he taught part-time at the college not far away. Because of his training, Dennis served as our family doctor and dentist, except when I was very ill, as I was two or three times; then Dr. Wilson was called in. But Dennis gave my father and me vaccinations and annual checkups. Luckily, I had strong teeth.

Dennis taught me how to swim, using the college pool, and he was my friend as well. He was the only person in our house who liked to laugh and to make me laugh. (Mrs. McG was too nervous to do more than smile, and even then it was a nervous smile.) Dennis had dark red wavy hair that he had cut every month or so; in between it grew almost to his shoulders. His freckled nose curved like a hawk's beak. Like my father, he was tall, around six foot three, but Dennis was stockier. He had a temper, too; he never hesitated to tell off Root when she was particularly rude or abrasive, and that made him a hero to me.

One late winter day when I was twelve, Dennis told me "the facts of life." He blushed when I asked him questions, but he answered every one. He patted me on the head when

I couldn't think of any more questions. After he'd gone back downstairs, I went to the bathroom mirror and looked at myself. Dark hair like my father's, blue eyes, pale skin. Something stubborn in my face.

Later that same afternoon I sat and watched the icicles that hung like awnings outside the living room windows slowly drip drip drip. For months the days had been one color: gray. Now I listened to the coming of a new season.

Outside, my father stood in the driveway. He seemed to be talking to himself. From time to time I'd see him there, oblivious to the weather, deep in conversation with no one.

Mrs. McG asked me once if I was lonely, and I had no idea what to answer. I knew from books that people had friends, children had playmates. But I had my father and Dennis and Mrs. McG (and Mary Ellis Root, alas), and I had all the books I wanted. So after a few seconds I replied that no, I wasn't lonely.

Mrs. McG apparently wasn't convinced. I heard her talking to Dennis about my "need to get out of the house." She went on, "I know how much he loves her, but overprotection can't be good."

And soon after that, I found myself in Mrs. McG's car one rainy afternoon. The idea was that I'd come to dinner at her house, meet her family, then be driven home well before my ten p.m. bedtime.

It was raining so hard that the windshield filmed with water immediately after the pass of the wiper blades. I remember Mrs. McG's hands clutching the steering wheel.

And I remember the calm when the car drove beneath an underpass—I marveled at how suddenly things could change from one state to another, then revert.

Was I excited? Frightened, more likely. I left the house rarely, only to be shepherded to periodic examinations at a local school. Today I had no idea what to expect. My father had told me that I had a weak immune system, that he himself had one, that it was better for us to stay away from crowds. I'd been a small, fragile-looking child, but now that I was twelve I seemed to myself sturdier, and my curiosity about the world had grown stronger, too.

Not to say that I wasn't "worldly." I'd read widely; I knew "the facts of life." But nothing had prepared me for Mrs. McG's house.

She lived on the south side of Saratoga Springs. The house was painted white—or had been, some time ago. Winters had worn away paint, and the house looked a little shabby.

Inside, a barrage of sounds, colors, and smells made me dizzy. This house smelled like people. Piles of shoes and boots of all sizes lay near the door, surrounded by puddles of melted snow. Damp coats and snowsuits hung from hooks, and the scents of sweat and wet wool mingled with those of hot chocolate and toast and something I couldn't identify, which turned out to be wet dog.

Mrs. McG led me down a corridor into the kitchen. There, up and down a battered table, sprawled her children. A boy about six years old paused in the act of spitting at one of his sisters to say, "We got company!"

The others stared at me. A large yellow dog walked over and stuck his wet nose against my leg.

"Hi." It was one of the older boys, dark-haired, wearing a plaid shirt.

"Who are you?" A small girl with green eyes looked up at me.

A taller girl flipped her long reddish braid over her shoulder and stood up. She smiled. "This is Ari," she said to the others. "I'm Kathleen," she said to me. "Mom said you were coming."

"Sit here." The girl with green eyes pulled another chair to the table next to her.

I sat. There were ten of them, altogether. They had bright eyes and flushed cheeks, and they watched me curiously. The dog curled up under the table at my feet.

Kathleen set before me a mug of cocoa with a large marshmallow melting in it. Someone else gave me a plate of toast splotched with cinnamon and butter. I took a sip and a bite. "It's delicious," I said, and they looked pleased.

"Take your time and settle in," Mrs. McG said. "Later you can try to learn their names. You'll never remember so many."

"Even Mom can't remember sometimes," Kathleen said. "She calls us 'girl' or 'boy.'"

"Do you like sledding?" another dark-haired boy asked.

"I've never tried it," I said. I licked marshmallow foam from my lips.

"Never tried sledding?" His voice was skeptical.

"Miss Ari hasn't spent much time outdoors," Mrs. McG

said. "She's not a ruffian like you all are."

"I'm not a ruffian," the girl with green eyes said. She had a tiny nose with two freckles on it. "I'm too petite to be a ruffian."

"Petite!" Some of the others repeated the word in mocking voices.

"Bridget's plump, not petite. Plump as a piglet," said the older boy. "My name is Michael," he said, while Bridget protested.

"When Michael goes to bed at night, he sleeps like a soldier," Kathleen said. She stood up straight and rigid, hands at her sides. "Like that he sleeps. Never moves all night long."

"Not like Kathleen," Michael said. "She tosses all the covers off and then wakes up shivering."

They seemed endlessly fascinated by each other. New voices chimed in, talking about how this one woke up before dawn, and that one talked in his sleep. I ate my toast and drank my cocoa, listening to them as if they were faraway birds.

"You all right?" It was Kathleen's voice, close to my ear.

"I'm fine."

"We're a noisy bunch. Mom says we're worse than monkeys." Kathleen flipped her braid back again. It had a way of creeping back over her shoulder, no matter how hard she flipped it. She had a small face, rather plain, but it dimpled when she smiled. "Are you thirteen?"

"Twelve," I said. "Thirteen this summer."

"When's your birthday?"

31

Gradually the others left the room, and finally, only Kathleen and I were left at the table. She talked about pets and clothes and television shows, things that I knew little about—if anything, only from books.

"Do you always dress like that?" She said it without malice.

I gazed at my plain starched white-cotton shirt and loose-fitting starched dark pants. "Yes." I felt like adding, *Blame your mother. She buys my clothes.*

To be fair, Mrs. McG hadn't always bought me drab clothing. When I was very young, perhaps two or three, she bought a bright paisley playsuit, its colors a swirl of red and green and blue. My father winced when he saw it and asked her to take it off me at once.

Kathleen wore tight jeans and a purple t-shirt. I wondered, why weren't they starched?

"Mom said you need some color in your life." Kathleen stood up. "Come and see my room."

On the way to Kathleen's room we passed a cluttered space with a television set along one wall. "That's the big screen Dad bought us for Christmas," Kathleen said.

McGarritts were stuffed into two sofas and assorted chairs, others lying on pillows on the carpet; all eyes were on the screen, which displayed moving images of an odd creature.

"What is it?" I asked her.

"Space alien," she said. "Michael's big on the Sci-Fi channel."

I didn't tell her that I'd never seen a TV before. I said, "Ray Bradbury writes about space aliens."

"Never heard of him." She was climbing stairs now, and I followed. She opened the door of a room slightly bigger than my bedroom closet. "Enter," she said.

The room was crowded with things: a bunk bed, two small bureaus, a desk and chair, a fuzzy red carpet on the floor littered with shoes. It had no windows, and the walls were covered with posters and pictures cut out of magazines. A black box on top of a bureau boomed music; next to it were CD cases, but none I recognized; at home we had mostly classical music, symphonies and operas.

"What sort of music do you like?" I asked.

"Punk, pop, rock. This is the Cankers." She gestured at a poster over the desk: a longhaired man dressed in black, his mouth open in a kind of snarl. "I love them. Don't you?"

"I've never heard of them," I said.

She looked at me for a second and said, "Oh, never mind. I guess it's true what Mom said? That you've led a sheltered life?"

I said I thought the description fairly apt.

My first visit to the McGarritt house felt endless at times, but as we drove home it seemed to have lasted only minutes. I was overwhelmed by unfamiliarity. Mr. McGarritt, a large round man with a large bald head, had come home for supper; it was spaghetti, and Mrs. McG made a special nonmeat sauce for me, which tasted surprisingly good.

Everyone crowded around the long table, eating and

talking and interrupting; the younger children talked about school and how a boy named Ford was bullying them; Michael vowed he would take care of Ford; his mother said he would not do any such thing; his father said enough of that, and the yellow dog (they called him Wally, short for Wal-Mart, a store near where he'd been found) let out a howl. They all laughed, even Mr. and Mrs. McG.

"Is it true that you don't go to school?" Bridget asked me. She'd finished her food before anyone else.

My mouth full, I nodded.

"Lucky," Bridget said.

I swallowed. "Don't you like school?"

She shook her head. "People make fun of us."

The table fell quiet for a moment. I turned to Kathleen, who sat next to me, and whispered, "Is that so?"

Kathleen's expression was hard to read; she seemed angry and embarrassed, and ashamed of her feelings, all at once. "Yes," she said, her voice low. "We're the only ones who don't have computers and mobile phones." Then, in a clear voice, she said, "The rich ones make fun of all the scholarship kids. It's not just us."

Mrs. McG rose and began to clear plates, and everyone began to talk again.

It wasn't anything like the way conversations proceeded at home; here, they interrupted and disagreed, and shouted and laughed loudly and talked while they ate, and no one seemed to mind. At home sentences were always finished; dialogues were logical, evenly paced, thoughtful; they progressed in undulating Hegelian spirals, considering all alternatives before reaching syntheses. There wasn't much silliness at my house, I realized that night, as Mrs. McG drove me home.

After I had thanked her and come inside, I found my father reading in his chair near the fireplace, waiting for me. "How was your outing?" he asked. He sat back in his leather chair, his eyes invisible in the shadows.

I thought of all I'd seen and heard and wondered how I could possibly describe it all. "It was very nice," I said cautiously.

My father flinched at the words. "Your face is flushed," he said. "It's time that you went to bed."

When I'd left the McGarritts, Kathleen had flung her arms around me in an impulsive goodbye hug. I imagined crossing the room and hugging my father goodnight. Even the thought of it was ludicrous.

"Good night," I said, and headed upstairs, still wearing my coat.

Early the next morning, something awakened me. Still half asleep, I stumbled out of bed and went to the windows.

Then came a sound—a high-pitched howl—like nothing I'd ever heard. It seemed to come from the back garden. More alert now, I went to the window that overlooked it, peering down, seeing nothing but a faint gleam of snow in the darkness.

The noise stopped. A second later I heard a thud, as if something had hit the house. A shadowy form of a person strode out of the garden toward the street. I followed the figure with my eyes. Was it my father?

I must have fallen asleep again, because the next thing I heard was Mrs. McG, screaming. The room was light. I raced down the stairs.

She stood outside, trembling slightly, in her winter coat (with the imitation-fox collar) and an imitation-mink hat. She seemed to shrink when she saw me. "Don't look, Ari," she said.

But I'd already seen Marmalade lying on the steps, the snow near her splotched with blood.

Mrs. McG said, "Poor cat. Poor innocent creature. What kind of animal would do such a thing?"

"Get back inside." Mary Ellis Root hissed the words at me. She lifted me by my shoulders and set me down in the corridor beyond the kitchen. Then she brushed past me and shut the kitchen door firmly behind her.

After a few seconds I flung open the door. The kitchen was empty. I went to the back door, and through the window next to it I saw Root lifting the cat. Marmalade's body was rigid; her neck had been broken, and the sight of her jaw facing skyward made me want to scream.

Root carried the carcass past the window, out of sight, but as she passed me I saw her face, her fleshy lips curved in a tight smile.

I never told Mrs. McG about the shadow-figure I'd seen earlier that day. Somehow it was clear to me that telling would only make things worse.

Later that day, as I waited in the kitchen for my father to begin the day's lessons, I heard voices from downstairs.

"Congratulations," Root said.

My father's voice said, "Indeed. And for what?"

"For showing your true nature," she said, her voice crooning satisfaction. Then she added, "I buried the cat."

I ran into the living room, not wanting to hear more.

— Two —

The year I was thirteen, I learned that almost everything I'd been told about my father was a lie. He did not have lupus. He was not a vegetarian. And he'd never wanted to have me. But I learned the truth gradually, not in one moment of blinding revelation—which I would have preferred, dramatically. That's the trouble with writing about your life: somehow you have to deal with the long boring bits. Thankfully, most of those are in Chapter One. My childhood was by and large so uneventful that, looking back, I seem to have been sleepwalking. Now I want to move more into the wakeful moments, the real time of my thirteenth year and what followed. It was the first year I had a birthday party. In other years, my father would give me a present at dinner, and Mrs. McG would make a sodden cake with runny icing. Those events happened this year as well, but in addition Mrs. McG took me home with her on July 16, the day after my birthday. I was to have dinner and spend the night:

another first for me. I'd never slept anywhere but home. From the living room I'd overheard my father discuss the plans with Mrs. McG. He'd had to be convinced that I'd be all right in a strange house. "The child needs friends," Mrs. McG had said firmly. "She's still brooding over the death of the neighbor's cat, I think. She needs to be distracted."

My father said, "Ari is fragile, Mrs. McGarritt. She's not like other children."

"She's overprotected," Mrs. McG said, with a strength I hadn't thought she possessed.

"She's vulnerable." My father's voice was quiet, but authoritative. "I can only hope that she won't share my affliction, since we lack the means to know for certain."

"I hadn't thought about that," Mrs. McG said, her voice contrite. "I'm sorry."

After a pause, my father said, "I'll consent to Ari spending the night, so long as you promise me you'll keep watch and bring her home if anything happens."

Mrs. McG promised. I quietly shut the living room door, wondering what my father was so worried about. In his excessive concern he reminded me of the princess's father in *The Princess and the Goblins*, terrified that his daughter would be kidnapped by beastly things that stole into her room at night.

Michael was playing loud rock music when we arrived, and Mrs. McG's first words were "Turn it down!" Kathleen came dancing down the stairs to greet me. She still wore her school uniform: a dark green plaid jumper over a

short-sleeved white blouse, white knee socks, and penny
loafers. She had to attend summer school because she'd
failed World History.

"Look at you!" she said.

For my birthday I had requested, and received, a new
outfit, which I was wearing: a pale blue t-shirt and matching
corduroy jeans; both fit more tightly than my usual clothes.
And I'd been growing out my hair, which before had been
cut by Dennis into a chin-length bob.

"What do you think?"

"Sexy," she said, and her mother said, "Kathleen!"

But I knew she wasn't lying when Michael came into the
room. He took one glance at me and fell backward onto a
sofa, in a mock swoon.

"Ignore him," Kathleen said. "Come up while I change."

Upstairs, I lay on Kathleen's bed while she put on jeans
and a T-shirt. She rolled her uniform into a ball and kicked
it into a corner. "It was my sister Maureen's," she told me.
Maureen was the oldest, and I rarely saw her because she
attended business college in Albany.

"Who knows who wore it before her? I wash it every
other day, and it still smells funny." Kathleen made a face.

"I'm so lucky I don't have to wear a uniform," I said, beating her to it, because she told me that two or three times a
week.

We'd taken to talking on the phone each night for an
hour, more if no one complained, and the curse of the
uniform was a regular topic. So was a game we played
called "Gross out," in which we tried to outdo each other in

imagining doing the nastiest possible things in the name of love; the winner so far: "Would you eat your lover's used dental floss?" Kathleen had come up with that one. She was also very interested in my father's lupus, which her mother had told her about. At one point she'd asked if I thought I had it, too.

"I don't know," I said. "Apparently they can't test for lupus." Then I'd told her I didn't want to talk any more about it, and she'd said she understood.

"So what did you get for your birthday?" She sat on the floor, unplaiting her hair.

"These new clothes," I reminded her. "And shoes." I lifted my pants leg and extended my ankle.

"Converse All-Stars!" Kathleen picked up one of her penny loafers and threw it in my direction. "You're cooler than me now." She pretended to sob into her arms, then looked up and said, "Not really."

I tossed a bed pillow at her.

"And what else?" she asked.

"What else did I get? Um, a book."

"About?"

I hesitated, because I suspected that her mother was behind the book. "It's sort of a guide to womanhood." I said it fast to get it over with.

"Not *On Becoming a Woman*?" I nodded, and she let out a yip of laughter. "Oh, poor Ari. Poor us."

I'd already skimmed the book, a paperback with an aqua cover published by a manufacturer of "women's hygiene products" (a free sample of which came in a plastic bag

41

taped to its cover). It had sentences like this one: "Your body is very unique, a real miracle, deserving to be treasured and protected every day." And this: "You are about to enter the sacred realm of Womanhood!" Its tone, relentlessly cheerful, worried me. Would I have to assume a similar attitude in order to enter the sacred realm?

"So have you started yet?" Kathleen peered at me through a curtain of hair.

"Not yet." I didn't say it, but I couldn't imagine experiencing the monthly ordeal that the book tried to make sound so worthwhile. What with the cramps and the general mess, I felt I'd rather avoid the whole business.

"I started five or six months ago." Kathleen pushed her hair back, and suddenly she seemed older to me. "It's not so bad. The cramps are the worst. Mom told me what to expect, and she was a lot more honest than that dumb book."

I thought of my mother, and Kathleen looked closely at me. "Do you miss your mom?"

"I never knew her," I said. "But I miss her anyway. She disappeared when I was born."

"Mom told us," Kathleen said. "She said she went into the hospital and never came out again. You know, Ari, sometimes women go a little crazy after they have babies."

This was news to me. "Are you saying my mother went mad?"

Kathleen came over and touched my arm. "No, no. I have no idea if that's what happened. But it's a possibility. It happened to Mrs. Sullivan down the street. She had a baby and a few days later they took her away to Marcy. You know, the mental asylum. Once you go in, you never come out."

Mrs. McG shouted for us to come to dinner, and I felt more than ready. But Kathleen had given me a new image of my mother, a most unwelcome one: a faceless woman wrapped in a straitjacket, locked in a padded cell.

They'd laid the table in a special way, setting at my place a cream-colored plate painted with tiny green leaves, instead of the chipped white china the others had. And next to the plate were presents: five or six small wrapped packages with foil bows on top. Several of the bows had been chewed slightly by Wally the dog.

I'd never expected anything like this. At home we had no giftwrap, no special china. Even at Christmas (which Dennis made us celebrate, with indifferent participation by my father and Root), we didn't bother to wrap gifts, and each person received one thing, always practical.

"Open them now," Kathleen said, and the others urged me on. I ripped through the paper to find barrettes for my hair, scented soap, a votive candle inside a blue glass flower, a CD (the Cankers, of course), and a disposable camera.

"For you to take pictures of your house, to show us," Michael said.

"But you can come and see it for yourself," I said.

He shook his head. "Mom said no."

Mrs. McG was in the kitchen, so I couldn't find out why she'd said that. I told myself I'd ask her later.

"Thank you all so much," I said.

When they lit the birthday candles and sang to me, I

nearly cried—but not for reasons you might think. Standing behind the heat of the small pink candles, watching them, I was struck by how united they were, how they all, down to the mongrel dog, belonged together. For the first time in my life I did feel lonely.

After dinner, the McGarritt family congregated in the living room to watch TV. They squabbled about what to watch, then compromised: first, a documentary for everyone; then the adults would take the younger McGarritts to bed and leave the three of us to watch what we liked.

An odd experience, watching television for the first time at the age of thirteen. The enormous screen flickered with colors and forms; it seemed alive. The sound didn't seem to come from the screen, but from the walls around us. When a lion fought with a hyena, I had to close my eyes; the images were too vivid, too real.

The sound that broke the spell of the TV was Michael's voice. He sat behind me (Kathleen and I were on floor cushions), and he had the habit of interjecting comments, as if the animals themselves were speaking. A soulful-looking lion on a hill gazing down on grazing antelope said, "Can I have fries with that?"

We all laughed, Even when I didn't get the joke, I laughed. But Michael's father found it annoying and made him stop.

When the documentary ended, Mr. and Mrs. McG gathered up the young ones and left the room. I sat up.

"Where're you going?" Michael said. "The fun is about

to begin." He took the control mechanism and made the TV change images. Next thing I knew, we were watching my first vampire movie.

Maybe it was the closeness of the room, or the dominance of the enormous screen, or the large slice of cake I'd had after a large dinner. Or maybe it was the movie itself: the pale creatures with fangs who slept in coffins, rising at night to drink human blood. Whatever the cause, about ten minutes into the movie a wave of nausea came over me.

I ran to the bathroom and had shut the door when the second wave hit. Clutching the sides of the toilet, I shut my eyes as I retched. I didn't open them until my stomach was empty, and the spasms subsided.

The tap water was cold, and I splashed some onto my face. In the mirror over the sink I saw a wavering image of my face, white, beaded with perspiration, my eyes dark and large. I opened my mouth and splashed water over my teeth and tongue to take away the sourness, and when I looked again, the face in the mirror wasn't mine.

Have you ever seen, in your reflection, someone else's face? It boldly stared back at me: beady animal eyes, a snout for a nose, a mouth like a wolf's, canine teeth long and pointed. I heard a voice (my voice) pleading, "No, no."

Then, just as suddenly, it was gone. My own frightened eyes gazed at me; my dark hair lay damp around my face. But when I opened my mouth, my teeth had changed; they seemed larger, the canine teeth more pointed.

"Ari?" Kathleen's voice came from outside.

I flushed the toilet, washed my hands, pushed back my hair. "I'm okay," I said.

Too much party—that was Kathleen's diagnosis. "You don't want to go home, do you?"

"Of course not." But I didn't want to talk all night, either. "I need some sleep," I said.

What I really wanted was time to think. But once Kathleen turned out the lights, I fell asleep almost at once, and didn't dream, and didn't waken until morning, when the house came alive with the sounds of floorboards creaking, doors banging, water rushing through pipes, and a petulant voice saying, "But it's *my* turn."

I had the lower bunk (Bridget was spending the night in one of the others' rooms), and I looked up to see that Kathleen wasn't in bed. Then I lay back again, thinking about the night before. I didn't want to think about the mirror yet, so I focused on the movie. It was the way the vampires moved, I decided, that had got to me. None of the other stuff— the sleeping in coffins, the crosses and garlic, the stakes in the heart—had bothered me at all. But the effortless glide, the graceful sweep to and from rooms, reminded me of my father.

Kathleen came in, fully dressed. "You have to get up, Ari," she said. "Otherwise we'll miss the horses."

Kathleen said she knew me well enough now not to ask if I'd ever been to the track before. "And I'll bet you can't ride a bicycle, either. Am I right, Ms. Sheltered Life?"

"Sad but true," I said.

The morning was bright but clouds of fog misted the air, cold against my bare arms. We moved briskly down the street. At six a.m. almost no one was stirring. "This is the best part of living in Saratoga Springs," she said. "You'll see."

We walked for several blocks past small houses—modern rectangles, most of them, nothing like the grand Victorians in my neighborhood—then cut across a wide lawn.

"The racetrack is over there." Kathleen waved her hand toward more fog. "Here's where they exercise the horses."

She led us along a white fence. A few other people were standing, sipping coffee, waiting for something.

We heard them before we saw them. Soft thuds of hooves on turf, like muted drumbeats, and then they emerged from the smoky fog, running flat out, jockeys curved low along their necks. Two white horses, two darker ones, flashed by us and disappeared into the fog again.

"It's a shame we can't see more," Kathleen said.

I was too thrilled to tell her I disagreed, that seeing a momentary manifestation of horses was far more magical than a clear view could be. Now came another one, moving more slowly—white mist parting to reveal a dark brown beauty with a black mane. Her jockey bent low, toward her ear, singing to her in a soft voice.

Kathleen and I looked at each other and grinned. "This," I told her, "is the best birthday present of all."

We began our walk back to the McGarritts', heading across the grass near the stables. Kathleen was telling me about a boy she had a crush on at school; then I stopped listening.

Someone was watching me. My skin tingled, telling me so. I looked around, but saw only fog and grass.

"What's wrong?" Kathleen said. She sounded so worried that I made a face at her, and then she laughed.

"Let's run," I said.

We raced each other back to the street. By then the sensation was gone.

Later that morning, Mrs. McGarritt drove me home, and Kathleen came along. Apparently Mrs. McG had reconsidered her ban, because she stayed in the car and let Kathleen help me carry my stuff inside. As always, our house was cool; the windows' shades had been drawn against the heat.

"You have so much space," Kathleen said, looking around my room: pale blue walls, ivory wainscotings and crown moldings, dark blue velvet drapes looped back from the windows. "And you don't have to share with anyone. Even your own bathroom!"

She especially liked my bedside lamp, which had a five-sided porcelain shade. Unlit, the shade seemed like bumpy ivory. Lit, each panel came to life with the image of a bird: a blue jay, a cardinal, wrens, an oriole, and a dove. Kathleen turned it off and on again, several times. "How does it do that?"

"The panels are called lithophanes." I knew because I'd asked my father about the lamp, years ago. "The porcelain is carved and painted. You can see it if you look inside the shade."

"No," she said. "It's magic. I don't want to know how

it's done." She switched off the lamp. "You're so lucky," she said.

I tried to see it with her eyes. "I may be lucky in some ways," I said, "but I don't have as much fun as you do."

It was the simple truth. She squeezed my arm. "I wish we were sisters," she said.

We were coming downstairs when, below, my father passed, a book in his hand. He gazed up at us. "What a relief," he said. "It sounded like a herd of elephants."

He shook Kathleen's hand. She couldn't stop staring at him. Then he went on, toward the library.

We headed for the door.

"Why didn't you tell me," Kathleen whispered, "that your father is such a hunk?"

I didn't know what to say.

"What a shame that he has lupus." Kathleen opened the door, then turned back to me. "He looks like a rock star. Our dad looks like a butcher, which is what he is. Count your blessings, Ari."

After she left, the house seemed larger than ever. I went to find my father in the library. He was sitting at the desk, reading. I looked at him, his chin resting on his long, narrow hand, his beautiful mouth that always seemed slightly disappointed, his long dark eyelashes. Yes, my father was a hunk. I wondered if he ever felt lonely.

"What is it, Ari?" he said, without looking up. His voice was low and musical, as ever.

"I need to talk to you," I said.

He raised his chin and his eyes. "About?"

I took a deep breath. "About a bicycle."

At first my father said he'd think about it. Then, a few days later, he said he'd talked it over with Dennis, and Dennis thought the exercise would be beneficial.

"I know you're *growing up*," my father said, on the day we went to buy the bicycle. "And I know you need to have more independence." He took a deep breath, then released it. "I know these things, and yet it's hard for me not to want to keep you safe at home."

We were driving in his old black Jaguar—a rare event, let me tell you. He used the car once a month, if that, and he almost never took me with him.

It was a warm summer afternoon in late July. He was wearing his usual dark suit—his suits and shirts were made in London, he'd told me when I asked why he never went shopping—and he'd put on a wide-brimmed hat, dark glasses, gloves, and a scarf for protection from the sun. Someone else might appear freakish, dressed that way, but my father looked elegant.

"I'll be ever so careful," I said.

He didn't reply.

The bicycle store was near a shopping mall; Kathleen and I had taken the bus to the mall the previous week, and she'd pointed it out. She and Michael had also debated the merits of various models and styles, and they'd narrowed their recommendations down to three. I had the list in my pocket.

But once we were in the store, I saw that I needn't have

bothered to bring the list. Browsing among the racks of bikes was Michael.

He blushed when he saw me. "Kathleen said today was the day," he said. "I couldn't let you make the decision by yourself."

"Afraid I might get it wrong?" I said, but he was gazing beyond me.

"How do you do, sir," Michael said, his voice oddly strained.

My father had come up behind me. "And how do you know Ariella?"

"He's Kathleen's brother," I said.

My father nodded, and shook Michael's rough hand with his gloved one. "And what do you think about these bicycles?"

Later that night on the telephone, Kathleen said she was mad at Michael for not telling her he was going to the bike store. "He says your father resembles a gothic prince," she said, her voice telling me what the words did not: that this was a good thing, an "awesome" thing, to use a word common at her house, unheard in mine.

I was struck by how easily and warmly the McGarritts liked people—even odd ones, like my father and me. Perhaps the snobbery they faced at school (and elsewhere in Saratoga Springs) made them that way? Or did something in their heritage make them instinctively friendly?

In any case, now I owned a bike, a blue and silver racer. And Dennis taught me to ride it in only a day, so that when

I rode up to the McGarritts' house, Michael was amazed. "You're a natural," he told me.

I hoped so. I was already thinking ahead, to the fall, when I planned to ask my father to let me take lessons in horseback riding.

With the bicycle, the whole city opened up to me.

At first I went out only with Kathleen. We had a weekday rendezvous at the racetrack to watch the horses exercise; then we'd go on downtown, where we sometimes had sodas and sandwiches, after which I'd pedal home for my afternoon lessons, and she'd head for the remedial history class at her school. Kathleen thought it unspeakably cruel that we were going to school in the summertime, but actually I looked forward to my time with my father. I liked learning.

Before I met Kathleen, I'd never even been in a restaurant. Could you imagine my father, Dennis, Mary Ellis Root, and me in an Olive Garden? We had plenty of food at home and no need to go out. But Kathleen showed me how much fun it was to choose a meal from a menu. Grilled cheese sandwiches in the soda shop tasted so much better than anything Mrs. McG made, although of course I didn't say that.

Kathleen also introduced me to the local library and to the Inter-net. She couldn't believe that I didn't use a computer at home. The two in the basement were devoted to my father's and Dennis's research, but I'd never thought of asking to use them.

And I didn't use them that summer. We had too many

other things to do. We took longer and longer bike rides, out to the Yaddo Rose Garden and beyond, to the lake. At first I couldn't go as far or as fast as she could, but my stamina grew over time. I suffered my first sunburn, which gave me a fever and a rash so severe that my father called in Dr. Wilson, who gave me a lecture and sent me to bed for two days; after that, I religiously applied the SPF 50 sunscreen from the enormous bottle Root had placed on my bedroom dresser, giving me a glance of utter contempt as she did so.

I had a less violent reaction to my first kiss. One evening a group of us went to the lake to watch fireworks. The others kept swatting at flies and mosquitoes, but insects never bothered me. I moved a little apart from the others, to see better, and when I took my eyes from the sky, Michael stood next to me. I saw the reflection of a shower of ruby-red stars in his eyes as he kissed me.

You're right—I haven't described Michael, have I? I think he was sixteen that summer—a boy of medium height, with dark brown hair, brown eyes, and tanned skin. He spent as much time as he could outdoors, biking and swimming. He was muscular, lean, with a deadpan expression that stayed on his face even when he told jokes, which was often. Occasionally he snuck cigarettes from his father's supply, and I remember the smell of tobacco. Is that enough? I think that's enough about him.

July melted into August, and all the McG kids were getting ready to return to school—shopping for notebooks and pens, getting dental exams, having their hair cut, talking about teachers. One day a cold wind blew in from Canada, bringing Saratoga Springs an unmistakable hint that summer wouldn't last forever.

Perhaps that knowledge made me irritable, I thought. Or perhaps I was missing Dennis, my father's assistant; he was in Japan conducting research that month. Since I'd been a baby he'd had a special fondness for me. I thought of how he'd carried me around on his broad shoulders, pretending to be a horse, and how he'd made me laugh. He called himself my "fine freckled friend." He'd be back with us in a few weeks, and that thought would have to console me for now.

I forced myself to read a collection of poetry by Edgar Allan Poe, and it was tough going. I'd suffered through *The Narrative of Arthur Gordon Pym*, which seemed to me painfully overwritten. But the poetry was even worse. In an hour my father would be upstairs, expecting me to have insights into meter and rhyme, and all I could think about was that Michael (and Kathleen) were out shopping, and that I wouldn't see them at all that day.

Mrs. McG had made me an omelet for lunch, so watery and tasteless that I couldn't make myself eat more than a few bites of it. I wondered why her cooking tasted so much better at her house.

When I met my father in the library at one, I said, "You know, I don't think much of Poe's poetry."

He was sitting at the desk, and one of his eyebrows lifted. "And how much of it have you read, Ariella?"

"Enough to know that I don't like it." I talked quickly, to hide the truth: I'd read the first and last stanzas and

skimmed the rest. I tried to explain. "The words are just …
words on the page."

"Which one were you reading?" How like him, to know
I'd read only one.

I opened the book and handed it to him. "'Annabel Lee,'"
he said, his voice caressing the name. "Oh, Ari. I don't think
you've read it at all."

And he read the poem aloud to me, barely glancing at
the book, never pausing between the lines or stanzas, and
the words were like music, the saddest song in the world.
When he read the final lines ("And so, all the night-tide, I
lie down by the side / Of my darling—my darling—my life
and my bride / In her sepulchre there by the sea— / In her
tomb by the sounding sea."), I was crying. And when he
looked up from the book, I saw tears in his eyes.

He recovered quickly. "I'm sorry," he said. "Poe was a bad
choice."

But I couldn't stop crying. Embarrassed, I left him and
went upstairs, lines of the poem still sounding in my head:
"For the moon never beams, without bringing me dreams /
Of the beautiful ANNABEL LEE; / And the stars never
rise, but I feel the bright eyes / Of the beautiful ANNABEL
LEE."

I fell onto my bed and cried as I'd never cried before—
for my mother and father and me, and all that we'd been
and might have been, and all that had been lost.

I slept through until early morning, waking from a vivid
dream. (Nearly all of my dreams since have been vivid, and

I remember every one of them. Is it like that for you?) In my dream were horses, and bees, and a woman's voice, singing: *When evening falls beyond the blue, the shadows know I wait for you.*

The song still in my head, I got up and went to the bath-room— and discovered that, while I'd slept, my body had "entered the sacred realm of Womanhood." I cleaned myself up and went down to tell Mrs. McG., who blushed. She in turn must have said something to my father, I thought later, because that afternoon he seemed more distant and dis-tracted than he'd ever been with me before. His eyes were wary when he looked at me.

We were working on geometric proofs (a subject I secret-ly adored), and I was engrossed in proving that the opposite sides of a quadrilateral inscribed in a cyclic quadrilateral are supplementary. When I looked up, my father was staring at me.

"Father?" I said.

"You were *humming*," he said.

The shock in his voice struck me as almost comical. "Is that so wrong?" I asked.

"The song," he said. "Where did you learn it?"

It was still playing, in my head: *Where water flows be-yond the blue, along the shore I wait for you.*

"I dreamed it, last night," I said. "I even dreamed lyrics."

He nodded, still visibly upset. "It was one of her favor-ites," he said finally.

"My mother's?" But I didn't need to ask. I thought, *Why*

can't you say that, Father? Say it was my mother's favorite song?

He looked as crushed as if I'd spoken the words, not merely thought them.

Later that afternoon we took our usual break for yoga and meditation. I went through the yoga poses without even thinking about them, but when we got to the meditation part, all I could do was think.

My father had taught me a meditation mantra: "Who am I? I don't know." I repeated the phrase again and again, and normally it led me to a place where I had no consciousness of self, where my mind became empty and open, and I felt at peace. But today, the mantra in my head abbreviated itself and sounded angry: "I *don't know*, I *don't know*, I *don't know.*"

One Saturday afternoon in late summer, Kathleen sprawled across an oversized towel spread across a patch of our back lawn. I sat in the shade of the horse chestnut tree, breathing in the scent of dandelions baking in the sun. Cicadas sang, and although the sun was hot, the breeze carried a faint tang of winter. We both wore bathing suits and sunglasses. Kathleen's skin glistened with baby oil, while mine was coated in sunscreen.

"Michael will have his license in October," she said. "Dad is going to let him have the Chevy on weekends, provided he doesn't stay out late. So he can drive us around."

"We should buy him a uniform," I said lazily.

Kathleen looked momentarily puzzled. Then she grinned,

"Our personal chauffeur," she said. "Picture that."

"We'll sit in the backseat." I pulled back my hair, which had grown past my shoulders that summer, and coiled it against my nape.

"What's that smell?" Kathleen sat up suddenly.

A faint, familiar odor of something burning grew stronger as I sniffed.

Kathleen got to her feet. She walked toward the house, pausing a few times to breathe again. I followed.

The smell emanated from the basement. An opaque casement window had been propped open, and Kathleen went right to it. She knelt to peer inside.

I felt an instinct to warn her, but I said nothing. Silently I knelt beside her.

We were looking into the room I called the night kitchen. Mary Ellis Root stood at a wooden table, chopping meat. Behind her a stew pot had been placed over high heat on the gas stove, and she flung chunks of meat into it with one hand, over her shoulder. She never missed once.

I put a hand on Kathleen's shoulder to draw her back before we were seen. We retreated to the chestnut tree. "Who is that witch, and what was she making?" Kathleen said.

I explained that Root was my father's housekeeper. "He has a special diet," I said, thinking, *which I always assumed was vegetarian, like mine*.

"It looked as disgusting as it smells," Kathleen said. "It looked like liver or hearts."

* * *

Later, we went back to my room to change clothes. Kathleen picked up the disposable camera from my dresser and snapped a photo of me while I was putting my shirt on. I grabbed the camera from her.

"No fair," I said.

She grabbed it back from me, laughed, and ran out into the corridor with it. I finished buttoning my shirt before I followed her.

But the long cedar-paneled corridor yawned at me, empty. I began to open bedroom doors, sure that she was hiding.

The house, so familiar, such a *given*, suddenly seemed strange to me. I was seeing it through Kathleen's eyes. The worn carpets and Victorian furniture suited the house, and I knew somehow that my mother had chosen them.

Here was the room my parents once shared; they had lain on that four-poster bed. I didn't dwell long on the thought. I focused on the wallpaper—the sprigs of lavender, patterned against an ivory background, that alternated from clusters of six blossoms to those of two with monotonous regularity from ceiling to floor— and on the place near the baseboard where a strip of paper curled away, revealing an olive-colored pattern beneath it. I wondered how many layers of paper I would need to peel away before I found a pattern that pleased me.

Room after room was empty. I even checked the closets. I'd entered the last bedroom when I sensed movement behind me, and when I spun around, Kathleen snapped my picture.

"Gotcha," she said. "Why do you look so scared?"

"I don't know," I said. But I did know. I'd been frightened that something—what, I didn't know—might have happened to her.

"Let's ride over to the pharmacy and get this developed," she said, waving the camera.

"But we haven't used all the film yet."

"Yes, we have." She grinned. "While you were wasting time up here, I took some shots downstairs. Including one of hunky dad that I plan to hang on my wall."

"Really." I hoped that she was joking.

"Don't worry," she said. "I didn't disturb him. He was so deep into his reading that he never even saw me."

On the way downstairs, Kathleen paused to examine a painting on the wall. "Creepy," she said.

It was a still life of a tulip, an hourglass, and a skull—so familiar to me that I rarely noticed it. "It's called *Memento Mori*," I said. "It means: Remember that you're mortal."

Kathleen stared at it. "Creepy," she said again. "Creepy, but cool."

I wondered who'd chosen that picture, and who had hung it there.

While we waited for the film to be developed, we meandered through the air-conditioned pharmacy aisles. We sampled makeup and perfume, and we opened bottles to smell several brands of shampoo. We read magazines out loud, shrieking at the exploits of Hollywood stars. The clerk at the cash register shot looks of hatred at us whenever we sauntered past.

The store wasn't busy that day, and within half an hour the prints were ready. The clerk said, "Hallelujah!" as we left. We headed for the park to look at them. Kathleen ripped open the package as soon as we'd sat on a bench.

To my utter humiliation, the first one showed me in jeans and a bra, shirt in hand. "I'll kill you," I said. My only consolation was that the picture was blurred; I must have been in motion when she snapped the shutter.

I tried to take the photo, but Kathleen snatched it away. "Michael will pay to see this one."

We scuffled back and forth until I managed to tear the photo in two and crumple the halves in my hand. Kathleen's dejection made me laugh.

The other photos lay forgotten on the bench, and we dove for them simultaneously. As usual, Kathleen got there first.

"No more partial nudity shots, sad to say." She riffled through the stack. "See? I wanted to show the gang what your mansion's like."

An unconfident photographer, she'd taken several shots of the same places, and we went through them, one by one: The front stairway. The alcove with the stained-glass window. The entryway. The outer library. The living room. And then, my father's green leather chair, with a kind of shimmer over it.

"Where is he?" she said. "What happened?"

"Something's wrong with the camera," I said. But I was thinking about the vampire movie we'd seen—the scene with the mirror that didn't reflect Dracula. And though she didn't say it, I had a sense that Kathleen was thinking about the same scene.

The last photo was of me—taken just before she'd said I looked frightened. But the photo was so blurred, you couldn't tell what I might have been feeling.

In my mind, that day in August was the last day of the last summer of innocence.

When Kathleen called later that evening, we didn't talk about the photographs. We went out of our way not to mention them.

Kathleen's first day of school was coming up, and she said she felt nervous. She said we both needed "new images." It would be a fine idea for us to have our ears pierced at the mall. But we needed to have parental consent, since we weren't sixteen yet.

"How's your hunky dad?" she said, her voice artificially bright. "Will he let you get your ears pierced?"

"Hunky dad is sad," I said. "And I doubt it."

"We'll work on him. First we need to cheer him up. He should start dating again," Kathleen said. "Too bad I'm not older."

I made a disgusted sound. But we were both acting, playing roles that had been natural behavior only yesterday.

"Tomorrow at seven," she said, her voice tinny. "Our last date of the season with Justin and Trent." Those were our pet names for our favorite horses.

"Sleep tight," I told her, and hung up. I went to say goodnight to my father, who was, as ever, reading *The Poe Journal* in the living room. I tried to envision him as a mere sheen of ectoplasm. He met my stare with level eyes that held a hint of amusement.

After he'd told me to sleep well, I turned back to ask, "Do you ever get lonely?"

He turned his head to one side. Then he smiled—one of his rare, lovely smiles that made him look like a shy boy. "How could I ever be lonely, Ari," he said, "when I have you?"

— Three —

The Germans call it *Ohrwurm*, or earworm: a song stuck in one's brain. All the next morning, as we watched the jockeys exercise the horses, my mind played the song from my dream. But today, the lyrics sounded slightly different:

> *When evening falls*
> *Beyond the blue*
> *The blue beyond*
> *Is calling you*

I didn't mind the song's playing and replaying. My mind often played little games with me, a welcome distraction for an only child. Earlier that summer I'd begun dreaming crossword puzzles (does this happen to you?), dreaming clues and grids that came to me piecemeal, so that filling in more than one word at a time was barely possible. I'd awaken with a few clues—"tropical evergreen" (eight letters) or "islands of earth" (eight letters)—still in my head, frustrated that I couldn't reconstruct the grid. But "The Blue Beyond" didn't affect me one way or the other; it seemed a natural background, somehow.

The other onlookers at the track must have been used to the sight of us by now, but no one ever spoke to us. I supposed they were wealthy horse owners, most of them. Even their casual clothes, however rumpled, looked expensive. They leaned against the white railings, not talking much, sipping from large aluminum cups; the smell of their coffee floated toward us through the damp morning air, along with the smells of horses and clover and hay— the green and golden essence of summer mornings in Saratoga Springs. I breathed it in, trying to hold it in my lungs. In a few days the season would be over, and everyone here would be someplace else. And the perfume of summer gradually would be replaced by scents of fireplace smoke and dead leaves steeped in rain, later supplanted by the icy white essence of snow.

Separated from the rich ones only by yards was an entire community of workers: exercise riders, trainers, grooms, and "hot walkers." Many of them spoke to each other in Spanish. Kathleen had told me they came to Saratoga Springs for the racing season, July through Labor Day. Then most of them moved on, who knew where.

But Kathleen and I didn't talk much, that morning. We seemed a little shy of each other. After we'd sent "see you next summer" messages to Justin and Trent, the horses we loved best, we headed downtown on our bicycles.

We wound up at the library. Besides the library, the pharmacy, and the park, there weren't many options for two teenaged girls without much cash. The shopping mall was a little far to go to on bikes, as were the lake and the Yaddo Rose Garden.

Downtown Saratoga Springs catered to upscale shoppers; along and off Broadway you could find coffee shops, clothing stores (Kathleen called them *yuppie dudstores*), several restaurants and bars, and an overpriced thrift shop full of moth-eaten cashmere cardigans and out-of-style "designer jeans." Sometimes we'd go through the racks of old clothes, making fun of them, until the store owners told us we'd better move on.

It was worse at the jewelry store; if the owner was there, we wouldn't even enter, because he'd say, "On your way, ladies." But if only the young saleswoman stood behind the counter, we'd swagger in and pore over the cases of glittering rings and necklaces and brooches. Kathleen favored diamonds and emeralds; I went for sapphires and peridots. We knew the name of every jewel in the store. If the saleswoman said anything to us, Kathleen had a bold reply: "You'd better be nice to us. We're your future customers."

No one ever asked us to leave the library. We went straight to the computers to surf the Internet. Kathleen coached me. She sat at one terminal, checking her email and searching for the perfect boots, while at another I moved from website to website, determined to learn about vampires.

Searching for "vampires and photographs" yielded more than eight million links to sites ranging from the fantastic to the obscene (which I couldn't have accessed had I wanted to, thanks to the library's built-in censorship system). However, I was able to visit a few websites that posted requests from vampires seeking other vampires for solace, instruction, or more arcane needs. A quick scan of the postings suggested many factions in the vampire community; some drank blood and others refrained (termed "wannabes" by one site, "psychic vampires" by another); some advertised themselves proudly as selfish and aggressive, while others sounded merely lonely, offering themselves as "donors." But I found no mention of vampires in photographs.

As I continued my research, I occasionally glanced over at Kathleen, but she seemed intent on her own quest and didn't meet my eyes.

The Wikipedia site offered a wealth of information. It talked about the origins of vampirism in folklore and fiction, and it linked to topics such as "Hematophagy" and "Pathology," which I made a mental note to visit when I had more time. In terms of photographs, however, it offered only this: "Vampires typically cast no shadow and have no reflection. This mythical power is largely confined to European vampire myths and may be tied to folklore regarding the vampire's lack of a soul. In modern fiction, this may extend to the idea that vampires cannot be photographed."

I sat back in my chair and glanced toward Kathleen. But her terminal was vacant. Then I felt her breathing, right behind me, and when I glanced over my shoulder, her eyes, full of questions, met mine.

* * *

I carried those questions home to my lessons that day, but I couldn't bring myself to ask my father any of them. How do you ask your own father about the state of his soul?

For that was one of the early definitions I'd found: upon becoming a vampire, a mortal sacrificed his soul.

Of course I wasn't sure I believed in souls. I was an agnostic—I believed that there was no proof of God's existence, yet I didn't deny the possibility that he might exist. I had read selected chapters of the Bible, Quran, Kabbalah, Tao Te Ching, Bhagavad Gita, the writings of Lao-Tse—but I had read all of them as literature and philosophy, and my father and I discussed them as such. We had no ritualized spiritual practice—we worshipped ideas.

More specifically, we worshipped virtue, and the idea of the virtuous life. Plato talked of the importance of four virtues in particular: wisdom, courage, temperance, and justice. A disciplined education would allow one to learn virtue, according to Plato.

Every Friday, my father asked me to summarize the various lessons of the week: history, philosophy, mathematics, literature, the sciences, art. Then he would synthesize my summaries, finding patterns and parallels and symmetries that often dazzled me. My father had the ability to trace the historical evolution of belief systems, linking them to politics, arts, and sciences in a cogent and comprehensive manner that I'm afraid I took for granted then; my actual experiences of the world have shown me over time that, sadly, few minds are capable of such thinking and such articulation.

And why do you suppose that is the case? An argument could be made that only those who are free of the fear of death are able to truly apprehend human culture.

Yes, I'll get back to the story now. One day we met as usual in the library, and I think we were meant to be talking about Dickens. But I wanted to talk about Poe.

After all my complaints, I'd decided on my own to take down *The Essential Tales and Poems of Edgar Allan Poe* from the library shelf. During the previous week I'd read "The Tell-Tale Heart" without much interest, and "The Black Cat" with considerable unease (it conjured images of the unfortunate Marmalade), but "The Premature Burial" gave me a nightmare about being buried alive, and "Morella" caused me three sleepless nights.

"Morella" is the name of a wife who tells her husband, "I am dying, yet shall I live." She dies in childbirth, and her daughter grows up unnamed. When the daughter is at last baptized, her father names her "Morella," whereupon she replies, "I am here!" and promptly dies. He carries her to her mother's tomb, which is of course empty—because the daughter *was* the mother.

Note how italics have crept into these pages. Blame Poe.

In any case, I had questions about "Morella," and about myself. I wondered how like my mother I was. I didn't think I was my mother; from my first conscious thought, I'd had an intense, if sometimes conflicted, sense of self. But since I'd never known her, how could I be sure?

My father, however, was not to be sidetracked. Today we

would indeed talk about Dickens's *Hard Times*. Tomorrow, if I insisted, we would return to Poe—but only after I'd read his essay, "The Philosophy of Composition."

Accordingly, the next day (having set aside Dickens) we did return to Poe—rather gingerly at first.

"I approach this lesson with a certain trepidation," my father began. "I hope that we'll have no tears today."

I gave him a look that made him shake his head.

"You're changing, Ari. I appreciate that you're growing older, and I know we'll need to consider modifications in your education."

"And in the way we *live*," I said, with emotion that sounded uncharacteristic even to me.

"And the way we live." His voice had a skeptical-sounding inflection that made me look hard at him. But his face was as composed as ever. I recall gazing at his crisply starched shirt—deep blue, that day—with onyx cufflinks securing the precise folds of its cuffs, and recall wishing that, just once, I could find some small sign of disorder.

"In any case, what did you make of the tales of Edgar Allan Poe?"

It was my turn to shake my head. "Poe seems to have a grave fear of acts of passion."

He raised his eyebrows. "And you received that impression from which tales?"

"Not so much from the tales," I said. "By the way, they're all overwritten, in my opinion. But his essay seems to me a flagrant rationalization, possibly premised on his fear of his own passions."

Yes, we really did talk that way. Our dialogues were conducted in precise, formal English—with lapses on my part only. With Kathleen and her family, I spoke a different language, and sometimes words from that language cropped up during my lessons.

"The essay discusses the composition of 'The Raven,'" I said, "as if the poem were a mathematical problem. Poe maintains that he used a formula to determine his choices of length, and tone, and meter, and phrasing. But to me, his claim isn't credible. His 'formula' seems a desperate plea to be considered logical and reasoned, when in all likelihood he was anything but."

My father was smiling, now. "I'm glad to see that the essay provoked your interest to such an extent. Based on your reaction to 'Annabel Lee,' I'd anticipated something far less"—here he paused, as he sometimes did, as if trying to think of the most appropriate word; in fact, I think now, the pause was for emphasis and effect only—"far less *engaged.*"

I smiled back, the sort of scholarly half-grimace I'd learned from him—wry, tight-lipped, nothing like his rare, shy smile of genuine pleasure. "For me, Poe will remain a taste to be acquired," I said. "Or not."

"Or not." He interlaced his fingers. "I agree, of course, that the writing style is florid, even overblown. All those italics!" He shook his head. "As one of his fellow poets said, Poe was 'three-fifths genius and two-fifths fudge.'"

I smiled (a real smile) at that.

My father said, "Nonetheless, his mannerisms are designed to help the reader transcend the familiar, prosaic world. And for us, reading Poe provides a sort of comfort, I suppose."

He'd never before spoken of literature in such personal terms. I leaned forward. "Comfort?"

"Well." He seemed at a loss for words. "You see." His eyes closed briefly, and while they were shut, he said, "I suppose, one might say, he describes the way I sometimes feel." He opened his eyes.

"Florid?" I said. "Overblown?" He nodded. "If you feel that way, you certainly don't show it." Part of me was marveling: *My father is talking about his feelings?*

"I try not to," he said. "You know, for all practical purposes Poe was an orphan. His mother died when he was very young. He was taken in by John Allan's family, but never formally adopted. His life and his work exhibit classic symptoms of a bereaved child: an inability to accept the loss of a parent, a longing for reunion with the dead, a preference for imagination over reality.

"In short, Poe was one of us."

Our conversation ended abruptly when Mary Ellis Root knocked loudly at the library door. My father went outside to confer with her.

I felt on fire with so much unexpected information: *One of us?* My father was a "bereaved child" too?

But I learned no more about him that day. Whatever issue Root had brought upstairs carried him down to the basement with her. I wandered up to my bedroom, my mind spinning.

I thought of my father reading "Annabel Lee," and I

recalled Poe's words in "The Philosophy of Composition": "The death then of a beautiful woman is unquestionably the most poetical topic in the world, and equally is it beyond doubt that the lips best suited for such topic are those of a bereaved lover."

And I thought of Morella, my mother, and me.

Only a short time later, Kathleen telephoned. Her school year had begun, and I hadn't seen much of her since that last day at the racetrack. School was over for the day, she said, and she needed to see me.

We met in the belvedere at the foot of the back garden. I haven't mentioned that place before, have I? It was an open, six-sided structure with a small cupola and rotunda roof that mimicked the larger ones at the top of the house. Cushioned benches were its only furniture, and Kathleen and I had spent many afternoons sitting there, "hanging out," as she phrased it. Belvedere means "beautiful view," and ours was well named; it looked out at an ascending slope covered in vines and overgrown rosebushes, their dark crimson blossoms turning the air pink with perfume.

I was lying across one of the benches watching a dragonfly—a Common Green Darner, though it seemed anything but common as its translucent wings slowly pulsed the air— poised on a cornice, when Kathleen raced in, her hair flying free and her face pink from the bicycle ride. The air was humid, promising one of the thundershowers that punctuated many late summer afternoons.

She stared down at me, panting to catch her breath,

then began to laugh. "Look ... at ... you," she said between breaths. "Lady ... of ... leisure."

"And who are you?" I said, sitting up.

"I'm here to rescue you," she said. She pulled a plastic bag out of her jeans pocket, opened it, and handed me a small blue flannel bag on a string. It smelled strongly of lavender.

"Put it on," she said.

She wore a similar bag, strung around her neck.

"Why?" I asked. The dragonfly, I noticed, had flown away.

"For protection." She fell back against the cushions of the bench facing mine. "I've been doing some research, Ari. Do you know anything about herbal witchcraft?"

I didn't. But Kathleen had spent some time at the library, and now she was an expert. "I got the lavender from your garden and marigold from a neighbor," she said. "They'll protect you from evil. I put basil from my mother's kitchen in mine—spells work best if the herbs come from your own house. Oh, and the flannel? It's from an old pillowcase. But I sewed the bags with silk thread."

I was skeptical of all superstitions, but I didn't want to hurt her feelings. "It's very thoughtful of you," I said.

"Put it on," she said. Her eyes flashed at me.

I slid the string over my head.

She nodded vigorously. "Much better," she said. "Thank goodness. I don't sleep some nights, thinking of you. What if your father crept into your room some night and bit your neck?"

"That's ridiculous." The idea was too preposterous to make me angry.

She held up her hand. "I know that you love your father, Ari. But what if he can't control himself?"

"Thank you for worrying about me," I said, feeling she'd gone too far, "but your worry is misplaced."

She shook her head. "Promise me you'll wear it."

I planned to take it off the minute she left. To placate her, I'd wear it for now. At least it smelled good.

But I kept the amulet on—not because I feared my father, but because I wanted to please Kathleen, and the little bag of lavender was a token of her love for me. There, I've said it—*love*. What existed between my father and me was something else, involving intellectual discourse and mutual respect and familial obligation— none of which should ever be underestimated—but love? If we felt it, we never used the word.

— Four —

Only when you look directly at a thing, can you truly see it. Most people go through life unaware of the limitations of their eyes. But you will never be among them.

Focus on the word *pine* in this sentence. At the same time, try to read the other words to the right and the left. You may be able to decipher *word* and *in this*, depending on how far the page is from your eyes. But *pine* will be the clearest, since the center of your field of vision is directed at it.

That center is called the fovea, and it's the part of the eye where cones are most tightly packed together. The fovea occupies roughly the same percentage of your eye as the moon occupies the night sky.

Everything else is peripheral vision. Peripheral vision is

effective in detecting motion, and it helps locate predators in the dark. Animals have a much stronger sense of peripheral vision than humans. Vampires fall somewhere in between.

From the corner of my eye, I sensed motion. But I saw no one, when I turned to look.

It was a gray morning in early October, and I was in my room upstairs, getting dressed for the day. Even though I'd be seeing no one but Mrs. McG and my father—and perhaps Dennis, if he ventured out of the basement—I took trouble with my appearance, and I'll admit to spending long minutes before the mirror, admiring myself. That summer my hair had grown rapidly, nearly halfway to my waist, and it had developed a slight wave. My body had changed as well—I felt embarrassed by it, to be honest. Even my lips seemed fuller, more womanly. Perhaps I should note here: my mirror image was wavering, indistinct—as if it I were viewing it peripherally. It had always been that way. I knew from reading the term "mirror image" in books that reflections were ordinarily clearer, more distinct; mine wasn't, but then all the mirrors in our house were old. I blamed the mirrors.

When my skin began to tingle, I turned around again. No one was there.

Dennis returned from Japan one night, and his jovial careless vitality enlivened the house. I'd been seeing less of Kathleen since her school resumed; she'd made new friends among her fellow eighth-graders, and although she telephoned once or twice a week, I sensed distance grow-ing between us. Spending time alone didn't feel as natural to me as it once had, and for days now I'd been feeling rather listless.

Dennis had walked into the living room, wearing a wrinkled suit that smelled faintly of alcohol and perspira-tion, his face ruddy, eyes bloodshot. My father sat in his usual chair, sipping Picardo, reading. My father, I realized, did not smell. He had no odor whatsoever. His face never flushed, his eyes were never streaked with red. His hands, the few times when mine had brushed against them, were cool, while Dennis seemed to radiate heat.

Dennis took one look at me and said, "Wow."

My father said, "Meaning?"

"Meaning that Miss Ariella has grown up just in the month I was away." Dennis bent to squeeze my shoulders. "It must be all that bike riding, Ari. Am I right?"

I hugged him back. "Obviously the bike riding," I said. "You could use a little of that yourself, am I right?"

He patted his stomach lightly. "The middle-age spread continues," he said, "aided and abetted by exotic cuisine and some fine Japanese beer."

Dennis was in his early forties at that time, and his face and body had creases that my father's entirely lacked.

"How was Japan?" I asked.

"Japan was fantastic," he said. "But the work didn't go quite as we'd hoped."

"What exactly were you working on?"

Dennis looked at my father.

After a moment's silence, my father said, "We're conducting some research into a class of compounds known as perfluorocarbons."

I must have appeared puzzled. "We're attempting to emulsify them," he went on, "to enable them to carry oxygen."

Normally I would have asked a hundred more questions, but this level of technical detail was beyond me. All I said was, "How nice."

Dennis changed the subject abruptly. "Tell me, Ari. What's that thing around your neck?"

I pulled the little flannel bag away from my neck for him to inspect. "It's lavender. It's meant to bring me good luck."

My father said, without emotion, "I had no idea that you were superstitious."

For weeks I'd been hoping that my father would resume our conversation about Poe and bereavement, but he always directed our lessons elsewhere. I'd arrive at the library armed with two or three provocative remarks guaranteed to re-engage him in personal revelations. Within seconds we'd be deep in a very different conversation—about Alexis de Tocqueville or John Dalton or Charles Dickens. An hour or so after lessons ended, I'd remember my resolve and marvel at his ability to deflect it. At times I was convinced that he hypnotized me. Other times, I realized later, he distracted me by extended metaphors; he launched into them easily, spinning them as he spoke.

"In *Hard Times*, Louisa looks into fire and contemplates

her future," he said one afternoon. "She imagines herself spun by 'Old Time, that greatest and longest-established Spinner of all,' but acknowledges that 'his factory is a secret place, his work is noiseless, and his Hands are mutes.' But if his factory is secret, his work and hands are mute, how does she know Old Time? How indeed do any of us know time, except through our imagining it?"

He seemed to have made an extended metaphor of an extended metaphor. *Was there a special name for that?* I wondered. *Perhaps metametaphor?*

Sometimes he made my head ache.

Nonetheless I was a persistent student. Finding out something, anything, about my parents and their past seemed far more important than Dalton or Dickens. So I concocted a plan.

On a Wednesday afternoon, when Dennis was scheduled to lead me through a zoological lesson focusing on eukaryotic cells and DNA, I said that I had a related topic to discuss: hematophagy.

Dennis said, "Oh yeah?" He gave me a quizzical look.

"Yeah," I said—a word I'd never use around my father. Dennis's teaching style was considerably more relaxed.

"I read about it at the library," I said. "You know, animals who drink blood. Like worms and bats and leeches."

Dennis opened his mouth to interrupt, but I pressed on. "The encyclopedia said hematophagy has two classifications: obligatory and optional. Some animals feed only on blood, while others supplement blood with additional fluids. What I need to know is—"

Here I hesitated, not sure how to proceed. *I need to know what sort my father is,* I thought. *I need to know if hematophagy is hereditary.*

Dennis put up his right hand—the gesture he'd used to signal me to stop when he taught me to ride a bicycle. "That's a topic you'll want to broach with your father," he said. "He's worked with leeches and such. In that area, he's the expert."

In frustration I raked my hands through my hair—and I noticed how closely Dennis watched me. He noticed me noticing him, and his face reddened.

"Ari, what have you been up to while I was away?" he said.

"I had my first kiss." My words weren't planned.

Dennis tried to smile. It was a little painful to watch. He clearly felt uncomfortable, but he wanted to hide his feelings.

"I know that you're growing up, and that you have questions," he said, sounding exactly like my father.

"Don't talk down to me," I said. "You're my friend—at least I always thought so."

He blushed again. "I'm your fine freckled friend." But his voice sounded doubtful.

"Please," I said. "Tell me something. Tell me something solid."

His face resumed its normal easygoing expression. "Let me tell you about Seradrone, about our research."

He talked about the growing need for artificial blood, as fewer people are willing to volunteer as donors. Although Seradrone had produced blood supplements, so far neither they or anyone else had been able to develop a clinically effective blood substitute.

"We thought we were onto a breakthrough," he said. "Unfortunately, what our studies in Japan showed was the potential for retention in the reticuloendothelial system."

I put up my hand, to stop him. "You've lost me."

He apologized. It was enough for me to know that the promise of perfluorocarbons had proven rather limited, he said. "Now we're back to looking at hemoglobin-based oxygen carriers—and so far none of them can replace whole blood, either; they merely supplement it."

I didn't want to ask any more questions. He'd told me more than I could understand.

Again, he was watching me closely. "Let's schedule a checkup for you tomorrow," he said. "You look pale."

The next day Dennis took a blood sample from me and ran some tests on it. He later re-emerged from the basement with a large brown bottle in one hand and a foil packet and a hypodermic needle in the other. He said that the test hadn't been conclusive for lupus. But I was anemic, he said, and I should take a tablespoon of tonic twice a day.

After he handed me the bottle, I unscrewed its top and sniffed. "Yuck," I said.

"Take it with a large glass of water," he said. Then he opened the packet, removed a swab, cleaned my skin, and gave me an injection. I asked him what it contained, and he said it was a hormone, erythropoietin. He said it would bolster my red blood count. I did feel a surge of energy afterward.

Later I remembered what Dennis had said: the test hadn't been conclusive for lupus. But hadn't my father told Mrs. McG that there was no blood test for lupus?

The following morning I got into trouble at the library.

On a rare October morning without rain. I'd ridden my bike downtown to use the computer. Why should I pester my father about hematophagy? He'd only change the subject.

It took me all of a minute to find a link to "human hematophagy," and two more to learn that many humans drink blood. African Masai, for instance, subsist largely on cow blood mixed with milk. The Moche society and the Scythians indulged in ritualistic blood-drinking. And stories of human vampirism were abundant, although whether they were fact or fiction was a matter of fierce Internet debate.

My next link took me to a series of sites related to "Real Vampires." These sites described some of the differences between the vampires of folklore and fiction, and those of contemporary reality. The sites disagreed about whether real vampires were dependent on drinking blood, about whether vampires could "evolve," about whether they could bear children, and if they could, whether the children would be vampires. In short, they didn't offer me any real answers.

One article by someone called Inanna Arthen concluded: "Furthermore, this article is not intended to mislead—real vampires, even evolved ones, do sometimes drink blood in order to obtain their energy. Those who understand the many ways that life 'gives way' to nurture more life will see this as no more unnatural than eating live vegetables or animals for food."

I was musing about this when the librarian put her hand on my shoulder. "Why aren't you in school?" she asked. She was an older woman with wrinkled skin. I wondered how long she'd been standing there.

"I'm home-schooled," I said.

She didn't seem convinced. "Do your parents know that you're here?"

I thought of telling her the truth: my mornings were my time in which to study as I pleased, before I met with my father after lunch. For some reason, I didn't think she'd believe me. So I said, "Of course."

"What's your home telephone number?" she asked. And like a fool, I told her.

Next thing she was talking to my father. While we waited for him to arrive, she had me sit on a chair before her desk. "I've seen you in here many times," she said. "Are you always Googling vampires?"

Like a complete idiot, I smiled. "I find them interesting," I said brightly.

I must confess that when my father finally swept into the library, his long black coat buttoned to the chin and black hat pulled almost to his eyes, the librarian's reaction was something to see. Her mouth dropped open, and she let us leave without saying another word.

But on the drive home, my father said plenty, ending with: "—and so you have managed to disrupt an important experiment, whose results may now be compromised, and for what? To annoy a librarian with questions about *vampires*?" But his voice held no emotion; only his choice of words, and the slightly lower tone of *vampires*, let me know that he was angry.

"I never asked her questions," I said. "I was trying to do some research on the computer."

He didn't say more until we were back home, and he'd put the car away. Then he came into the front hallway and began to unwind the scarf from his neck. "I suppose it's time we talked"—he paused to remove his coat—"about giving you your own computer."

By the time Kathleen called a few nights later, I was the proud owner of a sleek white laptop with a wireless Internet connection. I told her the story of its acquisition; it was rare that I had anything interesting to talk about lately, and perhaps that's why her calls had grown infrequent.

Kathleen responded to the tale of the evil librarian with appropriate "You did not!"s and "Really?"s. "You should have lied," she said when I'd finished. "You could have given her the wrong phone number. You could have given her our number, since nobody's at home during the days."

I admitted that I hadn't been clever with the librarian.

"But it all worked out," Kathleen said. "Your dad's not mad— he bought you your own computer. You're so lucky."

I didn't think luck was a factor, but I kept quiet. The computer, it occurred to me, was a convenient means for my father to avoid answering my questions. He seemed to want me to find the answers on my own.

* * *

It was around this time that I attended my first dance.

Michael telephoned (for the first time ever) to invite me, and he sounded nervous. "It's just a dance," he said, sounding needlessly argumentative. "It's the stupid school Halloween dance."

Halloween was not celebrated at our house. Every October 31, Root pulled all the window shades and locked the door. No one responded to the occasional pounding of the door knocker. Instead, my father and I sat in the living room playing cards or board games. (When I was younger, we'd also played with a *Meccano* set, which we used to build a machine that moved pencils from one end of the dining room table to the other.)

We were particularly fond of *Cluedo*, which we played in rapid games never lasting more than three turns each; at the McGarritts, I learned that others took much longer to solve the crimes.

I told Michael I'd have to ask my father's permission. When I did, my father surprised me. "It's your decision," he said. "It's your *life*." Then he turned back to his reading, as if I weren't there.

Kathleen found time to talk to me about what to expect at the dance. She said she was busy after school most days with rehearsals for a class play and with flute lessons. But as it happened, she would be free on Wednesday after school, and we could meet downtown at the thrift store to hunt for costumes.

I was examining a rack of dresses when she rushed in. She'd had her hair cut so that when she stopped moving, it fell to frame her face. "You look cool!" she said to me, and I said, "So do you."

But I thought that the Kathleen who met me at the thrift store wore too much makeup. Her eyes were rimmed with kohl, and her hair had been dyed black; it was darker than mine. "You've changed," I said.

She seemed pleased to hear me say it. "My new look," she said, lifting her hair to show me her ears. Silver hoops and studs punctured her lobes and upper ears—I counted seven on each ear.

We hadn't met for nearly two months, and I'd begun to think our friendship was at an end. But her eyes glistened with affection.

"I have so much to tell you," she said.

We worked our way through the clothes, pulling out hangers, nodding or grimacing, as she talked. The smell of mothballs, stale perfume, and sweat was intense, but some-how not unpleasant.

The news from the McG house wasn't all good. Bridget had developed asthma, and her wheezing kept Kathleen awake some nights. Mr. McG was being treated badly by the local supermarket where he worked; they made him work weekends now, because someone else had quit. And Mrs. McG acted "all worried" about Michael.

"Why?" I asked.

"That's right, you haven't seen him lately." Kathleen shook a pink satin dress, then shoved it back into the rack again. "He's let his hair grow, and he's got into some trouble at school. He's developed a major attitude."

I wasn't sure what that meant. "Do you mean he's a bully?"

"Michael a bully?" She laughed. "No, more kind of un-cooperative and intense. He's reading about politics a lot. He acts mad most of the time."

That could be interesting, I thought. "What's he wearing to the dance?"

"Who knows?" She pulled out a tight-fitting black sequined dress. "You are so trying this one on."

I ended up wearing that dress. Kathleen found one in red satin, v-necked front and back. She said we should wear masks, but I preferred not to.

On Halloween night, Michael showed up at our front door wearing black jeans and a black t-shirt with the word ANARCHY painted across it. He didn't wear a mask, either. We looked at each other with relief.

His hair had grown past his shoulders, and he was thinner than I remembered. His dark eyes seemed larger and his face smaller. We stayed in the doorway examining each other, not saying a word.

Some movement behind me made me turn around. My father stood by the wall, watching us; on his face was an expression of utter revulsion. I'd never seen that face before. His eyes and mouth turned downward at their corners; his shoulders pulled back, rigid, and his chin jutted forward. I said something inane ("Hello?"), and he twitched—an odd spasm that briefly convulsed his face and chest. I must have blinked, I thought then, because he suddenly wasn't there.

When I turned back to Michael, his eyes were still fixed on me. "You look," he said, "different."

Michael drove us to the school.

In the backseat, Kathleen and her friend Ryan, a short, blondhaired boy I'd met the previous summer, talked incessantly, often at the same time. Ryan wore a devil's mask.

"Bridget whined all through dinner. She really wanted to come tonight," Kathleen said from the backseat. "She felt she deserved it. This afternoon, when the school held the Halloween parade, she won a prize for best ghoul."

Kathleen said that some parents had wanted to cancel the school's Halloween events, claiming that they celebrated Satan. She and Ryan laughed loudly at that.

"It's all my work," Ryan said in a raspy voice, stroking the horns of his mask.

Michael and I didn't say much. Sitting next to him excited me. I stole glances at his hands on the steering wheel, at his long legs.

I noticed that Kathleen had put on plenty of makeup; her face was white, her eyes were ringed with black, but somehow tonight the makeup made her look younger. I felt I looked much older. The black sequins outlined my body, showing the world a self I'd barely glimpsed before. The previous night, I'd had fantasies of sweeping across a dance floor, enthralling everyone in the room with my presence. The fantasies seemed possible, now.

The dance was held in the school gymnasium, and an enormous statue of Jesus, arms outstretched, welcomed us. As we walked in, everyone did seem to watch us. Michael and I didn't look at each other.

The room was hot, and the smells of the people in it were overwhelming. It was as if every scent Kathleen and I had ever sampled at the pharmacy—the shampoos, the deodorants, the colognes, the soaps—simmered in the dimly lit room. I took shallow breaths, afraid that I might faint if I inhaled more deeply.

Michael steered me toward a row of folding chairs against one wall. "Sit here," he said. "I'll get us some food."

The music boomed from enormous black speakers set in the corners of the gym. The sound was too distorted for me to discern a tune or lyrics. Kathleen and Ryan were already gyrating on the dance floor. Kathleen's dress picked up the ever-changing glow from a color wheel on the ceiling. The fabric looked as if it were on fire, then doused by blue water, then engulfed again by yellow and red flames.

Michael came back with two paper plates and handed them both to me. "I'll get us drinks," he said, shouting slightly to be heard over the music. He went away again.

I set the plates on the chair next to me. Then I began to look around. Everyone in the room—even the teachers and chaperones— was disguised. Their costumes ranged from the hideous (Cyclops, demons, mummies, zombies, and other assorted freaks, sporting gashes and gouges and severed limbs) to the ethereal (fairies, princesses, goddesses of all sorts draped in shimmering fabric). Two boys with scars and blood etched on their faces stared at me.

They all looked terribly eager and naïve. Again, I was glad that Michael and I hadn't worn masks.

By the time he returned, I felt well enough to take a bite of the pizza he'd brought. A mistake, as it turned out.

The food in my mouth tasted strong and bittersweet, like nothing I'd ever eaten before. I swallowed it as quickly as I could and at once felt a swell of nausea. My face burned. I dropped the plate and ran toward the door, and I managed to make it to the edge of the parking lot before I fell to my knees and vomited.

When I'd stopped heaving, I heard someone laughing— a mean-sounding laugh—not far away. A few seconds later, I heard voices.

"What was it?" Kathleen was saying.

Michael said, "Pizza. Just pizza."

"The pizza has sausage on it," Kathleen said. "You should have known better."

She knelt beside me and handed me tissues, and I dried my face and mouth with them.

Later, Michael sat with me on the cold grass and said he was sorry.

I shook my head. "Normally I would have noticed the sausage. But it was dark, and all the smells confused me."

Michael hadn't seemed at all "grossed out," as Kathleen would have phrased it, by my nausea. "I should be the one apologizing to you," I said.

He put his hand awkwardly on my shoulder, then took it

away. "Ari, you don't need to apologize to me," he said. "Not ever."

And later that night, after I'd cried a little in bed about the disappointments of the evening, Michael's words came back to me and gave me unexpected comfort. But I wished I had someone to tell about the evening. I wished I had a mother.

"You said Poe was 'one of us.'"

Next day we sat as usual in the library. My father wore a dark suit that made his eyes seem indigo blue. I felt light-headed, but otherwise well. We didn't talk about the dance.

My father opened a book of T. S. Eliot's poetry. "Back to Poe, are we? Does that mean you've acquired the taste?"

I opened my mouth to reply and closed it without speaking. He would not deflect me today. "'One of us,' you said. Did you mean that in the sense of being a bereaved child? Or in the sense of being a *vampire*?"

There, I'd said it. For a moment the word seemed to hang suspended in the air between us—I could see the letters, floating and twisting like crimson dust motes.

My father tilted his head back and gave me a long look. His pupils seemed to dilate. "Oh, Ari." His voice was dry. "You know the answer already."

"I know the answer?" I felt like a puppet, responding on cue.

"Your mind is a fine one," he said, not pausing long enough to let me bask. "But it seems more comfortable with the prosaic than the profound." He laced his fingers.

"Whether we read Poe or Plutarch or Plotinus, we find meaning not on the surface, but in the depths of the work. The function of knowledge is to transcend earthly experience, not to wallow in it. And so, when you ask me simple questions, you're limiting yourself to the most obvious answers—ones you already know."

I shook my head. "I don't understand."

He nodded. "Yes, you do."

Someone began to bang on the library door. Then it opened, and Mary Ellis Root's ugly face appeared. She looked dismissively at me. "You're wanted," she said to my father.

Then I did something I hadn't planned, something I'd never even imagined. I ran to the door and slammed it shut.

My father stayed in his chair. He didn't even look surprised.

"Ari," he said. "Be patient. When the time is right, you'll understand."

Then he rose and left the room, closing the door so lightly that it didn't make a sound.

I went to the window. The Green Cross courier van was in the driveway, its engine idling. I watched as the driver carried boxes out of the basement and loaded them into the van.

— Five —

Do you ever have the sense that your mind is at war with itself?

Dennis had taught me about the brain stem—the oldest, smallest region in the human brain, lying at the base of your skull. It's sometimes called the "lizard brain," or "reptilian brain," because it's similar to the brains of reptiles; it governs our most primitive functions—breathing and heartbeat—and the base emotions of love, hate, fear, lust. The lizard brain reacts instinctively, irrationally, to ensure our survival.

Slamming the door in the face of Root? That was my reptile brain at work. Yet, I was ready to argue, it was provoked by a rational desire for knowledge—a desire that my father had dismissed as "prosaic."

I spent the morning trying to read the poetry of T. S. Eliot with half my mind, the other half struggling to understand what my father had told me and why I needed to know it.

* * *

After lessons that day, my father went down to the basement, and I headed upstairs. In my room, I avoided the mirror. I looked suspiciously at the bottle of tonic on my dresser and wondered at its contents. I sensed the presence of an *other* in the next room, and I told it to leave me alone. I picked up the telephone to call Kathleen and put it down again.

Then I called the same number and asked for Michael instead.

Michael picked me up in his father's old car, and we headed west. For half an hour or so we drove aimlessly, talking. Michael's hair looked even longer than on Halloween, and he wore old jeans and a black t-shirt under a moth-eaten sweater. I thought he looked wonderful.

Michael said he hated school. He hated America, too, but he also loved it. He talked on and on about politics, and I nodded from time to time, secretly a little bored. He handed me a paperback copy of *On the Road* by Jack Kerouac and said I must read it.

Finally he pulled the car into an old cemetery, the Gideon Putnam. "This place is supposed to be haunted," he said.

I looked out the car window. It was a bleak November day, the sky an opaque mass of gray clouds. The cemetery grounds were covered in dead leaves, interrupted by mausoleums, crosses, and statues. An obelisk served as monument for one grave, and I wondered idly who might be buried under such an imposing object. Who chose burial monuments? Were the wishes of the deceased taken into consideration? It was a subject I'd never considered before, and I was about to ask Michael's opinion when he leaned over and kissed me.

We'd had kisses before, of course. But today his lips felt unusually warm, and he held me harder and closer. It's not easy describing kisses without sounding soppy or stupid. What I want to convey is that this kiss was important. It left me feeling out of breath and dizzy (another stupid word, one that I use too often). When he initiated a second kiss, I had to pull away. "I can't," I said. "I can't."

He looked at me as if he understood. I didn't know why I'd said it, actually. But he held me not so tightly for a minute or so until we'd both calmed down.

He said, "I love you, Ari. I love you and I want you. I don't want anyone else to have you."

From reading, I knew that the first time someone declares love is meant to be special, almost magical. But in my head, a voice (not my own) was saying, "Ari, the whole world is going to have you."

"Someone is watching me," I told my father the next day.

He was wearing a particularly beautiful shirt, the color of smoke, with black enamel buttons and onyx cuff-links. It made his eyes seem gray.

He looked up from the physics book he'd opened, and his gray eyes looked shy, almost embarrassed, as if he'd heard my thought. "Someone is watching you," he said. "Do you know who it is?"

I shook my head. "Do you?"

"No," he said. "Are you able to define chromism and

isomerization?" In this way he changed the subject, or so I thought at the time.

The next morning I awoke from another crossword-puzzle dream with two clues—"sea cow" (seven letters) and "snakebird" (seven letters). I shook my head, trying to recover the grid, but I couldn't visualize it. So I dressed and went down for breakfast with a familiar sense of frustration at the limits of my intelligence.

For weeks I'd noticed that Mrs. McG seemed distracted. The morning oatmeal was more burnt than usual, and the evening casseroles some nights were inedible.

That morning, as she was taking a saucepan of oatmeal from the stove, she dropped it. The pan hit and bounced, and the glutinous cereal splatted against the linoleum and spattered her shoes. Aside from a quick inward breath, she barely reacted. She simply went to the sink and came back with towels.

"I'll help," I said, feeling guilty at my glee that I wouldn't have to eat the stuff.

She sat back on her heels and looked up at me. "Ari," she said, "I do need your help. But not with this."

She cleaned up the mess and came to sit with me at the kitchen table. "Why don't you spend time with Kathleen these days?" she said.

"She's too busy," I said. "With school stuff—you know, the play, and the band, and all."

Mrs. McG shook her head. "She dropped out of the play," she said. "And she quit her flute lessons. She's even stopped nagging me to buy her a mobile phone. She's changed, and she makes me worry."

I hadn't seen Kathleen since Halloween. "I'm sorry," I said. "I didn't know."

"I wish you would call her." Her hands scratched her forearms, on which I noticed a reddish rash. "I wish you'd come and spend the night. Maybe this weekend?"

I agreed to give Kathleen a call.

"Mrs. McG, have you ever seen a photo of my mother?" I hadn't planned to ask that question, but it was something I'd been thinking about.

"No, I never have," she said slowly. "But there might be something in the attic. That's where they put all her things. When I first started working here, Miss Root and Dennis were gathering them up for storage."

"What sorts of things?"

"Clothing and books, mostly. Your mother apparently was quite a reader."

"What sorts of books?"

"Oh, I don't know." She pushed her chair back away from the table. "You might want to ask your father about that."

I excused myself and headed upstairs. The staircase to the third storey was uncarpeted, and my footsteps sounded loud as I went up. But the attic door was locked.

So I went on up the final set of stairs, the air growing colder with each step. The top of the house was uninviting, always too hot or too cold, but today the cold didn't bother me.

Inside the cupola, I sat on a tall stool set before the oculus window—my round eye on the world—and looked out, over the rooftops of our neighbors and across the gray sky into the blue beyond. Beyond the houses, beyond the city of Saratoga Springs, lay a vast world, waiting to be explored.

I thought of the great-grandmother in *The Princess and the Goblin*, who lived in a rose-scented, transparent-walled room lit by its own moon, set high above the world. She gave her great-granddaughter, the Princess, a ball of invisible thread that led her out of peril, away from the goblins, back to the rose-scented room.

Like me, the Princess had lost her mother. But she had the thread.

"Do you ever dream crossword puzzles?" I asked my father when we met later that day.

For a second his face froze—the numb expression it normally wore when I tried to talk about my mother.

I answered my own question. "She did, didn't she? My mother. She dreamed crosswords."

"She did." He said such dreams were signs of an "overactive mind." He advised that I massage my feet lightly before retiring.

And then he launched into another physics lesson.

We were deep in a discussion of electromagnetic radiation phenomena when someone knocked on the door, then opened it slightly. Root's ugly face appeared in the crack.

"The delivery man needs to talk to you," she said. She kept her eyes on my father, not even glancing at me.

"Excuse me, Ari." My father rose and left the room.

When he didn't return, I went to the window and pushed aside its heavy drapes. A black car was parked in the yard near the house's rear entrance. On its side were the words "Sullivan Family Funeral Home."

About ten minutes passed before I heard the door open again. I was standing before a brass-framed oval Victorian shadowbox that hung on the wall. Inside it, encapsulated for eternity, were three brown wrens, a monarch butterfly, and two sheaves of wheat. But I wasn't looking at them—I was studying my wavy reflection in the convex glass that held them in.

Root's voice came from behind me. "He says to tell you he won't be back today," she said. "He says he's *sorry*."

As I turned around I thought that I should apologize to her, but her tone of voice was so contemptuous that I knew I never would. "Why can't he come back?" I asked.

"He's needed downstairs." Her breathing made a raspy sound.

"Why? For what?"

Her small black eyes flashed at me. "That's Seradrone's business. Why do you ask so many questions? Don't you realize the trouble you cause?" She moved toward the door, but as she opened it, she turned her head. "And why waste your time looking at your reflection? *You* know who you are."

She slammed the door as she left. For a moment I fantasized about going after her, yanking her chin hairs, slapping her—or doing something worse.

Instead, I went upstairs and called Kathleen.

"My school has been cancelled today," I told her.

*   *   *

As I pushed my bicycle along the gravel driveway that led from the garage to the street, I noticed that the car from the funeral home was gone. Perhaps my father was on his way upstairs again. I hesitated, but decided to press on. Kathleen was waiting for me.

It was a dull day in mid-November, the smell of dead leaves in the air. As I rode through the streets, the wind stung my face. Soon we would have snow, and the bicycle would stay in the garage until April, or even May.

As soon as I entered the soda shop I saw her, sitting in a booth. She wore a black sweater and black pants, and she was drinking coffee. I sat down and ordered a cola.

"That's an interesting necklace," I said. A round silver pendant hung from a silk cord, next to the flannel bag of herbs.

"It's a pentacle," she said. "Ari, I have to tell you. I've become a pagan."

The server brought my soda. I unwrapped the straw slowly, not sure what to say. "That could mean several things," I said finally.

Kathleen ran her hands through her hair. Her fingernails were painted black, and her hair looked freshly dyed. Next to her, in my fleece jacket and jeans, I felt dull and ordinary.

"We practice spells," she said. "And we're into role-playing."

I had no idea what role-playing meant. "Is that why your mother is worried about you?"

"My mother!" Kathleen shook her head. "She's impossible lately. She really doesn't have a clue." She took a long sip of coffee, which also was black.

I couldn't drink that stuff, and I watched her with awe.

"She found one of my notebooks and got all alarmed about it."

Kathleen reached into a battered backpack on the seat next to her, and pulled out a spiral notebook with a black cover. She opened it, and slid it across the table to me.

Under the heading *Magick Chants* was written what looked like poetry.

> *Oh, do not tell the Priest of our Art,*
> *Or he would call it sin;*
> *But we shall be out in the woods all night,*
> *A conjuring summer in!*

And on the next page:

> *When Misfortune is enow, wear the Blue*
> *Star on thy brow.*
> *True in Love ever be, Unless thy Lover be*
> *false to thee.*

I knew better than to ask what it meant. My father had taught me that one never asks what poetry means.

"I don't see anything so worrisome in that," I said.

"Of course not." Kathleen gave a withering look at the seat next to me, apparently imagining her mother sitting there. "It's really cool stuff. You'll see. We're going over to Ryan's house to do some role-playing."

"We are?" I said. "When?"

"Now," she said.

We left our bikes in the rack outside the soda shop and walked to Ryan's house, a few blocks away. It was a small shabby house, very like the McGarritts' place, but a new-looking greenhouse had been attached to one side. We paused for a moment to peer through the steamed-up glass walls, but saw only vague green shapes and purplish overhead lights through the condensation-beaded panes.

"Ryan's dad's hobby is growing orchids," Kathleen said. "He sells them to those rich old women on the other side of town. They even have an orchid club."

Ryan answered the doorbell. His short blond hair had been spiked with some sort of hair gel. Like Kathleen, he wore black. "Merry meet," he said.

"Merry meet," Kathleen said.

I said, "Hello."

Inside, all the lights were off, and candles burned on every available surface. Four people reclined on floor cushions; I recognized two from the dance. Michael was not among them.

"Who did you bring?" someone asked Kathleen.

"This is Ari," she said. "I thought the game needed some fresh blood."

The next hour seemed interminable to me, thanks to an interminable amount of dice-rolling, paced movements around the room, and shouts: "Vanquish!" or "My invisibility is almost depleted!" or "Regenerate!" or "My rage is empty!"

Two of the boys played werewolves (they had the letter *W* taped to their shirts), and the rest were vampires (wearing black t-shirts and rubber fangs). I was the only "mortal" in the room. Because it was my first time, they advised me to watch rather than play—and I sensed that they liked having an audience.

Nearly everything they said and pretended to do was consistent with what the Internet said about vampires. They shuddered at the sight of a crucifix; they turned into imaginary bats at will; they "flew"; and they used their virtual powers of agility and strength to scale imaginary walls and jump imaginary rooftops—all within a fifteen-by-twenty-foot living room.

They moved through the alleyways of an imaginary city, picking up cards representing coins and special tools and weapons, feigning at fighting and biting while barely touching. In fact, all five of the boys struck me as shy by nature, overacting in their attempts to socialize. Besides me, Kathleen was the only other woman present, and she moved around the room aggressively, as if she owned it. At times the others tried to gang up on her, and she fended them off almost effortlessly. She knew the most spells, and apparently she had the most detailed notebook.

Occasionally the players robbed one another and deposited their stolen coins in imaginary banks—ever the good capitalists, I thought. The game centered less on fantasy than on greed and domination.

The room's air grew stale with the intensity of their efforts and with the noxious smells of their orange-colored snack foods. I stood it as long as I could. Finally, claustrophobia and boredom drove me out of the room. I went through the kitchen, visited the bathroom, then followed a corridor that ended at a thick door with a glass window: the entrance to the greenhouse.

Once I opened the door, humid air washed over me, carrying a lush scent of vegetation. On table after table, potted orchids seemed to nod slightly in breezes generated by the slow revolutions of ceiling fans. The violet-tinged overhead lights made me a little dizzy, so I made sure not to stand directly beneath them. They turned the colors of the blooms luminous: deep violets and magentas, ivories veined in palest pink, yellows spotted with amber—all vivid against deep green foliage. Some orchids looked like tiny faces, with eyes and mouths, and I walked down the aisles, greeting them: "Hello, Ultraviolet. Bon soir, Banana."

At last, I thought, *an escape from the gray winter of Saratoga Springs. Ryan's father should charge admission.* As I breathed, the humid air circulated through my body, making me relaxed, almost drowsy.

Then the door swung open. A heavyset, freckled boy in black strode in. "Mortal, I am here to sire you," he said, his voice quavering. He opened his mouth to reveal fake fangs.

"I don't think so," I said.

I stared into his eyes—small and dark, but somewhat magnified by his eyeglasses—and held them steady.

He stared back. He didn't move. For a while I looked at him, at his reddened face, at the two nascent pimples eager to erupt on his chin. Nothing about him moved, and

I wondered if I'd hypnotized him. "Get me a glass of water," I said.

He turned and lumbered off toward the kitchen. As the door swung open, I heard the sounds of the others, biting and shouting, and as it shut I savored the tropical solitude, the only sound a slow dripping of water from a place I couldn't see. For a moment I entertained myself by imagining turning the tables on the boy—biting his throat amid the orchids. And, I confess, something like lust stirred in me.

A minute later the door opened again and the boy came back, a glass of water in his hand.

I drank it slowly, then handed him the empty glass. "Thank you," I said. "You're free to go now."

He blinked. He sighed a few times. Then he walked away.

As he opened the door, Kathleen pushed her way past him, into the greenhouse. "What was all *that* about?"

She must have been watching through the door's window. I felt embarrassed, but I wasn't sure why.

"I was thirsty," I said.

It was already dark when I left the game. Kathleen had run out of powers and was lying on a sofa while Ryan and the others stood over her, chanting, "Death! Death!" I waved goodbye, but I don't think she saw me.

I walked alone to the soda shop, unlocked my bike, and headed for home. Cars passed me, and once a teenaged boy shouted "Babe!" from a car window. Such things had happened before, and Kathleen advised me to "simply ignore them." But the shout distracted me enough to make my bike wobble and skid on the wet leaves, and it took effort to regain control. Out of vanity I wasn't wearing the bike helmet my father had bought, and as I pedaled on it occurred to me that I might have hurt myself.

After I put the bike away in the garage, I paused a moment and looked at the tall, graceful silhouette of the house, its left side traced by a woody vine. Behind those lighted windows were the familiar rooms of my childhood, and in one of them I'd find my father, no doubt sitting in his leather chair, reading. He might be thus forever, and the thought comforted me. Then, unbidden, a second thought struck me: he might be there forever—but what about me?

I recall vividly the smell of woodsmoke in the cold air as I stood, watching the house, wondering if I was, after all, mortal.

I looked up from a dish of milky macaroni and cheese. "Father?" I asked. "Am I going to die?"

He sat across from me, gazing at the food with visible disgust. "Possibly," he said. "Particularly if you don't wear your bicycle helmet."

I'd told him about the close call I'd had on the way home. "Seriously," I said. "If I had fallen and hit my head, would I be dead now?"

"Ari, I don't know." He reached across the table for a silver cocktail shaker, and poured himself a second drink. "So far you've recovered from the minor scrapes, yes? And that sunburn last summer—you were over that in a week, as

I recall. You've been fortunate not to have any more serious health issues so far. That might change, of course."

"Of course." For the first time, I felt jealous of him.

Later that night, while we were reading in the living room, I found I had another question. "Father, how does hypnosis work?"

He picked up his bookmark (shaped like a silver feather) and inserted it into the novel he was reading—I think it was *Anna Karenina*, because not long afterward he urged me to read it, too.

"It's all about dissociation," he said. "One person focuses intently on the words or eyes of another, until his behavioral control is split off from his ordinary awareness. If the person is highly suggestible, he will behave as the other prescribes."

I wondered how far I could have taken the boy in the greenhouse. "Is it true that you can't make someone do something they don't want to?"

"That's a matter of considerable debate," he said. "The most recent research suggests that under the right circumstances, a suggestible person can be made to do almost anything." He looked across at me, his eyes amused, as if he knew what I'd been up to.

And so I changed my focus. "Did you ever hypnotize me?"

"Yes, of course," he said. "Don't you remember?"

"No." I wasn't sure I liked the idea of anyone controlling my behavior.

"Sometimes, when you were very young, you had a tendency to cry." His voice was low and quiet, and it paused after the word *cry*. "For no apparent reason, you would make the most unearthly sounds, and of course I tried to placate you with formula, with rocking, with lullabies, and everything else I could think of."

"You *sang* to me?" I'd never heard my father sing, or so I thought.

"You truly don't remember?" His face was wistful. "I wonder why you don't. In any case, yes, I did sing, and sometimes even that had no effect. And so, one night out of sheer desperation, I looked steadily into your eyes, and with my eyes I told you to be at peace. I told you that you were safe, and cared for, and that you should be content.

"And you stopped crying then. Your eyes closed. I held you. You were so small, wrapped in a white blanket." He closed his eyes for a moment. "I held you close to my chest, and I listened to your breathing, until morning."

I had an impulse to get up from my chair and embrace him. But I sat still. I felt too shy.

He opened his eyes. "Before I became your father, I didn't know what worry was," he said. He picked up his book again.

I stood up and said good-night. Then I thought of another question. "Father, what lullaby did you sing to me?"

He kept his eyes on the page. "It's called *Murucututu*," he said. "It's a Brazilian lullaby, one that my mother sang to me. It's the name of a small owl. In Brazilian myth, the owl is the mother of sleep."

He looked up then, and our eyes met. "Yes, I will sing it to you," he said. "Sometime. But not tonight."

* * *

Do you see letters and words in color? Since I can remember, the letter *P* has always been a deep emerald shade, and *S* has always been royal blue. Even the days of the week have special colors: Tuesday is lavender, and Friday is green. The condition is called synesthesia, and it's been estimated that one in two thousand people is a synesthete.

According to the Internet, virtually all vampires are synesthetes.

And this is how I spent my mornings: surfing the Internet on my laptop computer, looking for clues, which I copied into my journal. (I've torn them out since, for reasons that will soon become clear.) Page after page of Internet lore I copied, and I realized I wasn't any less inane than Kathleen and her role-playing friends with their black notebooks filled with chants and spells.

But even though at times I doubted my research and questioned what I learned, I kept at it. I didn't know where it was going, but I felt compelled to proceed. Think of a jigsaw puzzle. Even when the puzzle isn't assembled, the pieces scattered in the box contain the picture.

Mrs. McG made a big point of insisting that I spend the weekend with Kathleen. She reminded me of it every day that week, and on Friday, when she drove home, I was with her. (For me, *Friday* is always vivid green. For you, too?)

Kathleen didn't seem different to me. By now I was accustomed to her dark clothing and excessive makeup. She looked a little more on edge, perhaps. We spent Friday night watching television and eating pizza with the family. Michael sat apart, not saying much, watching me, and I allowed myself to relish his attention.

On Saturday Kathleen and I slept late and then went to the mall, where we wandered for hours, trying on clothes and watching people.

It was an ordinary weekend until Saturday night. Mrs. McG insisted that we all go to Mass. Kathleen said we had other plans. Her mother said those could wait.

Without much more protest, Kathleen gave in, and I sensed that this fight was part of their weekend ritual.

"I've never been inside a church," I said.

The McGarritts stared at me as if I were a space alien.

Kathleen muttered, "Lucky you."

The church was rectangular, built of dingy bricks—not at all the imposing structure I'd expected. It smelled musty inside, like old paper and stale cologne. Behind the altar, several stained-glass windows depicted Jesus and his disciples, and I kept my eyes on them through most of the service. Stained glass always makes me daydream.

Among the congregation sitting in the pews, I saw three of Kathleen's friends from the vampire game, including the boy who had wanted to "sire" me. He saw me, too, but pretended he didn't. All of the role-players were wearing black, and it struck me as a little strange to see them mouthing the words of hymns and prayers.

Next to me, Kathleen kept crossing and uncrossing her legs and sighing. Later tonight the role-players would be meeting at Ryan's house for another session, and she'd promised me a real part to play. I wasn't much looking forward to it.

At the altar, the priest was quoting the Bible. He was an old man with a singsong voice, easy to ignore—until suddenly his words broke through my reverie.

"Except ye eat the flesh of the Son of Man, and drink his blood, ye have no life in you. Whoso eateth my flesh and drinketh my blood, hath eternal life." He raised a silver goblet in both hands.

And he went on about eating flesh and drinking blood, and people began filing down the aisle toward the altar. All of the McGarritts stood up and moved out of the pew, but Kathleen whispered to me, "Wait here. You can't take Communion."

And so I waited and watched as the others ate the flesh and drank the blood and were consecrated. The priest murmured, "Memento homo quia pulvis es et in pulverem reverteris" (*Remember, man, that thou art dust, and to dust thou shalt return*).

A strange buzzing began in my head. Was someone watching me? As the McGarritts filed back into the pew, the buzzing grew to a drone. Mrs. McGarritt's face looked refreshed, and she smiled with contentment. *You shouldn't be here*, a voice inside me said. *You don't belong.*

Michael had outpaced Bridget to sit next to me. While the others sang and prayed, he pressed his hand into mine, and the buzzing began to fade.

* * *

"Look at this garbage." Kathleen tossed a book onto my lap.

I read aloud the title: "*A Guide for Catholic Teens*. Is it better than *On Becoming a Woman*?"

We were in her room, and she was putting on her vampire makeup before we headed over to Ryan's house. I sat cross-legged on the bed. Wally the dog curled up next to me.

"It's exactly the same stuff." Kathleen had teased her hair into small mounds, to which she now applied gel, then twisted the mounds into spikes. The procedure fascinated me. "It's all this crap about saving your virginity until your honeymoon, and taking Jesus with you wherever you go."

I thumbed through the book. "'A woman's body is a beautiful garden,'" I read aloud. "'But this garden must be kept locked, and the key given only to her husband.'"

"Do you believe that crap?" Kathleen threw down the hair gel, then picked up a mascara wand.

I was still thinking about the image. "Well, in some ways our bodies are like gardens," I said. "Look at you—shaving your legs and plucking your eyebrows and messing with your hair and all. It's kind of like weeding."

Kathleen turned around and gave me her "Are you for real?" look: eyes bugged out, mouth open, head shaking. We both burst out laughing. But I thought what I'd said was true: in Kathleen's world, appearance mattered more than almost anything. Her weight, her clothes, the shape of her eyebrows—these were matters of obsessive concern. In my world, other things mattered more than appearance, I thought, somewhat smugly.

Kathleen turned back to the mirror. "Tonight will be

special," she said. "My horoscope said today is a red-letter day for me."

"Friday is green, not red." I said it without thinking.

Kathleen gave me another bug-eyed look, but I said quickly, "I didn't know you read horoscopes."

"They're the only thing worth reading in the daily paper," she said. "But I bet people like you prefer the editorials."

I didn't want to tell her the truth: at my house, no one read the daily paper. We didn't even have a subscription.

By the time we were ready to go to Ryan's house, the buzzing in my head had returned, and my stomach was churning. "I don't feel right," I told Kathleen.

She looked hard at me, and sick though I felt, I had to admire the thick tangle of her eyelashes and the impressive height of her hair.

"You can't miss the game tonight. We're all going out on quests," she said. "You need to eat something,"

The thought of eating sent me straight to the McGarritt bathroom to vomit. When I'd finished, and rinsed my face and mouth, Kathleen burst in without knocking.

"What is it, Ari?" she said. "Is it lupus?"

In her eyes I saw concern, even love. "I really don't know," I said.

But in a way I was lying. I had a strong hunch about the source of the problem. I'd forgotten to bring along my bottle of tonic. "May I borrow a toothbrush?"

Michael met us in the hallway outside the bathroom, a quizzical look on his face. He'd left the door to his room open, and a monotonous voice was singing, *"This world is full of fools. And I must be one…"*

Michael and Kathleen had an argument about whether I should stay at the McGarritts' or go to Ryan's house.

I settled it. "I want to go home." I felt like a fool.

Kathleen's face fell. "You'll miss the quests."

"I'm sorry," I told her. "But I won't be any fun to be around if I'm sick."

A car horn honked outside. Kathleen's friends had arrived to drive her to Ryan's.

"Go on, have fun," I said. "Bite someone for me."

Michael drove me home. As usual, he was quiet. After a while, he said, "What's wrong with you, Ari?"

"I don't know," I said. "My stomach tends to be delicate, I suppose."

"Do you have lupus?"

"I don't know." I was sick of the words, and of the mosquito-like drone in my head.

"Have you been tested?"

"Yes," I said. "The results were inconclusive." I was looking out the car window at the trees, gleaming with ice, and the icicles hanging from the eaves of houses. In a few weeks Christmas lights would be strung everywhere. *Another ritual that I won't participate in*, I thought with some bitterness.

Michael pulled the car to the curb and parked. Then he reached for me, and without thinking I went into his arms. Something happened, something electric, and then came an explosion of emotion.

Yes, I know that *explosion* isn't the right word. Why is it so hard to write about feelings?

All that matters here is to say it was my first real appreciation of our bodies. I recall at one point pulling back and looking at Michael in the streetlight, his neck so pale and strong-looking, and feeling the urge to burrow into him, to disappear in him. Does that make sense?

Yet part of me remained disengaged, watching as our hands and mouths went crazy. Then I heard my own voice say, calmly, "I don't intend to lose my virginity in the front seat of a car parked outside my father's house."

It was such a prim little voice that it made me laugh. After a moment, Michael laughed, too. But when he stopped, his face and eyes were serious. *Does he truly love me?* I thought. *Why?*

We said good-night, only good-night. No plans to meet the next day. No declarations of passion—our bodies had taken care of that.

As I came inside, I looked automatically toward the living room. But its doors were open, and no lamps were lit. I realized my father hadn't expected me back tonight, but somehow I'd thought he would be in his chair, as usual.

Just as well he wasn't around, I thought as I went up the staircase. One look at me, and he would have known how I'd spent the past hour.

I paused in the corridor upstairs. But I felt nothing, no sense of any other's presence. No one was watching me, that night.

— Six —

I awoke as if someone had called my name—opening my
eyes, saying, "Yes?" My father was in the room. It was
completely dark, but I felt his presence. He stood beside
the doorway.

"Ari," he said. "Where were you last night?"

I sat up, switched on the lamp next to my bed. The little
birds jumped out of the darkness. "What's wrong?" I asked.

"Mr. McGarritt telephoned a few minutes ago." My
father's eyes were large and dark. He wore a suit and shirt,
and I wondered: *Has he been up all night? Doesn't he wear
pajamas?*

"It's an odd time to call." I didn't want to hear any more.
I sensed bad news coming.

"Kathleen hasn't come home yet," he said. "Do you know
where she might be?"

And so I found myself telling my father about the role-
playing game. "Some people are werewolves, and others are

117

vampires," I said. "Everyone goes around chanting spells and pretending to drink each other's blood."

"How unseemly," my father said, his voice dry.

"And last night they were supposed to be going off on quests, whatever that means. They were meeting at Ryan's house. I felt ill after Mass, and Michael drove me home."

"After *Mass*?"

"Everyone was there," I said. "The McGarritts, and even some kids from the role-playing. They go every weekend."

"I see," he said, in a tone that implied he didn't. "The werewolves and vampires pray and are absolved before they feed."

"It's only a game," I said.

My father looked perplexed. "All right then, I'll call Mr. McGarritt back and tell him what you said. He may want to talk to you himself, if Kathleen doesn't come home soon."

"Doesn't come home?" I said. "What time is it?"

"Nearly four. Time for you to go back to sleep. I'm sorry that I had to wake you."

"They're probably still playing," I said, more to try to persuade myself than anything. It was dark and cold outside, and if they weren't at Ryan's house, where could they be?

My father left, and I turned out the light. But I didn't go back to sleep.

Mrs. McGarritt wasn't in the kitchen when I went downstairs that day. I made myself toast, and I was sitting at the table, eating, when my father came up from the basement.

He sat down opposite me and didn't speak at once. He

watched me chew and swallow, and I tried to find some reassurance in his eyes.

Finally he said, "They've found her."

Later that day I spoke with Mr. McGarritt, with the policemen who came to the house, and, after dinner, with Michael.

Kathleen had met the other role-players at Ryan's house. Each went off on a quest—a sort of scavenger hunt, I gathered. Kathleen was to bring back a lawn ornament, preferably a gnome. Their deadline was midnight, and by that time everyone except Kathleen had reconvened in Ryan's living room. The game broke up around one, and the players concluded that Kathleen had gone home early. At least that's what Michael told me later, and what they told the police.

The two policemen who came to our house sat awkwardly in the living room. They seemed apologetic, but their eyes scrutinized me, my father, and the furniture. I couldn't tell them much, and they told us less.

At some point one of them abruptly turned to my father. "What time was it when Ariella returned home?"

"Ten-fifteen," my father said.

I didn't look at him. I simply sat and wondered, *How did he know?*

"You were here all evening, sir?"

"Yes," my father said. "As usual."

Michael's voice on the phone that night was shaky. "It was Mr. Mitchell, Ryan's dad, who found her," he said. "She was in the greenhouse. I heard my dad tell Mom that she was lying there so peaceful-looking that Mr. Mitchell thought at first she was asleep. But when they moved her"—Michael began to sob—"they said everything fell apart."

I could barely hold the phone. I could see the scene: Kathleen lying amid the orchids, the purple fluorescence giving everything a blue-violet cast. I could see the odd tilt of her head, although Michael didn't describe it. And her body was sprinkled with parsley from the little bag she'd worn as a talisman.

When Michael could talk again, he said, "Mom's a mess. I don't think she'll ever be herself again. And nobody is supposed to tell Bridget, but she knows something bad happened."

"What did happen?" I had to ask. "Who killed her?"

"I don't know. Nobody knows. The other kids have been questioned, and they all say they never saw her after the first part of the game. Ryan is hysterical." He took jagged breaths between the words. "I swear I'll find who did this and I'll kill him myself."

I sat for a long time hearing Michael cry and rage and cry again, until we both were exhausted. Yet I knew that neither of us would sleep that night, or the night after that.

A few days later I turned on my computer and did an Internet search for Kathleen McGarritt. I came up with more than 70,000 hits. In the weeks to come, the number grew to more than 700,000.

The Saratoga Springs newspaper ran several articles

portraying the role-players as a Satanic cult, suggesting that Kathleen's death was a cult ritual. The editors printed few details about how she died, only that her body was found nearly bloodless and mutilated. They ran an editorial warning parents to keep their children away from role-playing games.

Other media ran less judgmental stories, reporting the facts without speculating about the motivation for the crime.

All of them agreed on one point: the identity of the murderer remained unknown. It was thought that she hadn't been killed in the greenhouse, but in a yard nearby, where bloodstains and pieces of a broken plaster gnome had been found in the snow. The local police had called in the FBI to handle the investigation.

If I hadn't been sick that night, I thought, *I'd have been with her. I might have prevented her death.*

Some of my search hits took me to MySpace.com, where three of Kathleen's friends kept blogs that talked about her death. I skimmed them, not liking the details. One of them said her body had been "cut up like sushi."

The next weeks passed, somehow. After a few days, my father and I resumed lessons. We didn't talk about Kathleen. One night he said, "Eileen McGarritt isn't coming back. Mary Ellis Root will be cooking for you now."

Until that moment I'd never known Mrs. McG's first name. "I prefer to cook for myself," I said. In truth I had no appetite.

"Very well," he said.

Once or twice a week Michael called. He wouldn't be

able to see me for a while, he said. The local media were hounding his family and Kathleen's friends, and it was better for him to stay home. Meanwhile, the police and the FBI kept silent, except to say that there were "persons of interest" in the case.

The McGarritts buried Kathleen. If there was a burial ceremony, they kept it private. A memorial service was held during the week before Christmas, and my father and I attended.

They held it in the school gymnasium—the site of the Halloween dance. Only now, instead of crepe paper streamers, the room was decorated for Christmas. A trimmed evergreen stood close to the statue of Jesus at its entrance, and the smell of pine was strong. Someone had set a photograph of Kathleen on an easel—a posed picture taken when her hair was long—near an open book that we all signed as we came in. Then we sat in uncomfortable metal folding chairs.

A priest stood at the front of the room, next to a white vase holding white roses, and he said things. I barely heard a word. I kept my eyes on the other people.

Mrs. McG had lost weight, and her face seemed collapsed upon itself. She didn't speak, and she didn't touch anyone, even to shake hands. She simply sat and nodded occasionally. She looked like an old woman, I thought.

Michael stared at me from across the room, but we didn't have a chance to talk. The other McGarritts didn't even make eye contact with me. Their faces were bonier than I remembered, and shadows lay beneath their eyes. Even little Bridget, who had finally been told about her sister's death, looked thinner and forlorn. Next to her, Wally the dog sat, his head on his paws.

Kathleen's "pagan" friends wore suits and ties, and they looked miserable. They glanced at one other with suspicious eyes. I can't begin to describe the tension in the room. The pink smell of the roses was sickening.

People filed to the front and said things about Kathleen. Platitudes, mostly. How she would laugh, if she could hear them! Again, I paid little attention. I wasn't going to speak. I couldn't believe she was dead, and I wasn't about to be a hypocrite—it was that simple.

My father sat next to me and later stayed by my side as we filed out. He shook Mr. McGarritt's hand and said something about how sorry we were. I didn't say a word.

Michael shot another look at me as we left, but I kept walking, like a zombie.

As we were about to leave the school, my father suddenly steered me away from the door, to a side exit. Later, when we were in the car, I saw why: the front door was mobbed by photographers and television cameramen.

My father started the car. I shivered, watching the media people surround Kathleen's friends and family as they left the school. It had begun to snow: large flakes like bits of gauze drifted through the air. Two clung to the car window for seconds before they began to melt, trailing down the glass. I wanted to sit still and watch the snow, but the car began to move. I sat back in the leather seat, and my father drove us home.

* * *

That night, we spent a silent hour pretending to read in the living room, and then I went upstairs to bed. I lay beneath the blankets, staring at nothing. Eventually I must have drifted into sleep, because I awoke with a start, once again thinking I'd heard someone call my name.

"Ari?" A thin, high-pitched voice came from somewhere outside. "Ari?"

I went to the window and pushed aside the heavy curtains. She stood below, bare feet in the snow, her black t-shirt torn, her figure lit by the lamppost in the driveway behind her. Worst was her head, which looked as if it had been pulled off and put back on at an impossible angle. She looked lopsided.

"Ari?" Kathleen called. "Come out and play?" Her body swayed as she spoke.

But it wasn't her voice—it was pitched too high, and it was singsong.

"Come out and play with me?" she said.

I began to shake.

Then my father strode out from the back entrance. "Go. Go back to your grave." His voice wasn't loud, but its power made me shake.

Kathleen stood a moment longer, swaying slightly. Then she turned and walked away, jerking like a marionette, her head bent forward.

My father didn't look in my direction. He went back to the house. A few seconds later, he was in my room.

Still shaking, I lay on the floor, knees to my chest, hugging myself as hard as I could.

124

He let me cry for a while. Then he picked me up, as easily as if I were a baby, and he put me back in bed. He tucked the blankets around me. He pulled a chair close to the bed, and he sang to me. "*Murucututu, detrás do Murundu.*"

I don't know Portuguese, but understanding the lyrics didn't matter at the time. His voice was low, almost a whisper. After a while I was able to stop crying. Eventually, he sang me to sleep.

I awoke the next day dry-eyed and determined.

When he came up to join me in the library that afternoon, I was ready. I waited until he'd sat down. Then I stood up and said, "Who am I, Father?"

"You're my daughter," he said.

I found myself noticing how beautiful his eyelashes were—as if he wanted me to notice, in order to distract me.

I would not be distracted. "I want you to tell me how it happened—how I happened."

He didn't speak for a minute or so. I stood still. I couldn't tell what he was thinking.

"Then sit down," he said, finally. "No, do. It's a rather long story."

He began this way: "I have no way of knowing how much you're like me, and how much like your mother." His eyes moved to the window, to the shadowbox on the wall, then back to me. "Often, because of the way you think, I've thought you were more like me—and that in time, you'd know without being told what you need to know to survive.

"But I can't be sure of that." He crossed his arms. "Any more than I can be certain that I'll always be able to protect you. I suppose it's time you were told everything, from the beginning."

He warned me that it would be a long story, one that took time to tell. He asked me to be patient, not to interrupt with questions. "I want you to understand how things ensued, how one thing caused another," he said. "As Nabokov wrote in his memoir, 'Let me look at my demon objectively.'"

"Yes," I said. "I want to understand."

And so he told me the story I've inserted at the beginning of this notebook, the story of one night in Savannah. The three men playing chess. The odd intimacy between my father and mother. The gate, the river, the shawl. And when he'd finished, he told me the story again, adding details. The men at the chess table were his fellow graduate students at the University of Virginia, visiting Savannah for the weekend. Dennis was one of the three. The other was called Malcolm.

My father had been born in Argentina; he'd never known his father, but had been told his father was German. His parents never married. His surname, Montero, came from his Brazilian mother, and she'd died soon after his birth.

I asked about my mother. "You told her you'd seen her before."

"An odd coincidence," he said. "Yes, we'd met when we were children. My aunt lived in Georgia. I met your mother one summer afternoon on Tybee Island, and we played in the sand together. I was six. She was ten. I was a child, and she was a child."

I recognized the line from "Annabel Lee."

"To live by the sea, after a childhood living inland in Argentina—well, it made a deep impression on me. The sounds and smells of the ocean gave me a sense of peace I hadn't known before." He looked away from me and stared again at the shadowbox, at the three small birds trapped inside.

"I spent every day on the beach, building sand castles and hunting for shells. One afternoon a girl in a white sundress came up to me and cupped my chin in her hand. 'I know you,' she said. 'You're staying in Blue Buoy Cottage.'

"She had blue eyes and red-brown hair, a small nose, full lips curved into a smile that made me smile. I looked into her face as she held my chin, and something passed between us."

He stopped talking. For a moment the only sound in the room was the ticking of the grandfather clock.

"So, you see, when we met in Savannah, it never occurred to me to wonder whether we would fall in love." His voice was low and soft. "I'd fallen in love with her twenty years before."

"Love?" I said.

"Love," he said, more loudly now. "'A form of biological cooperation in which the emotions of each are necessary to the fulfillment of the other's instinctive purposes.' Bertrand Russell wrote that."

My father leaned back in his chair. "Why so forlorn, Ari? Russell also called love a source of delight and a source of knowledge. Love requires cooperation, and human ethics are rooted in that cooperation. In its highest form, love reveals values that otherwise we would never know."

"That's so abstract," I said. "I'd rather hear about what you felt."

"Well, Russell was right on all counts. Our love was a source of delight. And your mother challenged every ethic I held."

"Why do you always say 'your mother'?" I asked. "Why don't you use her name?"

He uncrossed his arms, and laced his fingers behind his neck, looking across at me with cool appraisal. "It hurts to say it," he said. "Even after so many years. But you're right— you need to know who your mother was. Her name was Sara. Sara Stephenson."

"Where is she?" I'd asked this before, long ago, to no avail. "What happened to her? Is she still alive?"

"I don't know the answers to those questions."

"Was she beautiful?"

"Yes, she was beautiful." His voice sounded hoarse. "Yet she lacked the conceit that most beautiful women have. Then again, she was moody at times."

He coughed. "After we became a couple, she composed our time together. She planned days as if they were artistic events. One afternoon we went to Tybee Island for a picnic; we ate blueberries and drank champagne tinted with curaçao and listened to Miles Davis, and when I asked the name of her perfume, she said it was *L'Heure Bleue*.

"She talked about 'perfect moments.' One such moment

happened that afternoon; she'd been napping; I lay next to her, reading. She said, 'I'll always remember the sounds of the sea and of pages turning, and the smell of *L'Heure Bleue*. For me they signify love.'

"I teased her about being a foolish romantic. She teased me about being a dull intellectual. But she truly believed that the universe continually sends us sensory messages, which we can never quite decode. And she tried to send her own, back."

Then he said it was enough for one night—by now it was late, and very dark outside. He said he would tell me more tomorrow.

I did not object. I went upstairs to bed, and that night I did not cry, and I did not dream.

I'd expected my father to resume the story of his courtship of my mother, but the next day's lessons began in a rather different manner.

Instead of the library, he said, he preferred to meet in the living room. He had a glass of Picardo in his hand, even though he normally drank only when our lessons were concluded.

After we'd settled in our usual chairs, he said abruptly, "I miss some of the human qualities—the ones I see in the easy way you speak with Dennis. The banter, the casual affection.

"Of course, there are compensations." Here he smiled the tight-lipped scholar's smile. "One of which is memory. I remember everything. I gather from our conversations that you do not. But you have implicit memory—that is, you may lack conscious awareness of past events, yet your neural network retains distinct fragments of encoded experience.

"My expectations have always been that, in time, you would decode them. When an appropriate stimulus triggered the memory, you would consciously remember it."

I held up my hand, and he stopped speaking. It took me a minute or so before I could understand what he was telling me. Finally I nodded, and he continued his story.

My father's life had had five distinct phases. First, his childhood, which, he said, was monotonous: regular mealtimes, bedtimes, and lessons. He said he'd tried to structure a similar monotony for me, and he quoted Bertrand Russell's claim that monotony is an essential ingredient of a happy life.

When he left his aunt's house to attend the University of Virginia, my father entered another phase: his wild years, as he called them now. His classes weren't difficult, and he devoted considerable time to drinking, gambling, and learning about women.

Then he met my mother in Savannah, and a third phase began.

She left her husband and moved into an apartment in an old brick house across the street from Savannah's Colonial Cemetery. (And here, as if to prove the power of his memory, my father described to me the paths that led through the cemetery, embedded with broken oyster shells, and the patterns etched in the brick side-walks bordering it. They were spirals. He said he didn't like to look at them, but spirals are among my favorite symbols. Yours, too? They symbolize creation and growth if they curl clockwise from the center, and destruction if they twirl to the left. As it happens, hurricanes in the northern hemisphere twirl to the left.)

My mother took a job working for a business that harvested, packaged, and marketed honey. She'd refused to take any money from her husband. And she began divorce proceedings.

Every weekend my father drove eight hours from Charlottesville to Savannah, and every Monday he drove back again. He said he never minded the drive south. It was the drive back that he loathed.

"When you're in love, separations cause physical pain," he said. His voice was so low that I had to lean forward to hear.

I wondered what I might be feeling about Michael, if I weren't so numb. "Ari is numb." It was easy for me to think about myself in the third person during that time: "Ari is depressed," I thought often. "Ari prefers to be alone."

But when I was with my father, I forgot myself. Listening to his story was, I know now, the best way for me to come to terms with the death of Kathleen.

The house in Savannah where my mother lived had three storeys made of red brick, green shutters, and wrought-iron balconies and fences wrapped in wisteria vines. Her apartment was on the second floor. She and my father sometimes sat, drinking wine and talking, on the balcony facing the cemetery.

Locals said the house was haunted. One weeknight when my mother was alone, she awoke abruptly, sensing another's presence in the room.

The next day on the telephone she described it to my father: "I felt chilled to the bone, but I was under the quilt, and it wasn't a cold night. There was a mist in the room; I could see it twist in the light from the streetlamp outside. Then it condensed and began to take shape. Without even thinking, I said, 'God, protect me. God, save me.'

"And when I opened my eyes, the thing was gone. Completely gone. The room was warm again. I fell asleep feeling safe."

My father tried to console her. Even as he spoke, he thought she must be imagining things—her superstitions must be at work.

Soon he came to think otherwise.

"You've said before that my mother was superstitious." I found I was touching the little bag of lavender at my neck, and I took my hand away from it at once.

"She was." He'd seen my gesture, and he knew I was thinking of Kathleen. "She thought the color blue was lucky, and the letter S."

"S *is* blue," I said.

He said, "She wasn't a synesthete."

I listened to his story about my mother's ghost visitor without questioning it. My skepticism had been permanently suspended the night Kathleen stood outside my window.

* * *

One weekend when my mother and father returned to her flat after dining out, they both noticed an odd smell in the living room, a smell of mold and mildew. They opened the windows, but the odor persisted. Later, as they were about to go to bed, they saw a wisp of green smoke swirl into the bedroom. It spun around, vortex-like, and seemed to co-alesce—but its shape remained indistinct.

The room had grown cold, and my father held my mother as they watched the thing. Finally my mother said, "Hello, James." Thus acknowledged, the smoke dissipated. A few seconds later, the room was warm again. "How did you know his name?" my father asked. "He's been here more than once," my mother said. "I didn't mention it, because I knew you didn't believe me when I told you about his first visit."

My mother was convinced that the thing was the ghost of someone named James Wilde, and next day she led my father to his grave across the street. It was a windy day, and the Spanish moss draping the live oak trees in the cemetery seemed to dance around them.

While my father looked at the gravestone, my mother recited it from memory:

> *This humble stone*
> *records the filial piety*
> *fraternal affection and manly virtues*
> *of*
> *JAMES WILDE, Esquire,*
> *late District Paymaster in the army of the U.S.*

He fell in a Duel on the 16th of January, 1815,
by the hand of a man
who, a short time ago, would have been
friendless but for him;
and expired instantly in his 22nd year:
dying, as he had lived:
with unshaken courage & unblemished reputation.
By his untimely death the prop of a Mother's
age is broken:
The hope and consolation of Sisters is destroyed,
the pride of Brothers humbled in the dust
and a whole Family, happy until then,
overwhelmed with affliction.

Later, my father learned that Wilde's brother had commemorated his death in a poem, and he quoted lines from it to me:

My life is like the summer rose,
That opens to the morning sky;
And ere the shades of evening close,
Is scattered on the ground—to die.

At the time my father hadn't been convinced that the ghost was Wilde's, but my mother felt certain.

"So," he told me, "I was introduced into a new realm, where facts and science couldn't account for everything. As Edgar Poe knew too well. 'I believe that demons take advantage of the night to mislead the unwary—although, you know, I don't believe in them.' Do you remember that line of his?"

I didn't remember it.

Only much later I realized why my father told me the ghost story, and quoted all of the lines: he wanted both to distract me from, and to help me come to terms with, the loss of my best friend.

— Seven —

But I couldn't come to terms with her death until I knew who had killed her. The McGarritts indeed were "a whole Family, happy until then, overwhelmed with affliction," and they deserved to know—we all deserved to know—what had really happened.

On a bitterly cold day in January, I felt surprised but oddly relieved when my father told me an FBI agent would be calling on us that afternoon.

The agent's name was Cecil Burton, and he was the first African-American person we'd ever had in our house. Isn't that hard to believe? Remember, we led sheltered lives in Saratoga Springs.

My father led Burton into the living room, and the first thing I noticed about him was his smell: a rich blend of tobacco and men's cologne. Burton smelled good, and he looked at me as if he knew I thought so. His suit was beautifully tailored, and it managed to emphasize his muscles without being tight. His eyes had a weary expression, although he couldn't have been more than thirty-five.

Agent Burton stayed with us only an hour, but during that time he got more information from me about Kathleen than I'd known I had. He asked about our friendship, initially in the most casual way: "How did you two meet?" "How often did you get together?" Then his questions grew more focused: "Did you know she was jealous of you?" and "How long have you been involved with Michael?"

I answered every question honestly, although I didn't think we were getting anywhere at first. Then I tried to imagine what he was actually thinking as he talked, and I found I was able to read some of his thoughts.

You're looking into the eyes of another, and it's as if their thoughts are telegraphed to your mind: you know exactly what they're thinking at that moment. Sometimes, you don't even need to look; concentrating on the words alone is enough to bring you the thoughts.

Burton, I realized, was suspicious that my father and I were involved somehow in Kathleen's death. Not that he had any particular evidence—he simply didn't like the "setup" (a word I'd never used or even thought before). He'd done a background check on us; I could tell that because he kept making mental references to it, especially when he looked at my father. (*Cambridge, huh? Left there all of a sudden. That was sixteen years ago. How old is this guy? He doesn't look more than thirty. Dude must be doing Botox. Built like a marathon runner. But where's the tan?*)

Burton asked my father, "And where is Mrs. Montero?"

"We're separated," my father said. "I haven't seen her in years."

Burton thought, *Check separation agreement?*

All of this I knew he was thinking, but at other times, I couldn't gain access. The interference was caused by a kind of mental static, I thought.

Then I looked across at my father, whose eyes were eloquent. He knew what I was doing, and he wanted me to stop.

"What did you and Michael talk about when he drove you home that night?" Burton's question cut through my thoughts.

"Oh, I don't remember," I said. It was the first lie I'd told him, and he seemed to know that.

"Michael said things got"—his brown eyes seemed to relax at that moment—"a little hot and heavy." In a second his eyes were alert again.

My father said, "Is this *necessary*?" His voice, emotionless, somehow communicated distaste.

"Yes, Mr. Montero," Burton said. "I do believe it's *necessary* to establish what Ariella was doing that night."

I wanted to hear what he was thinking, but I refrained. Instead I tilted my head and looked hard at Burton without reading his eyes. "We were kissing," I said.

After he'd shown Burton out, my father returned to the living room. Before he'd had a chance to sit down, I asked him, "Do you remember Marmalade? The neighbor's cat? Do you know who killed her?"

"No."

He and I exchanged a look of mutual wariness. Then he left the room, headed toward the basement.

Had he lied to Burton? I wondered. If not, why hadn't he been in the living room when I'd come in that night? He was such a creature of habit, I thought. If he was lying, then where had he been that night?

And beneath all of those questions, the real one: had my father been involved in Kathleen's death? That was how I phrased it. I couldn't bring myself to think: had *he* killed her?

Yes, Burton was with us only an hour, but he altered the atmosphere of our house. He introduced an element never present before: suspicion. As I went upstairs, the sound of my feet on the steps, the shapes of the Moroccan cushions on the landing, even the paintings on the wall—all seemed strange and secretive to me, almost sinister.

I turned on my laptop and did an Internet search for Kathleen. I didn't find much new, except in the blogs, where someone said that one of the role-players had killed her, and several others responded. Their dialogue struck me as so stupid that I didn't read it.

On impulse I searched for "Sara Stephenson." More than 340,000 hits resulted. Adding the word "Savannah" to her name reduced the results to 25,000 hits. I scrolled through page after page of them, but none connected the name *Sara* and the name *Stephenson*— both names were mentioned in other contexts.

A search for "Raphael Montero" turned up references to

a character in Zorro movies. And "Montero" turned out to be the name of a sport utility vehicle. The indignity of it!

I gave up. I didn't want to think anymore. On my bureau lay the battered copy of *On the Road* that Michael had lent me, and I decided to spend the afternoon reading in bed.

An hour or so later, I set the book aside, dazzled by its style. Kerouac had an odd way with characters—none of his female characters struck me as authentic, and most of the men seemed wildly idealized—but his descriptions were beautifully detailed and sometimes almost lyrical. The book made me want to travel, to see the America that Kerouac saw. A vast world awaited me, I sensed, and no amount of reading or Internet research could teach me what experience would.

When I went downstairs again, my suspicions of my father had dissipated, and the house seemed familiar again. For the first time in weeks I felt hungry. In the kitchen I went through the cupboards and found a can of cream of asparagus soup. I looked for milk in the refrigerator, but the carton bought weeks ago by Mrs. McG had gone sour. I'd have to dilute the soup with water.

While it heated, I sat at the table, reading my mother's recipe book and making a grocery list. This was a first. Mrs. McG had always taken care of the shopping.

When the soup was ready, I poured it into a bowl and, on impulse, stirred in a dollop of honey from the jar in the pantry.

My father came in while I was eating. He looked at my

meal and then at me, and I knew what he was thinking: my mother had put honey in soup.

In the living room after dinner that night, my father resumed his story, without being asked.

The year that he turned twenty-seven, he was invited to conduct postdoctoral research at Cambridge University. His friend Malcolm also was invited, and the two of them arranged for Dennis to accompany them as a research assistant.

My father had mixed feelings about leaving my mother, but after some initial qualms, she urged him to go. "This will be the making of you," she told him.

So he went. After signing some papers, and unpacking his books and clothes in his new flat, he realized how alone he was. Malcolm and Dennis had taken off again, to attend a conference in Japan; he could have accompanied them, but he'd wanted some time alone to think.

He had a week before the Michaelmas term began, and he decided to take a brief tour of England. After a few days in London, he rented a car and headed for Cornwall.

His plan was to find a place where Sara and he might stay when she was able to visit him the following spring. First they would drive to Berkshire, so that she could visit a place she'd always talked of—the Celtic horse cut into a hillside near Uffington—then they'd drive on to Cornwall. He found a bed-and-breakfast inn at the top of a twisted road that led to the fishing village of Polperro. He spent three days in a room at the top of the house, reading and listening to gulls cry as they spiraled over the harbor below.

Every day he went hiking along the cliff paths. Having spent so much of the previous five years in classrooms and laboratories, his body craved exercise. And it lifted his spirits. As much as he missed my mother, he began to think that the separation could be managed.

En route back to Cambridge, he stopped in Glastonbury, a small town in the Somerset Levels, overlooked by the Tor, a sacred hill. Sara had described it as a center for "alternative thinkers," a place he must see.

Three strange things happened.

As my father was walking down Benedict Street, a black dog ran into the path of an oncoming car; the car swerved and hit a curb with such violence that its windshield shattered, casting shards of glass in all directions. My father stopped for a moment to watch passers-by ensure that the driver was all right—she huddled over the steering wheel, but seemed more shaken than injured—then walked on, glass crunching under his shoes.

When he saw a sign for the Blue Note Café, he thought at once of Sara. She loved the color blue, and anything with blue in its name she thought lucky. He imagined bringing her to Glastonbury in the spring, leading her down Benedict Street, watching her face light up at the sign. After he went inside and ordered a sandwich, he pictured her sitting across the table from him.

The woman who came to take his order said he'd "missed all the excitement." A few moments before, she said, a customer had finished his lunch, then stood up and methodically began to remove his clothing, which he folded and stacked on a chair. She pointed at a chair, at a small pile of folded clothes. Then, she said, the naked man ran out of the café and across the street.

"Someone's sure to call the police," she said.

Diners at other tables were talking about the incident; the man wasn't a local, they agreed.

"He must be mad," one said.

After my father had eaten and paid, he headed back to the car park. He was crossing a street when a blind man approached from the other side. He was a large man, rather fat, and completely bald; he tapped a white cane from side to side across the path before him. As he drew closer, my father noticed that the man's eyes were entirely white, as if the pupils had rolled back into his head. A second before they passed one another, the man turned his head toward my father and smiled.

My father felt a rush of adrenaline—and something else, that he'd never felt before. He sensed that he was in the presence of evil.

He quickened his pace. After a minute had passed, he looked over his shoulder. The man wasn't there.

Back on the road, he replayed the scenes in his mind but made no sense of them. He later told Dennis and Malcolm about seeing the man who'd feigned blindness, making a joke of it. He said he'd met the devil in Glastonbury. As they scoffed at him, he wished he still shared their skepticism.

*   *   *

143

Here my father paused.

"You believe in the devil?" I asked.

"It wasn't a question of belief," he said. "My instincts were immediate: I'd encountered *evil*—a word I don't think I'd even thought before."

I wanted him to go back, to tell me the things I most needed to know. Yet I loved the sound of his voice speaking my mother's name: *Sara*.

"You seem to have been different in those days," I said, to prompt him. "Hiking, and playing on the beach. You didn't have"— here I hesitated—"lupus when you were younger?"

He set his glass back on the marble-topped mahogany table next to his chair. "I was healthy then," he said. "Sunlight didn't bother me. Food wasn't a concern. I felt passion for Sara, and for my work. I had no financial worries, thanks to the legacy from my father that supports us. The future"— he smiled wryly—"looked *bright*."

The devil my father met in Glastonbury was nothing compared to the devil awaiting him in Cambridge.

His research initially was under the direction of Professor A. G. Simpson, a mild, rather shy fellow whose good manners didn't quite hide his intelligence. Simpson's research grants totaled in the millions of pounds, and the work focused on stem cell research.

But within a matter of months, my father and Malcolm were wooed—there's really no other word for it—by another professor in the Department of Haematology, John Redfern. Redfern's work was in transfusion medicine, and his laboratories were part of the National Blood Authority operations on the Addenbrooke campus.

I interrupted my father at this point. "You haven't told me much about Malcolm."

"He was my closest friend," my father said. "Malcolm was tall, only an inch or so shorter than me, and he had blond hair that he parted on the left and let fall across his forehead. He had very fair skin that reddened easily when he was embarrassed or angry. He was bright and he wasn't bad-looking, or so women at the time seemed to think. But he liked to play the part of misanthrope and habitual cynic. He didn't have many friends."

When Malcolm came to pick up my father that day, he wore a tie and a white shirt under his customary buttoned-up cardigan. He'd borrowed a car, and they met Redfern at an unfamiliar restaurant on the other side of town. It turned out to be a stuffy, smoke-filled place, where red-faced businessmen bent over plates of rare roast beef and two veg.

Redfern rose from a table when they came in. The room fell silent as the businessmen scrutinized the newcomers. Malcolm and my father often were stared at in public places. They didn't look British.

Redfern was five foot eight at most, with dark hair and eyes, a large nose, and ruddy skin. He wasn't handsome, but every time my father saw him on campus he walked in the company of someone beautiful.

Over red wine and red meat, Redfern explained his plan. He wanted to create a spin-out company to develop a database of serum samples for use in identifying diseases.

He spoke at length about how Malcolm and my father might enhance the potential of such a company, about how rich it could make them.

Malcolm said, "Right, what we're after is money."

The scorn in his voice seemed to surprise Redfern. He said, "I thought Yanks were all about the filthy lucre."

(I remembered my Latin—*lucrum* means avarice. And in Middle English, *lucre* meant profit, but also illicit gain.)

In any case, Redfern couldn't have been more wrong about Malcolm and my father. They both had too much money already. Malcolm's great-grandfather, John Lynch, had made a fortune in the American steel industry, and Malcolm was a millionaire. My father's money came from a trust established by *his* father, a wealthy German made even wealthier from some shady business conducted in Latin America after World War II.

After Malcolm spoke, my father looked across the bloody plates and splotched napkins on the table and saw anger flash in Redfern's eyes. In a second, his expression changed to one of sad appeal.

"Surely you'll think about my offer," Redfern said, sounding almost humble.

They let Redfern pay the bill, and they drove away laughing at him.

I moved restlessly in my chair.

"Are you sleepy?" my father asked.

I didn't know. I'd lost a sense of time. "No," I said. "I need to stretch my legs."

"Perhaps we should stop for tonight." He sounded eager.

"No," I said. "I want to hear it all."

"I wonder if you do," he said. "I don't want to upset you."

"I doubt anything will ever upset me again," I said.

A few days after the luncheon, my father met Redfern by chance, walking through the town center. Redfern was with a tall Swedish woman who worked in the Cavendish Laboratory. The three exchanged greetings. Then my father found he couldn't move.

His legs wouldn't budge. His eyes were locked on Redfern's, and when he tried to look away, he couldn't.

Redfern smiled.

My father tried again to look away, toward the woman. His eyes stayed where they were, fixed on Redfern's.

A full minute passed before my father found he could move again. Then he looked from Redfern to the woman, who didn't meet his eyes.

Redfern said, "I'll be seeing you soon."

My father wanted to run. Instead he walked away, down the street, followed by the sound of their laughter.

About a week later, Malcolm phoned to invite my father to his rooms for tea. My father said he was too busy.

Malcolm said, "I saw some amazing hemoglobin today."

Malcolm wasn't the sort to casually use a word like *amazing*. It was enough to entice my father.

As he climbed the stairs to Malcolm's rooms, he was struck by the strong smell of burnt toast. No one answered his knock, but the door wasn't locked, so he came inside.

As usual, Malcolm had a fire burning in the sitting room, and standing over it was Redfern, holding a poker, at the end of which smoldered a charred piece of bread.

"I like my toast burnt," he said, without turning around. "How about you?"

Malcolm apparently wasn't in.

Redfern invited my father to sit. Although he wanted to leave, he sat. He detected, beneath the smell of burnt bread, another odor, something unpleasant.

He wanted to leave. Instead, he sat.

Redfern talked. My father found him simultaneously brilliant and fatuous. *Brilliant* was a word tossed around Cambridge fairly casually, my father said—adding that he expected that things were similar at most large research universities. He said that academia reminded him of a badly run circus. The faculty members were like underfed animals—weary of their cages, which were never large enough to begin with—and they responded sluggishly to the whip. The trapeze artists fell with monotonous regularity into poorly strung nets. The clowns looked hungry. The tent leaked. The crowd was inattentive, shouting incoherently at inappropriate moments. And when the show was over, no one cheered.

(Extended metaphors were a device my father used from time to time, I suspect to keep himself amused as much as to elucidate. But I liked the image of the badly run circus, so I include it here.)

My father watched Redfern pace the room, talking about

philosophy—of all things. He said he wanted to know more about my father's ethics, but before my father could say anything, he talked about his own.

Redfern considered himself a utilitarian. "Would you agree," he said, "that man's sole duty is to produce as much pleasure as possible?"

"Only if the pleasure produced is equivalent to the diminution of pain." My father crossed his arms. "And only if one man's pleasure is as important as any other's."

"Well then." Redfern's face seemed redder than ever in the firelight, and he struck my father as exceptionally ugly. "You would agree that the amount of pleasure or pain produced by an action is a chief criterion for determining which actions to perform."

My father said he agreed. He felt as if he were attending a lecture in Ethics 101. "Many actions are wrong because they cause pain," Redfern said, waving his poker, the blackened bread slice skewered at its tip. "You would agree? And if it can be shown that an act will lead to pain, that in itself would be sufficient reason not to pursue it."

At this point my father noticed a small movement in the room, somewhere behind him. But when he turned to look, he saw nothing. The sickening smell seemed to intensify.

"It would follow, then, that there are cases in which it is necessary to inflict pain now to avoid greater pain later on, or to gain future pleasure that is worth the current pain."

My father's eyes were on Redfern's, trying to fathom his motives, when Malcolm came from behind, pulled back his head, and bit deeply into his neck.

* * *

"What was it like?" I asked my father.

"You don't feel a sense of disgust at hearing this?"

I felt simultaneously alert and numb. "You promised to tell me everything."

The pain burned, more fierce than anything my father had ever experienced. He struggled in vain to get away.

Malcolm held him in an awkward embrace that would have been unthinkable, had my father been able to think. He tried to twist his head to see Malcolm's face—and then he must have fainted, but not before he glimpsed that, from across the room, Redfern was watching the scene with blatant pleasure.

When my father regained consciousness, he lay across the sofa, and when he brushed his hand across his face, it came away dark with clotted blood. His *friends* weren't in the room.

He sat up. His head felt large and swollen, and his legs and arms felt weak, but he wanted more than anything to run away. The fire had gone out, and the room was cold, but the smells of burnt bread and the other unknown substance persisted. Now they seemed almost appetizing, as did an unfamiliar coppery taste in his mouth.

His nerves tingled. He felt empty, yet his veins seemed charged with something like adrenaline. He managed to stand and walk to the lavatory. In a dingy mirror over the sink, he saw the wound in his neck and a crust of blood around his mouth. His heartbeat echoed in his head like the sound of metal striking metal.

Opposite the lavatory was a closed bedroom door, and the unfamiliar odor came from behind it. Something dead must be in that room, my father thought.

Halfway down the steps, he saw Redfern and Malcolm approaching the staircase. He stood on the landing and watched them come.

He felt shame, anger, a desire for revenge. Yet, as they walked up the steps to the landing, he did nothing.

Redfern nodded. Malcolm glanced at him and looked away. Malcolm's hair fell over his eyes, and his face was pink as if he'd recently scrubbed it. His eyes looked dull, uninterested, and he smelled of nothing at all.

"Explanations are useless," Malcolm said, as if my father had asked for one. "But some day you'll realize that it happened for your own good."

Redfern shook his head and went on up the stairs, muttering, "Americans. Utterly incapable of irony."

"Did you know what you were?" I asked my father.

"I had an idea," he said. "I'd seen some of the movies, read some of the books—but that was fiction, I thought. And much of it *has* proven false."

"Can you change into a bat?"

He looked at me—that reluctant look of disappointment. "No, Ari. That's folklore. I wish it were true. I'd love to be able to fly."

I began to ask another question, but he said, "You need sleep. I'll tell you the rest tomorrow."

My legs had already gone to sleep, I realized. The grandfather clock struck the quarter hour: 12:15. I shook my legs and stood up slowly.

"Father," I said, "am I one, too?"

Of course he knew what I meant. He said, "It's beginning to look that way."

— Eight —

"Very little that people write about us is true," my father said the next afternoon. "Never trust those who claim to be vampire experts. They tend to be poseurs with morbid imaginations."

We sat again in the living room, not the library. I'd come to our meeting prepared, or so I thought, with pages of vampire lore I'd copied from the Internet into my journal. He'd skimmed a few pages, then shaken his head.

"Written by well-intentioned fools," he said. "It's a pity that more vampires don't write the facts. A few have, and I'd like to think that more will, as we learn better ways to cope with our condition."

"What about stakes in the heart?" I asked now.

He frowned, the center of his mouth pursed while its corners curled downward. "*Anyone* will die from a stake in the heart," he said. "And anyone will die if they're severely burned, including vampires. But sleeping in coffins, melodramatic costumes, the need for fresh victims—that's all bunk."

The world is home to hundreds of thousands, perhaps millions, of vampires, he said. No one knows for certain, because the question isn't likely to be listed on census forms. Most vampires live rather normal lives, once they've learned to cope with their special needs—not so much different from those of any other chronic ailment.

"Like lupus," I said.

"I lied to you about the lupus, Ari. I'm sorry. It's the story I devised in order to get by in the world. I wanted to be honest with you, but I felt I should wait until you were older. If you turned out to be mortal, I thought you might as well believe I had lupus. And if not—well, another part of me thought that you *knew* it wasn't lupus, all along."

Yet, he said, in some respects vampirism *is* like lupus— the sensitivity to sunlight, the tendency to experience joint pain and migraine headaches. Certain drugs and supplements that treat lupus help vampires, too, particularly in monitoring immune systems. Seradrone had developed blood supplements used by vampires and lupus sufferers alike, by-products of its research in the field of artificial blood.

"We're developing new drugs specifically for us," he said. "Last year clinical trials began on a new hybrid called Meridian Complex. It increases tolerance of sunlight and inhibits the desire for blood."

I must have looked uncomfortable. His eyes suddenly were sympathetic. "That part of the lore, unfortunately, is true."

"Did you kill my mother?" I said it without thinking first. More and more, that seemed to happen—words were spoken as they were thought.

"Of course not." Again, he looked disappointed.

"Did you ever drink her blood?"

"You promised to be patient," he said.

People have ridiculous names for the condition, but my father preferred *vampirism*, though the word's origins are in grim Slavic history. There are other names for the process of becoming a vampire: the role-players call it "being sired," while others call it "transformation" or "rebirth."

"You're only born once, unfortunately," my father said. "I wish it were otherwise."

He referred to his own initiation as a "change of state." "After the change of state, a period of ill health usually ensues," he said.

I tried to imagine what his "change of state" had felt like, and I couldn't.

Suddenly I found myself imagining what it would be like to bite him—yes, bite the neck of my own father. What might his blood taste like?

At that moment he gave me a look so dark, so threatening, that I said at once, "I apologize."

After a moment's awkward silence, he said, "Let me tell you how it was."

For days he lay in bed half awake, half dreaming, too weak to do more.

Malcolm came by once a day to feed him. The first time was the worst. Malcolm walked in, pulled an ivory-handled knife from his coat pocket, and without ceremony slit open his left wrist. He pushed my father's mouth into the wound, and like any newborn, my father sucked up nourishment.

After each feeding he felt stronger, and he always vowed to never do it again. But he wasn't strong enough to resist Malcolm.

One afternoon, while my father was feeding, Dennis walked in.

Vampiric lore talks of the erotic nature of the taking of another's blood. My father said there is some truth in those tales. He felt a sort of sickening pleasure as he drank.

Dennis's face showed shock and disgust. Although my father felt ashamed, he kept drinking. When he was full, and Malcolm had withdrawn his arm, they both looked at Dennis again. His expression had changed; it was pleading.

Malcolm opened his mouth, and my father knew he was ready to lunge at Dennis. With all his strength, my father shouted, "No!"

Malcolm made a noise like a snarl.

Dennis said, "I can help. Both of you, I can help."

For the next five days, Dennis was to prove himself my father's best friend.

My father lay in bed, almost delirious at times with the new hunger and with rage at Malcolm. He fantasized about murdering him. At that time he knew little about vampirism beyond fiction and film. Once he asked Dennis to bring him wooden stakes and a mallet.

Instead, Dennis brought blood from the hospital, which wasn't as potent as Malcolm's, but proved more easily digestible. My father felt less powerful after the injections, but also less agitated. Dennis read to him from current research into the development of artificial blood and hormones that stimulate bone marrow to produce red blood cells. Together they began to plan a protocol for survival that didn't require drinking live humans' blood.

During this time, Dennis introduced my father to the writings of Mahatma Gandhi and the Dalai Lama. He read aloud from their autobiographies. Both believed in the supreme importance of kindness and compassion. Gandhi wrote of the futility of revenge and the importance of non-violence. And the Dalai Lama wrote, "In the practice of tolerance, one's enemy is the best teacher."

I had to think for a minute before I understood the last sentence. "I think I see," I said, finally.

"It took me a while," my father said, "but when I understood, I felt comfort beyond measure. I had a sense that I'd always known these truths, but only when I heard the words did they begin to guide my actions.

"The next time that Malcolm came by, I told him I'd have no more of his cannibalistic nonsense. With Dennis's help, I was strong enough to return to my studies and to live with my affliction."

"Malcolm left you alone?"

"Eventually, he did. At first he tried to argue otherwise. He said that my place was in his lab, since he'd given me a chance to live forever.

"But vampirism is no guarantee of eternal life. Contrary to the Internet lore you've brought me, only a small percentage of those who've changed states lives more than a hundred years. Many get themselves killed through their own acts of aggression or arrogance. They die as painfully as mortals do."

"Surely there are compensations?"

My father had clasped his hands beneath his chin, and he gazed at me with an expression as close to love as I'd ever seen in his eyes. "Yes, Ari," he said, his voice soft. "As I said before, there are compensations."

My father paused to answer a knock on the door. Someone, probably Root, handed him a silver tray with two glasses of Picardo on it. He shut the door and carried the tray to me. "Take the glass on the left," he said.

Another first, I thought, taking the glass. My father set down the tray. He took the other glass and raised it in a toast: *"Gaudeamus igitur / iuvenes dum sumus."*

"So let us rejoice / While we are young," I translated. "I'll have that inscribed on my tombstone."

"Mine as well." It was our first shared joke. We clinked the glasses and drank.

The stuff tasted awful, and I guess my face showed that. My father almost laughed. "Another taste to be acquired," he said.

"Or not," I said. "What's in this stuff?"

He held the glass up and swirled the red liquid. "It's an aperitif. From the Latin *aperire*."

"To open," I said.

"Yes, to open the taste buds before a meal. The first aperitifs were made from herbs and spices, and the roots and fruit of plants."

"What makes it so red?"

My father set down his glass. "The recipe is a secret, created and kept by the Picardo family."

As we sipped our cocktails, my father resumed his story. Those who undergo the "change of state," as my father calls it, immediately are aware of their new nature. But when a vampire and a mortal beget a child, that child's nature is indeterminate.

"I've read atrocious accounts of parents exposing a half-breed child to sunlight—using ropes and stakes to tie it down, then leaving it to see if it burned," he said. "But photosensitivity isn't a certain sign of vampirism. Even in the general population, sensitivity to sun can fluctuate widely."

I wasn't sure I liked the term *half-breed*.

"I used the historical term," my father said. "Today, we prefer to use the term *diverse*."

I took a small sip of Picardo and forced myself to swallow it without tasting it.

"Isn't there a blood test for vampirism?" I asked.

"Not a reliable one." He crossed his arms across his chest, and I found myself noticing the muscles in his neck.

My father told me that vampires exist everywhere, in every country and in every profession. Not surprisingly, many of them are drawn to scientific research, particularly areas involving blood, but others serve as teachers, lawyers, farmers, and politicians. He said that two current U.S. congressmen reportedly were vampires; according to Internet rumors, one of them was thinking about "coming out of the box"—a euphemism for publicly acknowledging one's vampire nature.

"I doubt he'll do it anytime soon," my father said. "Americans aren't ready to accept vampires as normal citizens. All they know are the myths propagated by fiction and films." He picked up my journal and set it down again. "And the Internet."

I took a deep breath. "What about the mirrors?" I said. "And the photographs?"

"I wondered when you'd ask that question." He gestured toward the shadowbox on the wall and beckoned me.

We both stood before the picture. For a moment I didn't understand the point. Then I saw a faint reflection of myself in the domed glass. There was no reflection of my father. I turned to make sure he was still next to me.

"It's a protective mechanism," he said. "We call it emutation. Vampires emutate to varying extents. We can make ourselves entirely invisible to humans or produce a blurred or partial image by controlling our bodies' electrons, keeping them from absorbing light. It's a voluntary action that becomes so instinctive that it seems involuntary, over time. When your friend tried to snap my picture, my electrons shut down and let the light in the room—the electromagnetic radiation, to be more precise—pass through me."

I thought for half a minute. "Why didn't the photo show your clothes? And why aren't they in the mirror?"

"My clothing and shoes are made from 'metamaterials,'" he said. "The fabrics are based on metals, because metals respond so well to light; that's why they're used to make mirrors. When my body's electrons shut off, my skin temperature elevates, and the materials' microscopic structure is altered, allowing them to warp light, make it flow around me. So, when electromagnetic waves hit my clothing, they produce neither a reflection nor a shadow."

"Cool." I said it without thinking.

"Some British tailors are wizards," he said. "In any case, invisibility is one of the compensations that come with the affliction, if you want to call it that. Along with access to the world's best tailors."

"Do you call it an affliction?" I looked at the place in the glass where my father's reflection should have been.

He let me look for a few seconds more, then returned to his chair. "Hematophagy is only one aspect," he said. "Our *condition*, if you will, has more to do with physics—with energy conversion, with changes in molecules' temperatures and pressure patterns and movements. We need mammals' blood, or good substitutes, in order to endure. We can subsist on relatively small amounts—something I've learned through personal experience and experiment—but we become weak unless we're fed."

I nodded. I was hungry.

As I tried to eat dinner (my first attempt at making

vegetarian lasagna produced uninspiring results), my father sipped another cocktail and told me about the brighter side of vampirism.

"Before my change of state, I took so much for granted that now seems extraordinary," he said. "My senses became a hundred times more acute. Malcolm advised me to take the world in small doses, to avoid being overwhelmed by it. Our new state of sensory awareness was similar, he said, to that induced by LSD."

I set down my fork. "Did you ever take LSD?"

"No," my father said. "But Malcolm described his own experience of it and said he found it comparable. He said ordinary experiences now took on new appearances and meanings. A walk through King's College chapel while the organ was playing was almost too much for his senses to absorb. Colors became brilliant, sounds intensely true and pure, and all of the senses intermingled, so that he could simultaneously taste the texture of the stone walls, feel the smells of incense, see the sound of the carillon."

"I can do that," I said.

"Yes, I remember you telling me once that Wednesdays were always silver, while Tuesdays were lavender."

As he spoke, I admired his shirt, which managed to be three colors—blue, green, and black—and no color at all.

"I also became sensitive to patterns," he said. "Malcolm said not all of us share this trait. Certain designs—paisley, for instance, or the complicated patterns of Oriental carpets—are able to mesmerize me, unless I turn away. Needless complexity—complexity for no reason—arrests my attention, makes me look for the aberration that isn't there. Apparently it's related to my difficulty in opening things; it's a form of dyslexia. Have you experienced it?"

"No." For the first time I understood why none of the fabrics in the house was patterned, and why all of the door-knobs were oversized. "What about shape-shifting?"

"Another myth. I can become invisible, as I told you. I can hear others' thoughts—not always, but usually. And I can"—he paused and made a dismissive gesture with his hands—"I can hypnotize others. But so can you, and so can many humans. It's been said that Freud could control his family at the dinner table by the movement of his left eyebrow."

"Was Freud one of us?"

"Good heavens, no," my father said. "Freud was the fa-ther of psychoanalysis. No self-respecting vampire would have anything to do with that."

I looked up from my food and saw a glint of humor in his eyes.

"All in all, these qualities aren't what I consider assets, but rather unusual abilities that I choose to deploy as little as possible. The real assets are the obvious ones—never aging and enjoying potentially infinite longevity, immunity to many diseases and perils, and rapid recovery from limited exposure to the few to which we're vulnerable."

I pushed away my plate. "What are the few?"

"*Erythema solare*—that's sunburn," he said. "Fire. Severe heart injury."

"Father," I said, "am I mortal or not?"

"Part of you is, of course." He curled one hand around the base of his cocktail glass. His hands were strong, but not square, with long fingers. "We simply don't know yet how much. Matters will sort themselves out, as you age. Heredity is more than DNA, you know. Traits are also transmitted through behavior and symbolic communication, including language."

"As I age," I repeated. "Doesn't that mean I *am* mortal— the fact that each year I'm different, while you remain the same?"

He set down his glass. "So far, yes, you are aging as mortals do. There may come a time when you choose"—he stopped talking for a moment, his face falling into familiar lines of sadness, but his eyes close to despair—"when you choose, or the choice is made for you, to stop aging."

"I can choose?" This was something I hadn't considered.

"You can choose." He looked again at my plate and grimaced. "Your *food* is growing cold, with all these questions."

I didn't take the hint. "I have so many more to ask," I said. "How do I go about choosing? And what happened to my mother? Is she dead?"

He put up his hand. "Too many questions. I'll address them, but not in a piecemeal fashion. Let me tell you how it was between us, yes? And then, as I've said before, you'll be able to answer the big questions yourself."

I picked up my fork. He resumed his story.

During the time immediately after my father's change of

state, Malcolm told him that his new life would be better than his previous one.

"We'll never grow old," Malcolm said. "We'll survive anything—car crashes, cancer, terrorism, the infinite petty horrors of mundane life. We'll persist, despite all obstacles. We'll prevail."

In Western culture, aging always means diminished power. Malcolm said they'd enjoy freedom from pain—and from love, the curse of mortals. They would live without what he called *the ephemera*: transitory concerns based on mortal personalities and politics that, in the end, no one would remember.

Malcolm spoke of mortals as if they were vampires' worst enemies. "The world would be a better place if humans were extinct," he said.

I took another sip of Picardo, which sent a tingling sensation through my body. "Do you agree?"

"Sometimes I'm tempted to agree." My father waved his hand toward the shade-covered window. "When you walk around out there, you see so much unnecessary suffering, so much greed and malice. The abuse and murder of humans and animals—unnecessary, yet commonplace. Vampires— some of us—are always mindful of the ugliness. We're a bit like God in that respect; you don't recall that line of Spinoza's, that to see things as God does is to see them under the aspect of eternity?"

"I thought we didn't believe in God."

He smiled. "We don't know for certain, do we?"

But Malcolm didn't mention the problems, my father

said—the terrible urge to feed, the mood swings, the vulner-abilities, and all of the ethical implications of the change of state.

At first my father considered himself no better than a cannibal. Over time, he learned the truth of Bertrand Russell's belief: by ordering one's mind, happiness becomes accessible, even to an *other*.

One night when my father was half conscious, he called for Sara. Malcolm reminded him of it afterward. He said the only right thing was never to see her again.

"There's a history that you don't know yet," Malcolm said. "Other vampires have tried to live with mortals, and it never works. The only alternative is to bite her. You could use her as a donor, so long as you never let her bite you. I personally would be disheartened if you made a woman *one of us*." Malcolm was half-lying across a sofa in my father's room as he said this, very like a character in an Oscar Wilde play—the consummate misanthrope.

At the time, my father thought that Malcolm might be right—the kindest thing would be for him to end his relationship with Sara. He agonized over how to let her know what had happened. How could he tell her what had taken place? What sort of letter could he write?

My mother wasn't religious in a conventional sense, but she believed in a God among many gods, to whom she could pray in time of trouble. The rest of the time, she mostly ignored that God, as many mortals do. My father was afraid that his news could shock her into some irrational action. He considered never communicating with her again—

simply moving to a place where she'd never find him.

When Dennis took over Malcolm's role as caretaker, my father began to look at the problem differently. Perhaps there were other alternative actions. At any rate, it was clear to him that the matter couldn't be handled by a letter. No matter what he might write, she wouldn't believe it—and she deserved to hear an explanation face to face.

Some days, as he grew stronger, my father thought that he and my mother might be strong enough to weather the situation. Most times he felt otherwise. Malcolm had told him some odd tales while he was bedridden, and they persuaded him that any vampire union with a mortal was damned from the start.

So, for the time being, he told my mother nothing.

Surprisingly, Dennis raised the subject. "What will you tell Sara?"

"I'll tell her everything," my father said, "once I see her."

"Isn't that risky?"

For a moment my father wondered if Dennis had been talking to Malcolm. But then he looked across at his friend—the freckled face, the wide brown eyes—and he realized again all Dennis had done for him. Dennis was holding a vial of blood at the time, preparing to inject him.

"What's life without risk?" my father said. "Nothing but *mauvais foi*."

He reminded me that *mauvais foi* means "bad faith."

"We need to spend a little more time with the Existentialists, don't you think?" he said.

"Father," I said, "I'd be happy to spend more time with the Existentialists. And I do appreciate knowing these details. I do. But I can't bear the idea of going to bed tonight still not knowing about my mother, or whether I'm going to die."

He stirred in his chair, and looked over at my now-empty plate. He said, "Then let's move into the living room, and you shall have the rest of it."

In the end my father didn't have to choose a way to tell my mother what had happened. She took one look at him at the airport, and she said, "You've changed."

Rather than bringing her back to Cambridge, my father took her to the Ritz Hotel in London, and they spent the next five days trying to come to terms with each other. Sara had packed carefully for the trip; she had a distinctive style, my father said, recalling in particular a green chiffon dress that rippled like romaine lettuce.

But she didn't have any reason to dress up. Instead of going to the theatre, or even downstairs for tea, they stayed in their suite, ordered room service every day, and fought bitterly over their future.

When my father told her about his new state, she reacted as humans are said to react to news of a loved one's death: with shock, denial, bargaining, guilt, anger, depression, and finally, some sort of acceptance.

(He noted that I had not reacted in those ways to anything he'd told me. That alone, he said, suggested that I might be "one of us.")

168

My mother blamed herself for what my father had become. Why had she urged him to come to England? Then she blamed my father. Who had done this to him? Had he caused it to happen? Then she began to cry, and she wept for most of a day.

My father held her when she'd let him, but held her gingerly, worried that she might tempt him somehow. He didn't trust himself to relax around her.

He told her he regretted the day he'd been born—and then he apologized for using a cliché. He would get out of her life at once, he said, for both their sakes.

She refused to hear it. When her crying stopped, she grew insistent that they stay together. If my father left her, she said, she would take her own life.

My father accused her of being melodramatic.

"It's you who've turned our lives melodramatic!" she said. "It's you who managed to become a damned vampire." Then she began to cry again.

"Sara," my father told me now, "even at the best of times, which this was not, had little talent for reasoned argument."

By the end of the week, my father felt emotionally and physically exhausted.

Sara won. She went back to Savannah wearing an engagement ring: a replica of an Etruscan ring with a tiny bird perched on it, bought by my father when he'd first arrived in London. A few weeks later, he packed up his things and took a plane home.

He joined Sara in the brick house by the cemetery, which

indeed was haunted, and every day they learned new ways of accommodating what Sara called my father's "affliction." Dennis stayed in Cambridge, but he mailed my father freeze-dried "cocktails," the formulae for which were ever-evolving to more closely approximate fresh human blood. This work was the beginning of what would become Seradrone.

After a few months, my mother and father were married in Sarasota, a seaside town in Florida, and later they moved to Saratoga Springs. (Sara retained her fondness for the letter S, thinking it was lucky, and my father indulged her. He wanted to please her as much as he could, to compensate for his condition.)

They settled into the Victorian house. In time, Dennis finished his research at Cambridge and found a job at one of the colleges in Saratoga Springs, so that he and my father could continue to work together. They formed the company called Seradrone and recruited Mary Ellis Root as an assistant; her training in hematology was truly outstanding, my father said. The three of them developed a blood purification method that has enabled transfusions all over the world.

Sara kept busy at first, decorating the house, and tending the gardens and, later, her bees—she set up hives by the lavender patch in the garden. They were (my father spoke with some astonishment in his voice) *happy*.

But for one thing: my mother wanted a child.

"You were conceived in the usual way," my father said, his voice dry. "Your birth was a long process, but your mother came through it quite well. She had real stamina.

"You weighed only four pounds, Ari. You were born in the upstairs bedroom with the lavender wallpaper—your mother insisted upon that. Dennis and I handled the delivery. We both were concerned when you didn't cry. You stared at me with dark blue eyes— far more focused than we expected a newborn's eyes to be. You seemed to say hello to the world in a matter-of-fact way.

"Your mother fell asleep almost at once, and we carried you downstairs to run some tests. When we tested your blood, we found you were anemic—we'd anticipated this possibility, since your mother was anemic throughout the pregnancy. We spent some minutes debating the best treatment. I even called Dr. Wilson. Then I carried you upstairs again." Here he lifted both hands, in a gesture of helplessness. "Your mother was gone."

"Not dead," I said.

"Not dead. She simply wasn't there. The bed was empty. And that's when you first began to cry."

My father and I stayed up until four a.m., sorting out details.

"Didn't you look for her?" was my first question, and he said that yes, indeed they had. Dennis went out first, while my father fed me; they'd bought cans of infant formula in case my mother's breast milk wasn't adequate. When Dennis came back, he looked after me, and my father went out.

"She didn't take her purse," he said, his voice dark with memories. "The front door was ajar. The car was in the garage. We found nothing to suggest where she might have gone. Who knows what went through her mind?"

"Did you call the police?"

"No." My father left his chair and began to walk back and forth across the living room. "The police are so *limited*. I didn't see any point of calling them, and I didn't care to invite their scrutiny."

"But they might have found her!" I stood up, too. "Didn't you care?"

"Of course I cared. I do have feelings, after all. But I was sure that Dennis and I had a better chance of finding her on our own. And—" He hesitated. "I'm accustomed to being left."

I thought about his own mother, dying when he was a baby, and about what he'd said about bereaved children— how death informs them, marks them forever.

He said he sometimes felt as if a veil hung between him and the world that kept him from directly experiencing it. "I don't have your sense of immediacy," he said. "In that, you're like your mother. Everything was immediate to her.

"When the shock of finding her gone began to fade, I thought back on things she'd said during the last few months. Frequently she'd been ill, and she clearly felt de-pressed and unhappy. She said things that weren't rational, at times. She threatened to leave me, to leave you once you were born. She said she felt as if she were an animal trapped in a cage."

"She didn't want me." I sat down again.

"She didn't know what she wanted," he said. "I thought

172

that her hormones might be unbalanced. To be honest, I didn't know what else to think. But for whatever reason, she chose to leave." He looked at the floor. "Humans are always leaving, Ari. That's one thing I've learned. Life is all about people leaving."

For a few seconds we didn't speak. The grandfather clock struck four.

"I telephoned her sister, Sophie, who lives in Savannah. She promised to call me if Sara turned up. About a month later, she did call. Sara had told her not to let me know where she was. Ari, she said she didn't want to come back."

I felt empty inside, but the emptiness had weight and sharp edges. It hurt.

"If I hadn't been born, she'd still be here," I said.

"Ari, no. If you hadn't been born, she would have been even more miserable. She so much wanted you, remember?"

"And you didn't?" I looked at him, and I knew I was right.

"I didn't think it was a good idea," he said. He stretched his hands toward me, palms up, as if asking for mercy. "For all of the reasons I've told you, vampires aren't meant to breed."

The emptiness in me turned to numbness. I'd gotten the answers to my questions, all right. My head was filled with them. But instead of bringing me any satisfaction, they made me feel sick.

— Nine —

When animals and humans are babies, they tend to imprint—they instinctively note the characteristics of their parents, and they mimic them. Newborn foals, for instance, imprint and follow whatever large being looms above them at the time of birth. After I was born, my father was the only parent to loom above me, and so I learned to mimic him.

But in the womb, I must have listened hard to my mother. Otherwise, much of my later behavior couldn't be explained—except, perhaps, genetically. And that's a complicated matter that we'll consider at another time, yes?

Every January my father left the house for a week to attend a professional conference. Normally Dennis took over my lessons while my father was away.

The night before my father left, Dennis joined us at dinner. Root had prepared an eggplant casserole (surprisingly much tastier than anything ever made by poor Mrs. McG), but after a forkful I had no appetite for more.

Ari is depressed, I thought. Looking across at my father and Dennis, I knew they thought so, too. The worry on their faces made me feel a little guilty. They were pretending to talk about physics— in particular, electrodynamics, on which my next lessons would focus—but they really were talking about me.

"You'll begin with the review of atomic structure," my father said to Dennis, his eyes on me.

"Of course," Dennis said. He hadn't been around much since Kathleen's death, but whenever he came by, he put his hands on my shoulders as if to strengthen me.

Root came up from the basement with a large brown bottle in her hand. She set it on the table before my father, and he moved it to the side of my plate. Then she looked at me, and I looked back, and for a moment I saw a shred of sympathy in her black eyes. It disappeared almost at once, and she hurried back to the basement.

"All right, then." My father pushed back his chair. "Ari, I'll be back next Friday, and I expect by then you'll be ready to discuss quantum theory and relativity theory."

He stood there for a minute—my handsome father in his impeccable suit, his dark hair gleaming in the light from the chandelier over the table. I met his eyes for a second, then looked down at the tablecloth. *You didn't want me*, I thought, and I hoped he heard.

The new tonic tasted stronger than the previous one, and

after I took the first spoonful I felt a surge of unfamiliar energy. But an hour later, I felt listless again.

We didn't have a scale upstairs; there was one in the basement, I suppose, but I didn't want to go into Root's domain. I knew I'd lost weight only because of the way my clothes fit. My jeans were baggy, and my t-shirts seemed a size larger. It was around this time that my periods stopped. Some months later, I realized I'd been anorexic.

Dennis and I slogged our way through quantum theory. I listened to him without asking questions. At one point he stopped lecturing. "What's wrong, Ari?" he said.

I noticed that his reddish hair had a few strands of silver in it now. "Do you ever think about dying?" I asked.

He rubbed his chin. "Every day of my life," he said.

"You're my father's best friend." I listened to my words, wondering where they were heading. "But you're not—"

"I'm not like him." He finished my sentence. "I know. Too bad, huh?"

"You mean you wish you were?"

He leaned back in his chair. "Yeah, of course I do. Who wouldn't want the chance to be around forever? But I don't know if *he'd* like me talking that way around you. You're still kind of—"

He hesitated. I finished his sentence: "—up for grabs."

"Whatever that means." He grinned.

"It means I get to choose," I said. "That's what he told me. But I don't know how yet."

"I don't know, either," Dennis said. "Sorry. But I'm sure you'll figure it out."

"That's what *he* says." I wished I had a mother to give me advice. I folded my arms across my chest. "So where is *he*, anyway? Some big blood conference? Why didn't you go, too?"

"He's in Baltimore. Every year he goes there. But it's not about blood. It's something to do with the Edgar Allan Poe fan club, or society, or whatever they call themselves." Dennis shook his head and reopened the physics book.

We'd finished lessons, and I was doing yoga alone (Dennis had laughed when I suggested that he join me), when I heard the sound of the front door knocker. It was an old brass one with the face of Neptune on it, and I'd rarely heard it used before—mostly on Halloween nights, by trick-or-treaters whose expectations must have quickly deflated.

When I opened the door, Agent Burton stood on the porch. "Morning, Miss Montero," he said.

"It's actually afternoon," I said.

"So it is. How are you this afternoon?"

"I'm okay." If my father had been there, I'd have said *very well, not okay.*

"Great, great." He wore a camel's hair coat over a dark suit, and his eyes were bloodshot, yet energetic. "Is your father at home?"

"No," I said.

"When do you expect him?" He smiled as if he were a friend of the family.

"Friday," I said. "He's at a conference."

"A conference." Burton nodded, three times. "Tell him

I stopped by, won't you do that? Ask him to give me a call when he gets back. Please."

I said I would, and I was about to shut the door when he said, "Say, you wouldn't know anything about kirigami, would you?"

"Kirigami? You mean paper-cutting?" My father had taught me kirigami years ago. After folding paper, you made tiny cuts, then unfolded it to produce a picture. It was one form of design that he could tolerate, he said, because it was symmetrical, and it could be useful, too.

"Very skillful cutting." Agent Burton kept nodding. "Who taught you how to do it?"

"I read about it," I said. "In a book."

He smiled and said goodbye. He was thinking, *Bet her old man knows something about cutting*.

That night Dennis cooked dinner—vegetarian tacos with fake meat filling—and although I wanted to like them, I couldn't. I tried to smile after I said I wasn't hungry. He made me take two teaspoonfuls of tonic, and he gave me some homemade "protein bars" wrapped in plastic.

His face turned darker and redder when he was worried. "You're depressed," he said. "And it's no wonder. But it will pass, Ari. Do you hear me?"

"I hear you." The cheese melted into the glutinous fake meat on my plate, making me feel nauseous. "I miss my mother." Another sentence I hadn't planned. Yes, it's possible to miss someone you've never met.

I wondered why he looked guilty.

"Whatever happened to that boy you were seeing? Mitchell, was that his name?"

"Michael." I'd never mentioned him, I felt sure. "He's Kathleen's brother."

I could tell he hadn't known. "That's rough," he said. He took a large bite of his taco, which dripped tomato sauce onto his shirt. Normally I might have found that funny.

"Why don't you ask him over sometime?" Dennis said, still chewing his taco.

I said that maybe I would do that.

When I called the McGarritts' house that night, no one answered. The next morning I tried again, and Michael answered the phone.

He sounded neither pleased nor sad to hear my voice. "Things are okay," he said. "The reporters are pretty much leaving us alone now. Mom still isn't well."

"Do you want to come over?"

I heard him breathing. Finally he said, "I'd better not." Another pause. "But I'd like to see you. Could you come over here?"

After another stultifying physics lesson (Dennis preferred to work with me in the morning, so that he could go to the college in the afternoons), I went upstairs and looked at myself in the mirror. My wavering reflection wasn't impressive. My clothes were so loose that I looked like a waif.

Luckily, I'd received new clothes for Christmas (which we'd noted with even less fanfare than usual). An enormous box marked Gieves & Hawkes had been set next to my chair in the living room; in it were tailored black trousers and a jacket, four beautiful shirts, socks, underwear, even hand-made shoes and a backpack. I'd been too dispirited to try them on until now. They all fitted perfectly. In them, my body appeared lithe, not too skinny.

Feeling presentable, I trudged over to the McGarritts' house. The air wasn't too cold—the temperature must have been above freezing, because the snow on the ground oozed, and icicles on the houses dripped slowly. The sky was the same dead gray color it always was, and I realized how tired I was of winter. Sometimes it's hard to imagine why people choose to live in the places they live, and why anyone at all would choose Saratoga Springs. I found nothing quaint or picturesque about it that day, only row after row of in-creasingly shabby houses with peeling paint, framed by dirty snow and dreary sky.

I rang the McGarritts' doorbell—three ascending notes (C, E, G) that sounded inappropriately cheerful. Michael let me in. If I'd lost weight, he'd lost more.

His eyes looked at me without expecting anything. I put my hand on his shoulder in a sisterly way. We went into the living room, and we sat side by side on the sofa without talk-ing for nearly an hour. On the wall hung a calendar with a picture of Jesus leading a flock of sheep, showing the days of the month of November.

Finally I said, my voice close to a whisper, "Where is every-one?" The room was unusually tidy, and the house was silent.

"Dad's at work," he said. "Kids are in school. Mom's upstairs in bed."

"Why aren't you at school?"

"I'm looking after things here." He pushed back his hair, which by now was as long as mine. "I clean. I buy the groceries. I cook."

I hated the lost look in his eyes. "Are you okay?"

"Did you hear about Ryan?" he said, as if I hadn't spoken. "He tried to kill himself last week."

I hadn't heard. I couldn't imagine Ryan doing anything that serious.

"They kept it out of the papers." Michael rubbed his eyes. "He took pills. Are you reading the blogs? People are saying he killed her."

"I can't imagine Ryan doing that." I noticed reddish welts along Michael's forearms, as if he'd repeatedly scratched himself.

"I can't, either. But people say he did it. They say he had the opportunity and the motive. They say he was jealous of her. I never saw that." He looked in my direction, his eyes vague. "It makes you wonder how much you can ever know anyone."

There really wasn't anything left to say. I sat with him for half an hour more, and then, suddenly, I couldn't stand it a moment longer. "I have to go," I said.

He looked at me blankly.

"Oh, I read *On the Road*." I wondered why I'd said that. "Yeah?"

"Yeah. It was good." I stood up. "I'm thinking about going on the road myself."

Actually, I'd never thought of such a thing, except for my

vague yearning to see America. But suddenly it seemed like a fine plan, a necessary plan to counter the inertia all around me. I'd do what my father and Dennis hadn't done—I'd follow my mother's trail, find out what had happened to her.

Michael walked me to the door. "If you go, be careful."

We exchanged one last look. His eyes had no feeling left in them. I wondered if he took drugs.

On the walk home I began to reason it out. Why *shouldn't* I get away from this place for a while? Why not try to find my mother? I don't know if it was the weather, or seeing Michael, or the need to burst out of my depression, but I craved change.

My mother had a sister who lived in Savannah. Why not visit her? Maybe she could tell me why my mother had left us. Maybe my mother was still around somewhere, waiting for me to find her.

For all of my education, I didn't know much about land distances. I could tell you how far Earth is from the sun, but I had no idea how far Saratoga Springs was from Savannah. I'd seen maps, of course, but I didn't plan to look at them for the best route, or to calculate how many days it would take to travel. I figured I could reach Savannah in two or three days, meet my aunt, and then come back around the time of my father's return from Baltimore.

The most planning Kerouac had ever done was to make sandwiches to last his journey coast to coast, and even then, most of the sandwiches went rotten. The best way was simply to go, to initiate motion and see where it led.

By the time I reached home, my mind was made up. In my room I packed my new backpack with my wallet, journal, an old pair of jeans, and my new shirts, underwear, and socks. I packed quickly; the room felt claustrophobic to me now. I hated to leave my laptop, but it would add too much weight. As an afterthought I threw in a toothbrush, a bar of soap, my bottles of tonic, and sunscreen, sunglasses, the protein bars, and Michael's copy of *On the Road*.

I left Dennis a note: "I'm going away for a few days" was all it said.

In the kitchen pantry I found a piece of cardboard and with a marker wrote one word on it: *SOUTH*, in letters a foot high. I wasn't running away, I told myself. I was running toward something.

Part II

ON THE ROAD SOUTH

— Ten —

My first stop was the ATM downtown. My father had given me an account for clothing, food, movies, that sort of thing. It had a balance of $220, and I withdrew it all.

I figured it wouldn't be smart to hitchhike in the center of town, so I took a bus to the outskirts, then walked to the entrance ramp for I-87 South. It was late afternoon, and the sun emerged briefly from gray cloud blankets. I held up my sign, exhilarated to be out in the world, en route to an unknown destination.

My very first ride was lucky: a family in an old Chrysler New Yorker sedan stopped for me. I sat with three children in the wide backseat. One of them offered me cold french fries. The car was big and roomy, and it smelled as if they lived in it.

"Where you headed?" The woman in the front passenger seat turned around and looked me over. One of her front teeth was missing.

I said I was going to visit my aunt in Savannah.

"I-95 gets you right there." She nodded, as if agreeing with herself. "Well, you can ride with us as far as Florence. We live outside of Columbia."

"Thank you," I said. I didn't know what states those places were in, but I was too proud to ask.

The father, a large man with a tattoo on his right arm, drove without talking. The children kept surprisingly quiet, too. Next to me sat a girl, around six, who said they'd been visiting their cousins in Plattsburgh. I didn't know where that was, either.

I pressed my face against the cold window and watched the landscape: snow-covered hills, and houses, mostly white, with square unlit windows like lithophanes waiting for inner light to illumine them. As the sky grew darker, I imagined families inside the houses, talking around dining room tables, like the McGs in the old days; I imagined the smells of roast meat and mashed potatoes and the soft sounds of television in the background. I let myself imagine what it might be like to be part of a normal family.

The girl sitting next to me offered me another french fry, and I chewed it slowly, savoring the salt and grease.

"My name is Lily," she said. She had dark brown hair in tiny braids, with a bead at the end of each braid.

"I'm Ari," I said. We nodded at each other.

"Want to hold hands?" she said. She slipped her hand into mine. It was small and warm.

As the big car moved through the darkness, Lily and I fell asleep, holding hands.

We stopped twice at highway rest stops for gas and bathroom breaks. When I offered to help pay for gas, they acted as if they didn't hear me. The mother of the family bought hamburgers and coffee, sodas and more french fries, and she handed me a wrapped burger as if it was my due. Besides my tonic and protein bars, I'd planned on eating only ice cream and apple pie in diners, in honor of Kerouac.

I tried to say no, but she said, "You look hungry. Eat."

So I had my second taste of meat. At first I thought I'd throw up, but I found that if I chewed each mouthful fast and thoroughly, I could tolerate it. And it didn't taste bad.

After eating, the family's father began to sing. After each song, he announced its title, for my sake. "That was 'I Saw the Light,'" he said. And later, "That was 'Blue Moon of Kentucky.'" He had a high tenor voice, and the children joined in on the choruses. When he stopped singing, everyone but him went to sleep again.

They stopped on an off-ramp in Florence, South Carolina, early the next morning to let me out, and they seemed genuinely sorry to see me go.

"You take care now," the woman said. "Watch out for the cops."

I stepped out into a cold clear morning, the sun rising over a flat maize-colored landscape marked by motels and gas stations. As the car moved away, Lily waved at me frantically through the rear window. I waved back.

I'd never see her again, I thought. My father was right: people are always leaving. They fall in and out of your life like shadows.

* * *

It took me more than an hour to get my next ride, which brought me only fifteen miles down I-95. I spent that whole day making slow incremental progress, and I began to realize how lucky the first ride had been. I told myself that every mile might bring me closer to my mother, but the romance of hitchhiking began to fade.

I remembered what the woman had said, and every time I saw a police car I ran into the trees near the road's shoulder. None of them stopped.

Most of the people who stopped for me drove old-model cars; the SUVs passed me by, as did the trucks. One man driving a tank-like SUV nearly ran me over.

The sky grew dark again, and I waited at an entrance ramp in the middle of nowhere, wondering where I could spend the night. Then a shiny red car (little silver letters on its side read *Corvette*) stopped for me. When I opened the passenger door, the driver said, "Ain't you a little young to be out here by yourself?"

He was probably in his early thirties, I thought. He was small and muscular, with a square-jawed face and greasy-looking black hair. He wore aviator sunglasses. I wondered why he wore them at night.

"I'm old enough," I said. But I hesitated. A voice inside me said,

You can choose not to get in.

"You coming or what?" he said.

It was late. I was tired. Though I didn't like his looks, I got in.

He said he was headed for Asheville. "That work for you?"

"Sure," I said. I wasn't sure if he'd said Nashville or Asheville. Either destination sounded sufficiently Southern.

He gunned the engine and barreled the car up the ramp onto the highway. He turned up the radio, which played rap music. The word *bitch* was in every other line. I focused on rubbing my hands. They felt stiff and cold despite my gloves, but I kept them on, for the illusion of warmth.

How long was it before I knew something was wrong? Not very. The route signs said I-26, not I-95, and we were headed west, not south. I'd have to double back to get to Savannah, I realized. At least I wasn't standing outside in the cold.

The driver held the steering wheel steady with his left hand and rubbed it repeatedly with his right. His fingernails were long and stained. The masseter muscle in his right cheek clenched and unclenched, clenched and unclenched. Once in a while he looked over at me, and I turned my head away, toward the passenger-side window. In the gathering darkness, I couldn't see much outside. The road stretched ahead, flat and pale, lit only by headlights. Then, gradually at first, it began to climb. My ears popped, and I swallowed hard.

Two hours later, the car swerved and headed down a ramp so fast that I never saw the exit sign.

"Where are you going?" I asked.

He said, "We need to get a bite to eat. I bet you're hungry, ain't ya."

But he turned the car away from the lights of the service station and fast food restaurant, and a mile or so later he turned sharply down a country road.

"Relax," he said, not looking at me. "I know just the place."

He did seem to know exactly where he was going, taking three more turns before driving onto a dirt road that twisted up a hillside. I saw no houses, only trees. When he stopped the car, I felt my stomach sink.

He used both arms to grab me, and he was strong. "Relax, relax," he kept saying. And he laughed, as if he found my struggling funny. When I pretended to relax, he used one hand to unbutton my trousers, and that's when I lunged and bit him.

I didn't plan it in any conscious way. Only when I saw his neck, exposed and bent before me, did it happen. I can still hear the sound of his scream. It sounded surprised, then angry, agonized, pleading—in the space of seconds. Then all I heard was my heart beating loud, and the sound of my sucking and swallowing.

What did it taste like? Like music. Like electricity. Like moonlight shining on rushing water. I drank my fill, and when I stopped, my own blood sang in my ears.

I spent the next hours walking through woods. I didn't feel the cold, and I felt strong enough to walk for miles. The moon overhead was nearly full, and it stared down with blank indifference.

Gradually, my energy began to fade. My stomach

churned, and I thought I would be sick. I stopped walking and sat on a tree stump.

I tried not to think about what I'd done, but I thought about it anyway. Was the man alive or dead? I hoped he was dead, and part of me was appalled at myself. What had I become?

I gagged, but I didn't vomit. Instead I tilted my head back and watched the moon, visible between two tall trees. I breathed slowly. The nausea passed, and I felt ready to walk again.

The hill inclined steeply. Walking wasn't easy, but without the moonlight, it would have been impossible. The trees grew close together. They were tall and bristly—some sort of pine, I supposed.

Father, I'm lost, I thought. *I don't even know the names of the trees. Mother, where are you?*

I came to a crest and followed another path that gradually declined. Through the leafless brush, lights glimmered from below— indistinct at first, then brighter. *Back to civilization*, I thought, and the phrase cheered me.

When I heard voices, I stopped walking. They came from a clearing ahead.

I stayed among the trees and moved quietly around the perimeter of the open space.

There must have been five or six of them. Some wore capes, others pointed hats.

"I am vanquished!" someone shouted, and a boy wearing a cape waved a plastic sword at him.

I moved into the clearing and let them see me. "May I play?" I said. "I know the rules."

* * *

For an hour we played on the hillside in the cold moonlight. This game differed from the one I'd watched at Ryan's house; here, no one consulted spell-books, and everyone ad-libbed their parts. No one mentioned banks, either.

The game focused on a quest: to find and steal the werewolves' treasure, which someone had hidden in the forest. The werewolves were the other "team," playing somewhere nearby, and they'd given my team (the wizards) a set of written clues. "Keep thy eyes far from the sky / What you seek is closer by" was an early one.

"Who are you?" one of the boys had asked me, when I entered the game. "Wizard? Gnome?"

"Vampire," I said.

"Vampire Griselda joins the Lounge Wizards," he announced.

The clues seemed too easy to me. Wizard Lemur, the one who'd announced me, also read the clues; he was the group's leader. Each time he read one, I moved instinctively as it directed. "Where the tallest tree doth grow / To its right side you must go." That sort of thing. After a few minutes, I felt they were all watching me.

The treasure turned out to be a six-pack of beer hidden in a pile of dead branches. As I lifted the beer, the others cheered. "Vampire Griselda secures the treasure," Lemur said. "Which we hope she'll share."

I handed him the six-pack. "I never drink," I said, "beer."

* * *

The wizards took me home with them.

I rode with Lemur (whose real name was Paul) and his girlfriend, Beatrice (real name Jane) in Jane's beat-up old Volvo. They looked like brother and sister: multicolored hair cut in layers, skinny bodies, even the same frayed jeans. Jane was a college student. Paul had dropped out of school. I told them I'd run away from home. They said it was cool if I "crashed" at their place—an old house in downtown Asheville. They said I could have Tom's room, since he was on tour with his band.

And crash is what I did, almost falling into the bed I'd been assigned. My body felt weary and excited at the same time, tingling from my head to my toes, and all I wanted to do was to lie still and take stock. I remembered my father describing his change of state, how he'd felt weak and sick, and I wondered why I didn't feel weak. Maybe because I'd been born half vampire?

Would I need to bite more humans? Would my senses become more acute? I had a hundred questions, and the only one who could answer them was miles and miles away.

The days passed in an odd blur. At times I was intensely aware of every detail of the place and people around me; at others, I could focus only on one small thing, such as the blood pulsing under my skin; I could see the blood move through my veins with each beat of my heart. I stayed still for long periods of time. At some point I noticed that my talisman—the little bag of lavender—no longer hung from my neck. The loss didn't matter much to me; one more familiar thing was gone.

The house was poorly heated and sparsely furnished with battered furniture. Paint was spattered on the walls, especially in the living room, where someone had begun to paint a mural of a dragon breathing fire, and quit before the dragon's tail and feet were finished. Others had penciled in telephone numbers where the rest of the dragon should have been.

Jane and Paul accepted me without questions. I told them my name was Ann. They tended to sleep late, until one or two in the afternoon, and stay up until four or five a.m., usually smoking marijuana. Sometimes they dyed their hair, using Kool-Aid; Jane's current color, lime green, made her look like a dryad.

Jane's school was "out on winter break," she told me, and she meant to "play hard" until classes resumed. Paul apparently lived this way all the time. Some days I barely saw them; others we spent "hanging out," which meant eating, or watching movies on DVD, or walking around Asheville— a pretty town, ringed by mountains.

We spent my second night in the house gathered around a small television with the other Lounge Wizards, watching a movie so predictable that I didn't pay attention to it. When it ended, the news came on—a signal for everyone to talk—but Jane nudged Paul and said, "Hey, check it out."

The newscaster said police had no leads in the case of Robert Reedy, the thirty-five-year-old man found murdered in his car the day before. The video showed police officers standing near the red Corvette, then a pan of the woods nearby.

"That's near where we were on Sunday," Jane said.

Paul said, "Blame it on the werewolves."

But Jane didn't let it go. "Annie, did you see anything weird?"

"Only you all," I said.

They laughed. "Kid's been in the South like three days and she's *y'alling* already," Paul said. "Go, Annie."

So his name was Robert Reedy, I thought. *And I killed him.*

They passed around a pipe, and when it came to me, I decided to try it to see if I could lighten my mood. But marijuana didn't work for me.

The others engaged in long, rambling conversations. One began with Paul's inability to find his car keys, the others chiming in suggestions for finding them, and ended with Jane repeating, again and again: "Everything is somewhere."

Instead of talking, I spent the rest of the night staring at the pattern of the threadbare carpet on the floor, sure that the design must contain an important message.

On subsequent evenings, I always declined the pipe.

Paul said, "Annie doesn't need to smoke. She's naturally stoned."

When I look back on my time in Asheville, I associate it with a song that Paul frequently played on the house stereo: "Dead Souls" by Joy Division.

I slept little, ate less, and spent hours doing nothing but breathe. Often, usually around three a.m., I wondered if I was ill, or even if I was going to die. I didn't have the energy to look for my mother. I wondered if I should go home and try to recuperate—but what would my father think of me?

Sometimes I wandered to the window, sensing someone out there. Sometimes I was too frightened to look. What if Reedy's ghost waited for me? When I did look, I saw nothing.

Each morning, the wavering reflection of my face in the mirror hadn't changed; if anything, I looked healthier than I had when I left Saratoga Springs. So, I spent most days alone in my haze, or hanging out with Jane.

Jane's idea of a good day was to sleep late, eat a lot, then stroll around Asheville, periodically talking to Paul on her mobile phone. (He had a part-time job in a sandwich shop, and each night he brought home free food.) She'd perfected the art of *thrifting* (scouting secondhand stores for treasure); she could walk into a store and scan racks of clothes so quickly, with such precision, that in seconds she'd say, "Velvet jacket, third aisle center," or "Nothing but rags today. We move on."

We'd move on to coffee shops or "New Age" bookstores, where we'd read books and magazines without ever buying any. Once, Jane shoplifted a deck of Tarot cards, and I felt something stir in me. Was it conscience? I found myself wanting to say something to her, tell her to take them back. Instead, I said nothing. How could a murderer preach right and wrong to a shoplifter?

A few times a week we went to the supermarket, and Jane bought groceries. When I offered to help pay, she usually said, "Forget it. You eat like a bird, anyway."

I normally didn't eat much, but once in a while hunger came over me in waves, and then I devoured whatever I could find. I'd been raised a vegetarian, but now I craved meat—the rawer and bloodier, the better. One night, alone in my room, I ate a pound of raw hamburger. Afterward, my energy surged, but a few hours later it plummeted. There must be a better way to manage things, I thought.

Sometimes we got together with wizards and werewolves to role-play. The players had crafted identities much more intriguing than their actual ones. Why identify yourself as a college dropout or a mechanic or a fast-food server, when instead you could be a wizard, werewolf, or vampire?

One night we met the group at a club downtown. The place was like a warehouse, a long building with high ceilings; techno music echoed off the walls, and dim blue lights illumined the dance floor. I leaned against a wall to watch, then found myself dancing with a boy no taller than me—a sweet-faced boy with beautiful skin and dark curly hair.

After we'd danced awhile, we walked outside into an alleyway. He smoked a cigarette, and I looked up at the sky. No stars, no moon. For a moment I lost all sense of who I was, or where I was. When I came back to myself again, I thought of the scene in *On the Road*, when Sal woke up in a strange hotel room and didn't know who he was. He said that his life felt haunted.

"What are you?" the boy with the curly hair asked me, and I said, "A ghost."

He looked confused. "Paul—I mean, Lemur, said you were a vampire."

"That too," I said.

"Perfect," he said. "I'm a donor."

I folded my arms, but my eyes were on his throat—his fine, white-skinned, narrow throat.

"Will you sire me?" he asked.

I wanted to correct his terminology. I wanted to reason with him, to scold him for playing with fire. But more than any of that, I wanted blood.

"Are you sure?" I asked.

"Definitely," he said.

My mouth opened instinctively as I bent toward him, and I heard him say, "Wow. You're the real thing!"

That was the night I learned restraint. I took only enough blood to dull my hunger. When I pulled away from him, he looked up at me, his pupils dilated, an expression of ecstasy in his eyes. "You really did it," he said.

I pulled away, wiping my mouth with my jacket sleeve. "Don't tell anyone." I didn't want to look at him. Already I felt ashamed.

"I'll never tell." His hand rubbed at the wound in his neck, and he pulled it away to look at his blood. "Wow."

"Put pressure on it." I found a tissue in my jacket pocket and handed it to him.

He pressed the tissue against his neck. "That was amazing," he said. "I—I love you."

"You don't even know me."

He held out his free hand. "I'm Joshua," he said. "And now I'm a vampire, like you."

No, you're not, I wanted to say. But I didn't contradict him. He was only role-playing, after all.

* * *

I might have stayed on in Asheville forever. I had a place to live, friends (of a sort), and a willing source of nourishment. But gradually, I began to emerge from the haze. The way we lived made me more and more uneasy; every day seemed the same, more or less. I wasn't learning or accomplishing anything. And every night, waiting for me, instead of sleep, was the fact that I'd killed a man.

I rationalized that he fully deserved it. The assurance with which he'd found the forest road and the way he'd laughed at my struggling persuaded me that he'd done to other women what he tried to do to me. Yet my behavior—purely instinctive—in the end could not be excused. Everything my father had taught me argued against what I had done.

At other times I questioned the value of that education. What did it matter to know history, literature, science, or philosophy? All that knowledge hadn't kept me from murder, and it wasn't serving me now in any practical sense. I'd survived; that was all that mattered.

During the months of haze, my dreams were murky, often violent, populated by beasts and shadows and jagged trees. In the dreams I ran, chased by something I never saw. Often I awoke with the sense that I'd been trying to call for help, but the words wouldn't come; sometimes I wondered if the inarticulate sounds that I made in my dreams were actually vocalized.

I'd open my eyes to the same untidy room filled with the possessions of someone I'd never met. No one ever came to see if I was all right. Those were the times when I longed for the mother I'd never met. But what would she think of having a vampire daughter?

Gradually, my dreams began to take on more structure—as if I were dreaming chapters of a story that continued, night after night. The same characters—a man, a woman, a birdlike other—moved through a deep blue landscape among exotic plants and gentle animals. Sometimes they traveled together, but more often they were separate, and I, the dreamer, was privy to each of their thoughts and feelings. They were each looking for something never specified; each felt lonely or sad at times, but they all were patient, curious, even optimistic. I loved them without knowing them well. Going to sleep now seemed more interesting than being awake—a good reason for thinking it was time to leave Asheville.

Joshua was another good reason. He called me his girlfriend, although we'd never kissed or even held hands. I thought of him as a younger brother—pesky at times, but part of the "family." He seemed always to be around, and he talked of moving into the house. I told him that I needed my space.

One night after dinner (a burrito for him, a half-pint of Joshua's blood for me), we sat on the floor of my room, both of us leaning against the wall, dazed. Years later I saw a movie about heroin addicts, and the characters evoked Joshua and me in Asheville, in our postprandial state.

"Annie," he said. "Will you marry me?"

"No," I said.

He looked so young, sitting by the wall in his scruffy jeans, pressing a paper towel against his neck. I tried to always bite in the same place, to minimize possible infection. I didn't know then that vampires are germ-free.

"Don't you love me?" His eyes reminded me of those of another faithful hound, Wally—Kathleen's dog.

"No."

I treated him terribly, didn't I? And no matter what I said or did, he stayed around for more.

"Well, *I* love *you*." He looked as if he might cry, and I suddenly thought, *Enough*.

"Go home," I said. "I need to be alone."

Reluctant, but ever obedient, he stood up. "You're still my girlfriend, Annie?"

"I'm nobody's girlfriend," I said. "Go home."

Spring arrived, and the whole world turned green. The lacy new leaves on the trees filtered sunlight, their patterns reminding me of a kaleidoscope; the air felt soft. I stretched my fingers close to my eyes and watched sunlight shine through them, watched blood pulse through them. I told Jane that the day was like a poem. She looked at me as if I were a lunatic. "I'm majoring in sociology," she said. "My days aren't like poems."

All I knew about sociology was what my father once said: "Sociology is a poor excuse for science."

"By the way," she said, "Joshua called this morning. Twice."

"He's annoying," I said.

"The boy makes me nervous," Jane said. "It's like you put a spell over him."

We were walking through downtown, wearing sunglasses for the first time that year, on our way to a shoe store. Jane always seemed to have plenty of cash, but it was likely that she'd steal a pair, anyway. I felt a sudden claustrophobic sense of oppression— by her, by Joshua, even by the harmless wizards and werewolves.

"I'm thinking of moving on," I heard myself saying.

"Where to?"

Where, indeed? "To Savannah," I said. "I have a relative there."

She nodded. "Want to go this weekend?"

As easily as that, the decision was made.

I didn't say goodbye to anyone but Paul. "Does Joshua know you're going?" he asked me.

I said, "No, and please don't tell him."

"Annie, that's cold," he said. But he gave me a goodbye hug, anyway.

Jane drove fast. The car sped down I-26, and I shuddered as we passed the ramp where Robert Reedy had picked me up.

"You cold?" Jane asked.

I shook my head. "Don't we turn onto 95 for Savannah?"

"We're stopping in Charleston first," she said. "I need to see the rents."

"The rents?"

"Parents," she said. And she turned the radio on, loud.

Within an hour we were in Charleston, and Jane stopped the car at a wrought-iron gate. "It's me," she said into a speaker, and the gate swung open.

We drove up a winding driveway bordered by tall trees studded with enormous dewy white blossoms; they're called Southern magnolias, I learned later. The car stopped before a white brick mansion. I suppose I should have been surprised that she was rich, but somehow I wasn't.

We ended up spending the night. Jane's parents were tight-faced blond-haired middle-aged people who talked and talked about money. Even when they talked about family—Jane's brother, a cousin, an uncle—they talked about how much money they had, and what they were spending it on. They fed us shrimp and grits, and enormous crabs whose shells they smashed with silver mallets in order to suck out the meat. They asked questions about Jane's schoolwork, which she answered ambiguously: "Not really," or "Kind of," or "Whatever." She made a point of checking text messages on her mobile phone several times during dinner.

Jane treated them even more contemptuously than I'd treated Joshua. By the next morning, I understood why she shoplifted: it was her way of expressing further contempt for her parents and their materialism.

Nonetheless, when her father handed her a wad of bills as we left, she took them and stuffed them into a pocket of her jeans.

"Well, that's done," she said. She spat out the window, and we drove on.

* * *

Jane took the Savannah Highway, Route 17, out of Charleston, and after we left the city I got my first sight of the "Low Country." On either side of the road, reddish-brown marsh grass rippled in the wind. Gray creeks shone like veins of silver in the fields of grass. I rolled down the car window and breathed in the air, which smelled of damp flowers. It made me a little light-headed. I opened my backpack to take a swallow of tonic.

"What *is* that stuff, anyway?" Jane asked.

"Medicine for my anemia." I lied without even thinking, these days. The bottle was three-quarters empty. I wondered what I'd do when it was gone.

Jane picked up her mobile phone and called Paul. I tuned out her voice.

We passed a sign for Bee Ferry Landing and a gift shop called Blue Heron; the names made me think of my mother. I hadn't thought of her much in Asheville, but this landscape evoked her, made me imagine her as a girl, growing up amid the marshes and the bittersweet smells. Had she driven down this road when she ran away from us? Had she seen the same signs I was seeing? Had she felt happy, as if she were coming home?

We passed the Savannah River, sapphire-blue, and arrived downtown by lunchtime.

Jane set down her mobile phone. "You hungry?" She looked eager to be on her way back to Asheville, and Paul.

"No." Of course I was hungry, but not for fast food, or even shrimp and grits. "You can let me out anywhere."

She pulled over near an intersection. I thanked her, but

she waved her hand. "The Lounge Wizards will miss you," she said. "And God, Joshua will probably kill himself."

"I hope not." I knew she was joking. I also knew Joshua might want to do such a thing. But I didn't think he was capable of carrying it out.

We both said "See you," without conviction.

I watched the gray sedan drive away, much too fast, and I wished her well. We hadn't been friends, really, but she'd offered me what companionship she could. For that I was grateful.

— Eleven —

In Savannah I learned how to be invisible. That first day I spent hours walking through the city, savoring the cool green squares, the fountains, the statues, the church bells. I memorized the names of streets and squares so that I wouldn't get lost, and I imagined the city's original architect trying to calculate how much street should lie between squares in order to offer respite from the humid heat. I commended him for an excellent design.

It was late May, and people passed through the city wearing cotton dresses or short-sleeved shirts, and carrying their jackets. My black trouser suit looked out of place among them. I sat on a bench in a square sheltered by live oak trees, and I watched the people as they walked past. Perhaps one of them was my aunt. I had no way of recognizing her. I could tell the tourists from the locals by the way they walked and by what they looked at; the locals moved with an easy familiarity, a languorous stroll.

In Savannah I began to wonder: *How does one vampire recognize another? Is there a secret gesture, a nod or wink or hand movement by which she proclaims herself "one of us"? Or does some instinct allow for instant identification? If I met another vampire, would he or she welcome or shun me?*

As the afternoon waned, I sat on my bench and watched for shadows. Everyone who walked by cast a shadow. I did not. Either Savannah held few vampires besides me, or all of them were inside, waiting for nightfall.

I made a pilgrimage to Colonial Cemetery, but I didn't go inside the gates. Instead I looked for the house where my mother had lived. And I think I found it: a three-storey red brick house with green shutters and black-iron-framed balconies. I stared up at the balcony facing the cemetery, and I imagined my father sitting there with a woman—a faceless woman. My mother.

As I walked away, I looked down at the brick sidewalk, at the patterns etched in the bricks. They weren't spirals—they were concentric circles, like little target signs. My father's memory wasn't perfect after all, or else his pattern dyslexia was to blame.

A few blocks later I saw an old hotel with wrought-iron balconies overhanging the street, and for a moment I fantasized about checking in, having a bath, spending a night sleeping on crisp clean sheets. But I had fewer than a hundred dollars left, and I didn't know how or when I'd have more.

I looked into the hotel's first-floor windows: a lobby, then a bar and restaurant. At the bar sat a tall man in a dark suit, his back toward me, and he lifted a glass that caught the candlelight and gleamed a familiar dark red.

Picardo. Suddenly, I missed my father terribly. Was he sitting now in his leather chair, raising a similar cocktail glass? Did he miss me? He must be worried, more worried than ever before. Or, did he know what I'd been doing? Could he read my thoughts from that distance? The notion alarmed me. If he knew what I'd done, he would despise me.

The mirror behind the bar reflected the cocktail glass— but not the man who held it. As if he sensed my stare, he turned around. Quickly I walked on.

The sky had darkened by the time I found the river. My feet ached, and my hunger turned to dizziness. I walked among the tourists on River Street, past gaudy shops and restaurants that promised raw oysters and beer. When I saw an Irish imports shop, I stopped walking. In my mind, I saw my father go inside and come out with a shawl, which he wrapped around the faceless woman.

My neck tingled—a sensation I hadn't had in so long that at first I didn't recognize it. Then I knew. Someone was watching me. I looked in all directions, but saw only couples and families, intent upon themselves. I took a deep breath and looked around again, more slowly. This time my senses focused on a stone staircase, then on the first step, where mist from the river seemed to have gathered.

So you're invisible, I thought. *Are you the same other who watched me at home?*

I heard a laugh, but no one around me was laughing.

My face felt hot. *It's not funny.*

And for the first time, I tried to make myself invisible.

It's not difficult. Like deep meditation, it's a matter of concentration; you breathe deeply and focus your awareness on the immediate moment, the experience of here and now, then you let it all go. Your body's electrons begin to slow down as you absorb their heat. Deflecting light feels as if you're drawing all energy into your deepest core. A sense of freedom and lightness spread through me; later I learned that it's called *qi* or *chi*, a Chinese word for "air" or "life force."

As a means of proof, I held my hands before my face. I saw nothing. I looked down at my legs, and saw right through them. The tailor-made trousers had disappeared. So had my backpack. My father's claims about metamaterials had not been exaggerated.

After that, I had no sense of the *other*. I moved on, down River Street, as if I were floating. I walked into a restaurant, toward the kitchen, where plates of food waited to be collected and served. No one even looked in my direction. I took a plateful of rare filet mignon, went out the back door with it, and sat on a stone wall to devour it, using my hands as utensils. A few minutes later, two servers from the restaurant came out to smoke cigarettes, and one of them noticed the empty plate on the wall, right next to me. He sauntered over to pick it up, standing so close that I saw flakes of dandruff in his hair.

"Somebody must have dined al fresco, huh?" he said.

The other server laughed. "Al Fresco? Who's that? You mean the wino who sleeps by the Dumpster?"

I tucked a ten-dollar bill into his back pocket as I left, to pay for my dinner.

I drifted on, through the alley to River Street again, giddily dodging tourists. Being invisible must be almost as good as flying. Once I brushed by a plump man in a suit; he recoiled and furtively glanced around to see who had touched him. He gasped. It took me a second to figure out why: he'd been bumped by my invisible backpack.

For the first time in a long while, I was having fun, and I wondered what else I might do. But the physical strain of maintaining invisibility is as exhausting as running or biking for miles. It was time to find a place to stay the night.

I walked up the steep cobblestone street toward the city again, headed toward the hotel I'd seen earlier.

Checking into the Marshall House was easier than you might imagine; I pulled myself up a wrought-iron brace to the balcony, passed a row of empty rocking chairs, and climbed through an unlocked bathroom window. After making sure that the room was empty, I locked its door, shed my clothes, and ran a bath. They even provided a fluffy robe. On the counter I found a small vial of lavender-scented bath oil, but its top was so tightly screwed on that I couldn't remove it—until I used my teeth. I poured the oil into the running water.

Into the tub I sank, and slowly let the light escape me, let myself become visible—as if anyone could see. I scrubbed my legs and my hair—which, I noticed, had grown past my waist.

I nearly fell asleep in the bath. Exhausted, I toweled off,

wrapped myself in the robe, braided my hair, and climbed into a king-sized bed. The sheets smelled improbably of roses. I dreamed of flowers, and birds, and crosswords.

In the *Aeneid*, Virgil calls sleep "Death's brother." To us, sleep is as close to death as we're likely to come—barring catastrophe, of course. Always barring that.

Sunlight woke me, streaming in golden bands through the window over the balcony. I sat up in bed, my mind fresh and alert for the first time in months. I felt as if I'd been asleep since I left home. In a second I realized how much I'd missed my orderly mind. Perhaps my earlier education had some use after all, not so much in terms of what I'd learned as in teaching me how to think.

Finding my aunt now seemed a perfectly straightforward process. First I consulted the telephone directory on the bureau; more than twenty Stephensons were listed, but no Sophie or even S.

But she might have married and taken another name, or have an unlisted number. I thought back on the little my father had told me about my mother's background: she'd been raised in the Savannah area, but I didn't know where she'd attended school. I knew, or thought I knew, her former address, and I knew she'd had a job keeping bees.

I left the hotel room exactly as I'd found it, minus one small bottle of lavender bath oil. The old wooden door creaked as it opened. I tiptoed down the corridor and down a flight of stairs. In the lobby I sat at the guests' computer station. Thanks to the hotel's Internet access, it took me seconds to search for *Savannah* and *honey* and to find what I needed: the address and phone number of the Tybee Bee Company.

I walked out through the lobby as if indeed I were a paying guest.

The doorman opened the front door for me. "Mornin', babe," he said.

"Good morning," I said. I slid on my dark glasses and strutted down Broughton, feeling, in my London-tailored black trouser suit, very much the babe.

Some days, it seems as if you're one with the universe. Do you feel that way, too? With every step you take, the ground rises to meet your feet, and the air caresses your skin. My long hair floated in the breeze behind me, smelling of lavender shampoo. Even my back-pack felt light.

The Tybee Bee Company was situated on the outskirts of the city in a warehouse—not a pretty place, and not easy to find. Being invisible helped; I didn't want to hitchhike, but at a gas station I slipped into the backseat of a car with a Tybee Island sticker on its rear window. A teenaged girl was the driver, and she headed out the Island Expressway. When she neared the President Street exit, I began to whine, sounding as much like an ailing engine as I could. She obediently pulled over, and I (and my backpack) slipped out while she was looking under the car's hood. I mouthed a silent thank-you.

No, I didn't feel guilty about my pranks at the time; I felt the end would justify the means, whatever the end might be. Only much later would I come to a full moral reckoning with myself.

I made myself visible for the last stretch, and I stopped twice to ask directions before I found the warehouse. Inside, half a dozen young people were working. One was attaching labels to tall bottles of golden honey. Another packed small jars into cartons for shipping, and someone else used a spatula to cut squares of honeycomb. The room had tall windows and a high ceiling, but its air felt thick and sweet.

They all looked up as I came in. "Hi," I said. "Are you hiring?"

A sleek woman in a suit interviewed me in an upstairs office. She said they had no openings at the moment, but that she'd keep my application on file. When I filled out the paperwork, I said I was eighteen, and I left the address section blank. I explained that I was en route to visit a relative. I asked if she'd known my mother, who had worked here about fifteen years ago.

She said, "I've only been here a year. You may want to talk to the owner. He's out on Oatland Island with the bees."

One of the packagers lived on the island and was headed home for lunch, so she drove me to the hives. They stood at the edge of a nature preserve, near an old wooden boat that rested on cement blocks. She pointed them out, then turned to head back to her car.

"I'm afraid of bees," she said, over her shoulder. "Walk slowly, and they should leave you alone."

Thus warned, I moved across a lawn toward the hives, which looked from a distance like ramshackle wooden filing cabinets. A man in a white suit and hood was pulling what seemed to be a drawer out of one of the files. On the ground next to him was a metal device emitting pine-scented smoke. I came up slowly behind him. A bee buzzed over me, as if checking me out, then flew away. A steady stream of bee traffic came and went from the hives. The sky had clouded over, and the place was utterly still but for the sound of bees.

The beekeeper turned to look at me. He slid the drawer back into the cabinet, then motioned me back toward the boat. When we'd reached it, he pulled off his hood and veil. "That's better," he said. "The girls are a little wild today."

He had a shock of pure white hair and eyes the color of aquamarines.

Have I mentioned my interest in gemstones? It began with an old encyclopedia at home. I can still see the plates of cabochon- and emerald-cut gems: jade, aquamarine, cat's-eye, emerald, moonstone, peridot, ruby, tourmaline, and my favorite: the star sapphire. Diamonds, to me, are boring, unsubtle. But the sapphire's six-legged ivory star radiated against a Prussian blue background like fireworks or lightning in a night sky. Years later, I saw a real star sapphire, and it proved even more subtle: the star wasn't visible until you looked at the gem from a particular angle, and then it emerged, like a ghostly sea creature surfacing in deep water, thanks to an optical phenomenon called asterism. I pored over the descriptions of the stones and their mythology, then flipped the page to the next entry: *Genealogy*, which included a "chart of blood relations," explaining how a great-grandparent ultimately connected to a first cousin once-removed. I never read that entry, but its accompanying chart—a series of small circles, connected by lines—will always be associated for me with the gleam and fire and mystery of gemstones.

"You're not from around here," the beekeeper was saying.

I introduced myself, using my real name for the first time in months. "I think my mother worked for you," I said. "Sara Stephenson?"

His face changed from quizzical to sad. "Sara," he said. "I haven't thought of her for years. Whatever happened to her?"

"Your guess is as good as mine," I said.

His name was Roger Winters, and when he heard I'd never met my mother, he shook his head. After a few seconds, he said he'd known her fairly well. "She worked part-time for me when she was in high school, and then later she came back, after she got her divorce. You knew she was married before?"

I said, "Yes."

"I was glad she left him, and glad to have her back. She was a good worker," he said. "She got on real well with the bees."

His voice was soft and slow, with inflections and muted vowels that I'd never heard before. I thought of the harsh way most people talked in Saratoga Springs (my father a notable exception). I could listen to Mr. Winters talk for hours.

"I do see the resemblance now," he said, looking at me. "You've got your mother's eyes."

"Thank you!" He'd given me my first physical link to my mother.

He shrugged—an odd twist of his right shoulder, only. "She was a great beauty," he said. "And funny? That woman could always make me laugh."

I told Mr. Winters I'd come to Savannah to find my mother, any trace of her, or her relations. "She had a sister, Sophie."

"Sophie's nothing like Sara," he said.

"Is she here?" I could hardly believe my luck.

"Lives a couple miles from here, back toward the city. At least she did. I haven't heard mention of Sophie for years. Used to see her in the papers with her roses, every time they had a flower show."

My disappointment must have shown, because he said, "That don't mean she ain't still here, now. You might want to give her a call."

I told him I hadn't found her name in the telephone directory. He shrugged again. "She's a spinster. Lives alone. Like to have her number unlisted. Yes, that's the sort of thing Sophie *would* do." He bent to pick up his hood and veil, which he'd set next to the smoker device on the grass. "Tell you what. It's about time for my lunch break anyway. I'll run you over there after lunch, and we'll see if she's still at that house on Screven Street."

"That's very kind of you," I said.

"Seems like I could do that much for Sara's daughter.

How old are you, anyways? Seventeen? Eighteen?"

"More or less." I didn't want to have to explain why a thirteen-year-old was traveling alone.

Mr. Winters drove an old blue pickup truck with a yellow honeybee logo on both its doors. The windows were rolled down, and I was glad; the sun had emerged from the clouds, and the air swept into the truck, humid and hot.

He stopped at a restaurant on the way back to town— nothing fancy, a roadside shed—and, sitting at a picnic table outside, overlooking a marsh, I had my first taste of raw oysters.

Mr. Winters carried out a plateful of them, half-shells of various sizes embedded in shaved ice. He went back for a soup plate holding a bowl of crackers and a bottle of red sauce. He removed them and set them strategically, midway between us.

"Never had one?" he said, his face as baffled as if I'd said I never breathed. "Yankees," he muttered.

He demonstrated the proper oyster-eating technique: he sprinkled two drops of sauce on the round gray oyster, lifted the shell, tipped it toward his mouth, and sucked it down. He set the empty shell in the soup bowl. Then he took a few soda crackers and tossed them back.

I picked up a shell, already planning ways in which to hide my distaste—subtly coughing it out into a paper-towel napkin, for instance. The little ivory and gray bodies looked inedible, and in any case, these days I had no appetite for anything that wasn't red. I held the shell as he had, so that it didn't spill any liquid, and I gamely sucked it into my mouth.

How to describe that first taste? Better than blood! The texture was firm, yet creamy, and it yielded a mineral essence that seemed to shoot oxygen right through my veins. Later I found out that oysters—the ones that haven't been polluted, that is—are full of nutritious minerals, including oxygen, calcium, and phosphorus.

Mr. Winters was watching me—I felt it, even though I'd closed my eyes. I heard his voice say, "Of course some folks can't abide the things..."

I opened my eyes. "The best thing I ever tasted."

"That right?" He laughed softly.

"Ever." We looked at each other with complete understanding.

Then we stopped looking and talking, and settled down to eating. We went through four dozen in no time.

You know, there are some things in life we either love or hate. No middle ground. Oysters are such things. By the way, they taste blue—the muted, salty shade of a London blue topaz.

Back in the truck, thoroughly sated, feeling oxygen moving like elixir through me, I said, "Thank you."

He made his funny shrug again and started the truck. As we drove off, he said, "I had a daughter, once."

I looked over at him, but his face in profile didn't show emotion. "What became of her?"

"She married an idiot," he said.

We didn't speak for a minute. Then I found myself

asking, "Did you ever meet my father?"

"Oh yes." He turned the truck off the highway, into a neighborhood of old houses. "Met him three or four times. Liked him the first two."

I didn't know what to say.

He drove onto a quiet street of old houses, and pulled up close to a corner, under an enormous magnolia tree. Some of its blossoms weren't open yet, and they were conical, the color of pale straw. Hard to imagine them opening into saucer-shaped white blooms, but the tree held plenty of evidence that they could, and would.

"So we're here." He looked across at me, his blue eyes serious. "Now, your auntie, if she's home, is someone you'll need time to get to know. She's one of them ... ladylike women, if you know what I mean."

I didn't know.

"She would never in her life eat a raw oyster," he said. "She's the kind you see in tearooms, eating little sandwiches on white bread with the crusts cut off."

We left the truck. The house was gray, with two stories, symmetrical and plain in design, with a large, empty yard off to its left.

"That's where she had the rose garden," he said, speaking to himself. "Looks like it got dug up."

He stood slightly behind me on the front porch as I rang the bell. The porch was well swept, and the windows above it were hung with lace curtains and Venetian blinds.

I rang the bell a second time. We heard it echo inside.

Mr. Winters said, "Well, you know—"

Then the door opened. A woman in a shapeless house-dress looked at us with eyes that were the same color as mine. She was shorter and stouter than me. We stared at each other. She smoothed back her chin-length gray hair, then rested her hands on her neck.

"Good heavens," she said. "Are you Sara's girl?"

Mr. Winters left us soon afterward, but he wrote his telephone number in pencil on an old gas station receipt and handed it to me, with a wink, as he went out.

It wasn't an easy reunion.

Aunt Sophie, it became clear within minutes, had been thoroughly disappointed by life. Again and again, people had let her down. She had been engaged once, to a man who later left town without saying goodbye.

While her accent was similar to that of Mr. Winters in its treatment of vowels, hers was higher and harsher in tone and more correct in grammar. I much preferred to listen to Mr. Winters. In fact, as I sat on the overstuffed, uncomfortable sofa in the parlor, lace doilies perched precariously on its arms and head, I wished Mr. Winters were related to me, instead of this person who clearly loved to talk and didn't care or know how to listen.

"Your mother"—she paused to widen her eyes and shake her head—"hasn't been in touch with me for years. Can you imagine a sister like that? But of course you're an only child, Arabella. But not even a Christmas card. Not even a call on my birthday. Can you *imagine*?"

If I hadn't recently consumed the best lunch of my life,

I might have told her that yes, I could imagine. I might have added that my name wasn't Arabella. I might even have walked out. She was boring, and repetitive, and condescending, and selfish. Within minutes I knew she'd been jealous of Sara all her life, and I suspected she'd treated my mother badly. But the joy of discovering oysters lingered, made me forgiving and tolerant. The world wasn't such a bad place that afternoon, even if Aunt Sophie was in it.

She sat on the edge of her chair, ankles in pale nylons neatly aligned above low-heeled black pumps, as if she were the guest in the house. She looked to be in her late fifties; her mouth had a permanent downcast purse, and her skin a sallowness that I'd expect to see in a much older, thinner woman. Yet her eyes suggested that once she'd been pretty.

Her hands were jammed into her apron's pockets, and her elbows looked dry and red. The room was decorated in beige and white, the furniture square and uncomfortable. A glass-fronted curio cabinet imprisoned porcelain figurines of impossibly cheerful children. Not one thing in the room felt genuine.

She had a way of beginning a story, then interjecting irrelevant comments of disapproval ("Your hair is so *long*" was one). After a while I stopped trying to make sense of it and simply let the words wash over me, knowing I'd sort them out later, if ever.

When she invited me to spend the night it was with such reluctance, such an odd, questioning note in her voice, that I was tempted to leave. But she was my aunt. She knew things about my mother, even if they were half-articulated.

So I decided to stay.

We dined on chicken salad scooped onto leaves of iceberg lettuce, with green seedless grapes for dessert. Afterward, in the spare bedroom, I felt disappointed and deflated. I took a hefty swig of tonic and reminded myself that, besides Aunt Sophie, the world contained oysters, Roger Winters, and my mother—that is, if my mother was still alive. I pulled out my journal and began to write.

Sophie had last seen my mother thirteen years ago, soon after my birth. (She didn't say that, but I figured out the dates, lying in bed.)

My mother had shown up on her doorstep one afternoon.

"Just the way you did," Sophie told me. "I guess people are too busy to call first."

"Was your phone number unlisted then, too?" I asked.

"Oh," she said, making the word last three syllables. "I don't remember that. You know, I had to have my number taken out of the telephone directory. A man kept calling here, and he *said* he dialed the wrong number, but I knew from his voice what sort he was. It's not an easy life, living alone." And off she went on a rant about the sorrows of spinsterhood, and being too poor to live in a gated community, and how she'd had to buy her very own revolver.

Anyway, my mother had arrived in sorry shape, Sophie said. "She looked terrible, and she hadn't even packed a bag. And she wouldn't tell me a thing—she wanted some money, and of course I don't have any."

For three minutes I heard about the loss of the family fortune two generations back, and the sorry circumstances that forced Sophie into a menial job at a local rose nursery.

The thing about my aunt's mind—its meandering was infectious. Soon I found myself thinking in weird loops and tangents, Sophie-style. So it took considerable effort, as I lay in bed that night, trying to pull together the facts.

My mother had shown up. She'd looked ill. She'd asked for money. She said she'd left Saratoga Springs for good, that she was headed for a new life. She asked Sophie not to tell anyone she'd been there.

"Well, of course the second she left, I was on the phone to your father," Sophie said. "He'd called me a month or so before, to see if she was here. Can you imagine—running away from a newborn baby?"

What could I say to that? But it didn't matter, since she was already talking again.

"Your father, he's a strange fellow. Don't you think so? Such a handsome boy he was, and so full of life. All the girls were half in love with him—why he chose Sara I never will know, she had such a temper. Raphael—we called him Raff—was such a good dancer. So full of life. Then he went off to England. Something must have happened to him over there. By the time he came back, all the fire was gone out of him." She nodded emphatically. "England," she said, as if the nation itself were to blame.

The next morning, after a meager breakfast of stale biscuits and butter that tasted old, I thanked Sophie for her hospitality and told her I planned to move on. "My mother didn't tell you anything about where she was going?"

"She said she was headed south." Sophie adjusted the crocheted tablecloth, whose irregular loops and bumps suggested it was home-made. "Does your father know where you are?" She looked up at me, her eyes suddenly sharp.

I'd taken a sip from my juice glass—ruby-red grapefruit juice from a can—and its tart yet saccharine flavor made me want to spit it out. Instead, I swallowed. "Of course," I said. Then, to deflect her, I asked, "Do you have any photos of my mother?"

"I threw them away," she said, her voice matter-of-fact. "I mean, all those years of never hearing from her—not even a birthday card, only that cheap postcard—"

"She sent you a postcard?"

"It was a picture of an animal, some sea creature. Vulgar-looking."

I tried to be patient. "Where was it sent from?"

"Someplace in Florida." She pressed her hands against her forehead. "You can't expect me to remember everything. Aren't you going to finish your juice?"

I said I thought I'd better be on my way.

"Don't you want to call your father?" Again, her eyes changed from vague to sharp.

"I spoke to him yesterday," I lied.

"Oh." Her eyes went vague again. "You have one of those mobile telephones?"

"Yes." I picked up my backpack and moved toward the door, hoping that she wouldn't ask to see it.

Although Aunt Sophie's attitude toward me had been

close to indifferent, it now blossomed into a wavering show
of affection. She put her hand on my shoulder, staring dis-
approvingly at my hair. "Where are you going today?" she
asked in a bright voice.

"South." I had no idea where I was going. "I'm going to
stay with friends."

"You know, it's a strange thing." Sophie patted her hair,
which didn't need patting—it seemed lacquered into place.
"Your mother always made a wish when she saw a white
horse. She was superstitious to a fault." Sophie's voice went
dark. "That ridiculous wedding, held in the dead of night."

"You were at their wedding?"

She turned and walked out of the room. I stood by the
door, my backpack on, wondering, *What now?* I wondered
if my aunt was senile, or if she'd always been this way. The
small, beige-walled dining room, antiseptically neat, looked
as if it had been rarely if ever used. Suddenly I felt sorry for
her.

Sophie came back, carrying a green leather photo album.
"I'd forgotten I had this. Come and sit in the parlor."

So we went back to the uncomfortable sofa, and this
time she sat next to me. She opened the album. And there
they were, my mother and father, looking back at me. My
mother—to finally see her face! She looked radiant—her
eyes wide, her smile joyous, her long auburn hair shining.
She wore a white evening dress that shimmered like a fire
opal. My father looked elegant in a tuxedo, but his face was
blurred.

"Can you imagine wearing a dress like that at your

wedding? And no veil." Sophie sighed. "Not a good picture of Raff. None of them turned out well."

She flipped the page. Another photo of my parents, this one taken by candlelight against a background of bamboo trees. "They had the wedding outdoors in a garden down in Florida." My aunt's voice sounded bitter. "Way down in Florida. Sarasota, it was called. They took us down there on the train."

"Sarasota?"

"She chose it because of the name." Sophie made a clicking sound with her tongue. "That was the way Sara did things. Did you ever?"

I turned the next page, and the one after it. In each photo, my mother looked beautiful and serene, my father indistinct. "She's so lovely." I had to say it.

Sophie didn't respond. "You can have it, if you want it."

It took me a second to understand. She thrust the album toward me.

"Thank you." I took the book, and looked across at my aunt. Her eyes were sad, but they changed even as I looked, sharp again.

"How are you traveling, Missy?"

I couldn't tell her my plan: to be an invisible hitchhiker again. "I thought I'd take the train," I said.

She nodded briskly. "I'll drive you to the station."

"You don't have to do that," I said, but she refused to listen.

I stood outside, watching her back her car out of the garage. It took a while. When I got in, I asked her, "Whatever happened to your rose garden?"

Her face turned sour. "It was a never-ending battle with Japanese beetles," she said. "I tried every kind of pesticide you can think of. Nothing fazed them. They made me so mad, I even shot some of them, but that damaged the rose-bushes. One day I decided it wasn't worth the struggle, and I pulled them up by the roots, every last one of them."

I'd thought Sophie would drop me off at the station, but instead she parked and came inside with me. So I joined the line at the tickets window, forced to choose a destination. "How much is a ticket to Florida?" I asked.

"Whereabouts in Florida?" the clerk asked.

"Um, Sarasota," I said.

"Train goes to Tampa or Orlando," he said. "And the rest of the way, you take the bus. Either way, a one-way ticket is $82."

He said that Tampa was further south. I counted out the bills. "When does the train leave?"

"It leaves at 6:50," he said, "a.m., tomorrow."

And so I had another night in the hard narrow bed at Sophie's, preceded by another lackluster dinner of chicken salad. Did she eat anything else? I wondered. I wished I could call Mr. Winters and have dinner with him, instead of being Sophie's captive audience. Tonight's topics included her noisy neighbors, the horrors of dogs, more evidence of my mother's spoiled and selfish nature, and Sophie's digestive problems.

I tried to listen only to the parts about my mother ("She had to have horseback riding lessons, even though they cost a fortune and she came home filthy afterwards. I couldn't bear the *smell*"), but it was hard to concentrate, because Sophie's thoughts kept interfering. Even when I tried to block her thoughts, they trickled through somehow. She had suspicions about me; she thought at first I'd "come looking for money," and when I didn't ask for any she grew suspicious that I had too much of my own. What was I doing, traveling alone at my age? She wondered if I was taking drugs. She didn't think my father had any idea where I was, but she wasn't about to call him after that last time, when he sounded so ungrateful.

I wanted to ask about that, but I kept quiet. The most interesting thing I learned was that for years my mother had given Sophie financial support; she sent money every week when she had her bee-keeping job (Sophie was too genteel to take a job herself), and when my parents married, they gave Sophie five thousand dollars to help her start a rose nursery. But Sophie's jumbled thoughts were bitter even about that: *a measly five thousand, when they had so much. If they'd given me ten, the business might have survived. Will you look at her hair? I'd like to cut it myself, make her look respectable.*

We said good-night, both of us weary yet wary. Sophie thought I might creep about the house, looking for cash or something else to steal. I worried that she might try to cut off my hair while I slept.

Next morning, she woke me at 5:30 and urged me to hurry. "You need to get to the station at least half an hour early," she said.

Sophie drove with both hands clenched on the steering wheel, slowing down whenever another car approached. "Only drunks out at this hour," she said.

We made it by 6:20. It was cold and not quite light outside, and despite my fleece jacket, I shivered.

Sophie also felt the cold, but she wasn't about to leave. She felt it was her duty to make sure I got on the train. In truth, if she hadn't been around, I would have asked for a refund and hitchhiked instead.

So we stood and shivered together, watching the train approach.

Saying goodbye to her was awkward. Clearly, we'd proven a mutual disappointment. But she presented her dry, powdered cheek, which I kissed lightly, and that seemed to suffice.

"You call me when you get there," she said, and I said I would, both of us knowing that I wouldn't.

The train's name was the Silver Star, and from the moment I saw it, I loved it. I looked around at the other passengers, many of them asleep, blankets pulled up to their chins, and I wondered where they'd come from and where they were going. The conductor who checked my ticket wore a navy blue uniform and a crisp white shirt, and he smiled at me and called me "Ma'am." I loved that, too.

Sometimes I felt like thirteen, not "going on thirty"—alive in all my senses, filled with curiosity and wonder. Today was such a day. As the train picked up speed, its horn blew, and we moved smoothly through a brightening landscape, through woods, past lakes and streams, past towns only beginning to waken. A few passengers stirred and wakened, and some passed me on their way to the dining car for breakfast. I felt content where I was.

I lay back in my leather seat, my feet extended on the footrest, and let the gentle sway of the car rock me to sleep. When I awoke, we were pulling into Jacksonville, Florida. The loudspeaker said we'd stop for ten minutes, and we could leave the train and find coffee and food in the station.

I didn't want coffee or food, but I decided to stretch my legs, so I walked along the platform, savoring the fresh air. Florida's air smelled different from Georgia's. It was still early morning, and the scent was faint but pronounced: a humid earthy odor, with hints of flowering citrus and rotting vegetation in it. Later I'd learn the smell is characteristic of land and vegetation that bake in intense sun, then sizzle in heavy rain.

A newspaper box stood outside the station, and one of its headlines read: "Reedy's Killer Strikes Again?" And that was the end of my morning of wonder.

I couldn't read much through the box window, but the first paragraph of the story said that last night in Savannah, a body had been found, its condition similar to that of Robert Reedy, murdered four months ago near Asheville.

I glanced at the passengers around me, sure that my face betrayed my guilt, but no one seemed to notice. Quickly I walked back to the train. I took a swallow of tonic to steady me; so little was left, perhaps enough for two more days.

Then what would I do?

The train began to move again, but I took no pleasure in its movements. All I saw ahead of me was an endless struggle to survive. Now I knew why my father called our condition an affliction.

South of Jacksonville, the landscape grew more tropical. Trees I'd never seen before grew profusely—a jungle of palms of various shapes and sizes interspersed with trees whose leaves grew in red-tinged clusters. Again, it bothered me that I didn't know their names.

Green-tinged ponds spotted with water lilies bordered plots of land covered by black plastic tarps, under which verdant vines grew profusely. What was growing there? Houses, some little more than sheds or shacks, and small churches had front doors facing the railroad tracks. We passed towns with exotic names: Palatka and Crescent City and Deland. (Although its station looked pretty and picturesque, I sensed something sinister about Deland. Later I learned that it was a frequent site of natural disasters, accidents, and murders. Why is it that some places are so much more prone to trouble than others?)

When I let my mind turn inward again, it was much calmer. It was grisly to think of another death like Reedy's, but whoever had done it would only deflect attention away from me. I didn't bother to speculate about who might have committed this murder—it could be any one of the thousands of vampires my father had told me were out there, getting by in whatever way they could. I let myself hope that whoever died had been a bad person, even though I'd been taught that there was no excuse for murder.

Then I thought ahead, to what might happen in Sarasota. I took the small book of wedding photos from my backpack and studied each picture. My mother's smile suggested that she'd never had a moment of worry or despair, yet from my father's stories I knew she'd known both, before and after the wedding. Why would she have chosen to return to the city where she was married? Wouldn't the memories be painful?

I studied the details: the tropical plants in the background, the candles and glowing paper lanterns used to light the ceremony. There were few guests; one photo showed a heavily rouged Aunt Sophie and a younger, thinner Dennis with my mother (I assumed my father had taken the picture); another showed my parents standing before a woman in a black gown; her back faced the camera, but from their positions it seemed she was pronouncing them man and wife.

I flipped the page, and a postcard fell from the album's binding. An image of a creature floating in turquoise-colored water stared up at me; I bent to pick it up. On the card's other side, a legend identified the animal as a *manatee*, also known as a sea cow. I'd heard that word before, in a crossword dream.

The message, written in right-slanted handwriting, read, "Sophie, I've found a new home. No worries, and no word to the others, please." It was signed simply, "S."

But it was the postmark that interested me most:

"Homosassa Springs, FL." I thought, *Five S's in one name*.

The next time the conductor made his way through the car, I flagged him down. "I've made a mistake," I said. "I bought a ticket to the wrong place."

The conductor shook his head. He seemed genuinely sorry that he couldn't change the ticket. The only person who could do that, he said, was a ticket agent, and he advised me to talk to one at the next station.

And so I left the Silver Star at the next stop, Winter Park. The agent in the small brick station told me three times that it said *no refund* on my ticket. Then he told me three times that Amtrak had discontinued service to the Gulf Coast.

I still had no idea where Homosassa Springs was, which probably was an asset in my negotiations. I kept saying "I need to find my mother," and he kept saying, "Amtrak doesn't go there," until finally a person in line behind us said, "She could take the bus!"

Someone else said, "Give the kid a break."

And that was how I got a refund of eighteen dollars and advice on how to find the bus station (which I had no intention of following). I headed down the main street of Winter Park, lined with shops and sidewalk cafés. The air smelled of stagnant water and women's perfume. As I passed a café, I heard a woman tell a server, "That was the best Bloody I've ever had."

I stopped walking, and went back to the restaurant. The server seated me on the patio. "I'd like one of those," I said, pointing at the woman's tall red glass.

The server said, "May I see your ID?"

I showed him the only ID I had: my library card.

"Uh huh," the server said. He came back with a tall glass that looked like the one my neighbor was drinking. Imagine my disappointment when it turned out to be nothing more than spicy tomato juice.

— Twelve —

Light and shadow: you need both to paint a scene or tell a story. To represent three dimensions on a flat surface, you need light to form the object and shadow to give it shape.

In composing a picture or a story, you pay attention to negative and positive space. The positive space is what you want the viewer's eye to focus on. But negative space also has substance and shape. It isn't the absence of something; it's a presence.

My mother's absence in my life was in many ways a presence. My father and I were shaped by it, even in the years when we didn't mention her name. The prospect of finding her tantalized me, yet made me anxious; it threatened to rearrange and displace everything familiar. If I found her, would I become the negative space?

The last leg of my journey was the easiest of all. Thanks to the United States Postal Service, I got a free ride to Homosassa Springs.

In Winter Park, I found a post office and asked the clerk whether a letter to Homosassa Springs would be transported directly there. He looked at me as if I were crazy. "I'm writing a paper about mail delivery," I said, as an excuse.

He said a letter addressed to Homosassa Springs would first go to the Mid-Florida Processing Center in Lake Mary. And so that's where I went, via postal truck.

I felt a little like an urban legend: the invisible guest in the passenger seat. But the driver never glanced in my direction, except to look at his side mirrors. The road was dull and flat from Winter Park to Lake Mary. Once we'd arrived at the processing center, it wasn't hard to find a truck being loaded with westbound mail. The driver whistled incessantly as the landscape changed from flatness to slightly rolling hills. By late afternoon the truck arrived in Homosassa Springs, which looked like any of the several small towns I'd seen: gas stations, strip malls, phone masts. I thought, not for the first time, *If you ever want to hide from the world, live in a small city, where everyone seems anonymous.*

When the driver left the truck, I pulled my backpack from under my seat and climbed out. Standing in the shadow of an oak tree, I willed myself visible and walked around the parking lot and into the post office. The clerk inside, a middle-aged woman with dark hair, stood with her back to the door. She was talking to someone in a room off to the left of the counter.

I pulled the photo album out of my pack and opened it.

When she turned around, I said, "Excuse me. Do you know this woman?"

The clerk looked from me to the picture, then back at me. "I may have seen her around," she said. "Why do you want her?"

"She's related to me." I couldn't say the words "my mother" to a stranger.

"Where are you staying?" The clerk was thinking, *What do you want with her?*

"I don't know yet. I just came into town."

"Well, when you find out, you can come back and leave a note for her. Ask for me—ask for Sheila. I'll make sure she gets it, if she happens to come by."

Slowly, I shut the album, and slid it into my backpack. I felt tired, and hungry, and out of ideas.

The woman was thinking, *Am I doing the right thing?* "Are you looking for a hotel?" she said. "There are two in Homosassa, right down the road."

She gave me directions. I thanked her and left. I walked along a busy highway, then turned onto a quieter road.

Trees overhung the narrow road on both sides, and I made my way along the roadside path, past small wood houses, a library, a restaurant, a school—all sleepy-looking. I felt that I was plodding, plodding toward nothing. Ahead a billboard advertised the Riverside Resort, where an invisible guest would shortly check in.

This time I entered the room through a balcony door. I had to try three balconies before I found a door unlocked. Inside, I drank the last of my tonic, and then I sat on the balcony and watched the sun set on the Homosassa River. The blue-green water was speckled with fiery orange, like a bloodstone.

Later, a visible me went to the hotel restaurant and ordered two-dozen oysters on the half-shell.

The restaurant had glass windows overlooking the river, and a nearby small island with a red-striped, fake-looking lighthouse on it. As I watched, an animal—large and dark—moved through the trees.

"Bob's restless tonight." The server set down a large silver tray of oysters, along with bottles of hot sauce and cocktail sauce.

"Bob?"

"The monkey," she said. "Anything else?"

"No, thanks." As I ate, I watched Bob the monkey pace the small island.

Once again, the oysters worked their magic. I wondered what gave them their subtle flavor, as fresh and electric as ozone after a thunderstorm. With every mouthful, my energy and spirits revived.

At least the postal clerk had recognized the photo, I thought. Of course, my mother would be in her mid-forties now, and she probably looked different—but how hard could it be to find someone in a town as small as Homosassa Springs?

The server asked me if I wanted anything else to eat. "Another dozen, please," I said. When they arrived, I asked her, "Are these oysters alive?"

"They're fresh-shucked," she said.

I looked lovingly down at the plate: the beautiful, plump gray morsels still attached to the mother-of-pearl colored shells. Whenever they died, I hoped their death wasn't painful.

"Anything else?" The server tapped her foot.

"More crackers, please," I said.

Yes, I did go back to the restaurant the next day for another three dozen. And I confess, this time I went as the invisible Ari, because my money was running low.

I wanted to wash my clothes, which were more grimy than I liked. One of the perks of vampirism is that we don't perspire, but our clothes still pick up lint and dust and dirt.

Washing them would be too risky—they'd need to be hung up to dry, and someone might rent my room in the meantime. So I put on my trousers and an almost-fresh shirt, and I folded the jacket and put it into my backpack.

On the balcony I looked for Bob the monkey; he had a playmate, I saw now, a smaller monkey swinging from a rope bridge strung between two trees. As I watched, two pedal boats approached the island, and the people on board took out their cameras. Bob and his friend stopped playing. They walked down to the island's shoreline. Standing side by side, they stared at the cameras.

Can't they swim? I wondered. I sent them sympathy and a silent farewell.

My strategy now was to return to the post office and tell the woman that I was staying at the Riverside Resort. But before I'd walked more than a hundred yards, I noticed small groups of people standing along the road, looking at the sky, as if they were waiting for something. Schoolchildren clustered around teachers, holding small pieces of cardboard. Everyone seemed to be talking at once.

I'd never seen an eclipse, except once, on television at the McGarritts' house. Now I stood close to one of the groups and listened to a teacher talk about the eclipse path, about the moon moving into the earth's umbra. She warned the children to use their cardboard pinhole cameras, and she urged them to watch for the "diamond ring effect."

When the teacher stopped talking, I asked her if she had an extra camera. She looked at me oddly, but she handed me two cardboard squares. "Don't forget to turn your back to the sun," she said. "Are you from around here?"

"I'm visiting," I said. But I heard her think, *She looks like Sara.*

"Do you know my mother?" I asked, but she'd already moved away. The sky began to darken, and the air was colder now. We all turned away from the sun, like obedient ducklings. I held the squares apart, so that the one with the pinhole filtered light onto the other. The sun appeared—a white dot.

As noisy as they'd been before, the people around me suddenly grew quiet. As the moon passed through the earth's shadow, the sun on my cardboard became a crescent—and for a moment, it did look like a diamond ring, a radiant gem attached to a thin band of light around a dark center. It was, to use Kathleen's words, *totally awesome*. And those words awoke my memories of her—racing ahead of me on her bicycle, or lying on floor cushions, flipping back her hair and laughing—a girl full of life, not yet a victim. Standing in the near-darkness, I wished she could have seen the eclipse, and I hoped that she was at peace.

How much time passed before the sun emerged? We stood silently as mourners in the faint light. I stood looking down at the cardboard long after I needed to. I hoped that no one saw me cry.

The noise of the others brought me back. I wiped my eyes with my sleeve, and when they were dry, I looked up again, straight into the eyes of my mother.

She stood at the edge of a group of children, watching me. Except for her clothes—faded jeans, a t-shirt—she looked like the woman in the wedding photos: fair skin, long hair that curled back from her forehead, eyes blue as lapis lazuli.

"Well," she said. "We wondered when you might drop in."

She held her arms out, and I ran into them. This time I didn't care if anyone saw me cry.

And this is the hardest part of all, wouldn't you agree? How to describe the first experience of your mother's love, without sounding like a bathetic greeting card?

Perhaps I needn't try. A phrase from the Bible conveys it: "peace that passeth all understanding."

Part III
THE BLUE BEYOND

— Thirteen —

The road to my mother's house was narrow, made of dirt, and bumpy. Her white pickup truck skirted the deepest ruts, but it still made for an exciting ride. She drove fast, and when I looked into the side mirror I saw clouds of dust behind us.

She left that road and turned right onto an even narrower one. Small white lights marked its curves. Finally she stopped at a tall aluminum gate, connected to a high aluminum fence that sprawled off in both directions.

"Ugly, isn't it?" she said. "But necessary, at times." She unlocked the gate, drove us past it, then locked it again.

I couldn't take my eyes off her. When she returned to the truck, I said, "Please? Tell me what I should call you."

She smiled at me. "Call me Mãe," she said. "It's Portuguese for mother, and a nicer sound than *mother*, don't you think?"

"Mãe." I extended the two syllables: *MY-yeh*.

She nodded. "And I'll call you Ariella. A name I've always loved."

Tall trees made a canopy over the road; some were live oaks, trailing Spanish moss; others, I'd learn later, were mangroves.

"The river is off to the west," Mãe said. "And to the east, we border a nature preserve. We have forty acres."

"We?"

"Dashay, and the animals, and me," she said. "And now, you."

I was about to ask who Dashay was, but we turned another curve and I saw the house. I'd never seen anything like it. The central structure was rectangular, but a dozen or more rooms and balconies had been added on. Skylights and round windows were set at angles and positioned high or low in the walls. The house was made of gray-blue stone; later I found out that the additions were stucco, painted to match. In the late morning sun (brighter than usual, it seemed; did it seem so because of the eclipse, or because of my finding my mother?), the walls seemed to glow.

We left the truck. Mãe carried my backpack. I paused to touch the wall near the front door; close up, I could see the stone's veins of silver, slate gray, and midnight blue. "It's beautiful," I said.

"Limestone," Mãe said. "Built in the 1850s. This part is all that's left of the original house; the rest was destroyed by Union soldiers."

Beside the front door stood a stone statue of a woman riding a horse, next to an urn full of roses. "Who is she?" I asked.

"You don't know her?" Mãe seemed surprised. "Epona, goddess of horses. Every good stable has a shrine for her." She opened the heavy wooden door, and beckoned me in. "Welcome home, Ariella."

The smell of home: wood polished with the oil of Meyer lemons, roses, a savory soup cooking somewhere, lavender, thyme, white geranium, and a hint of horses. Mãe removed her shoes, and I did the same, embarrassed at the sight of my socks, one of which had a hole in its heel. She noticed but didn't say anything.

My first visual impression of the place was a jumble of things: each wall (painted varying shades of blue) had a mural, or framed paintings, or a bookcase, or an alcove holding statues, flowers, and herbs. The furniture was simple, low and modern, most upholstered in white. Carpets and cushions were scattered everywhere. She led me down a corridor, into a room with periwinkle walls, a vast white bed, and an ivory chaise next to a floor lamp with a mother-of-pearl shade.

It was so different from the ornate Victorian furnishings of my father's house. I'd always assumed that my mother had decorated it, but now I wondered. And that thought brought me back to the one that kept me from happiness: why had she left us?

She looked at me, and I tried to hear her thoughts, but couldn't. "You probably have questions, Ariella. I'll answer them as best I can. But first, let me get you into some clean clothes and feed you. All right?"

"All right," I said. "Sorry about the socks."

She put her hand on my shoulder and looked into my eyes, and I wanted to melt into her arms again. "You need never apologize to me," she said.

My mother—Mãe—ran me a bath with rose petals floating in it. "To soften the skin," she said. Her own skin was like velvet. And while her voice shared Sophie's Savannah accent, its pitch and rhythm were more like those of Mr. Winters. Her voice was gentle and light, as hypnotic as my father's voice, but in a different way.

"You look like your wedding photo," I said.

"I thought your father would have put all of those things away."

"Sophie showed me. She gave me an album."

"So you've been with Sophie?" Mãe shook her head. "It's a wonder she didn't shoot you. You must tell me all about her, after your bath."

She left me in the bathroom—a hexagonal room with cornflower-blue walls, and a large stained-glass window over the tub depicting a white horse against a cobalt background. I shed my clothes and slipped into the water, rose petals floating over me, and I looked up at a skylight that framed the leaves of a vine-covered tree and a small patch of lazuline sky. On the wall over the tub, shelves held small green plants, each in a mother-of-pearl pot.

When I left the bathroom, wrapped in a fragrant towel (she added geranium or thyme oil to the laundry rinse water, I found out later), I saw that new clothes had been left on my bed: a shirt, pants, and underwear, all made of the same soft cotton, the color of blanched almonds. They looked comfortable—but they wouldn't protect me as the metamaterial suit had. Maybe I wouldn't need to be invisible, here.

I dressed, slathered on sunscreen—a ritual automatic by now as breathing. Humans and vampires alike need constant protection from the sun. I hope you will remember that. If more humans realized it, they wouldn't age as horribly as they do.

On the table next to the bed lay a wooden comb. I tried to unsnarl my hair, not altogether successfully.

Mãe knocked and came in, a small spray-bottle in her hand. "Sit," she said.

I did, and she sprayed something on my hair, then worked the comb through the tangles. "Do you recognize the smell?"

I didn't.

"Rosemary," she said. "Mixed with a little white vinegar."

"I know about vinegar," I said. "And I've read the word *rosemary*, but I never smelled it before."

She worked the comb gently through my hair. "What *did* he teach you?" she said.

"He taught me a great deal," I said. "History, science, literature, philosophy. Latin, French, Spanish. Some Greek."

"A classical education," she said. "But not Epona, or the smell of rosemary?"

"He didn't teach me about some things," I said slowly. "I'm not good with road maps. And I don't know much about goddesses."

"He didn't teach you mythology." She said it decisively. "There, your hair is like silk. Now let's have lunch."

The kitchen was another large, high-ceilinged room, with stone tiles of alternating shades of blue on the floor and walls of turquoise-colored plaster. Copper pans hung from the ceiling, and a saucepan simmered on a blue-enameled stove. Eight chairs were pulled up to a long, battered oak table.

I wondered how to tell my mother about my diet, for want of a better term. "I don't eat the same foods as most people," I said. "That is, I can eat them, but only certain foods make me feel strong."

She ladled soup into two large blue bowls and carried them to the table. "Try some," she said.

The broth was dark red, with a hint of gold in it. I took a cautious spoonful, then another. "Oh, it's *good*," I said. The broth had vegetables in it—carrots, beets, potatoes—but I couldn't identify the other flavors. It was thick and sultry, and it made me happy.

"It's red miso soup." My mother took a spoonful herself. "With beans, lentils, saffron, and some other things—fenugreek and lucerne and such—added for flavor. Plus some vitamins and mineral supplements. You haven't had this before?"

I shook my head.

"That's right, eat," she said. "You're too thin. What did he feed you?"

Her voice wasn't critical, but the references to "he" were making me nervous. "My father hired a cook especially for me," I said. "I was on a vegetarian diet. And he and Dennis monitored my blood, and gave me a special tonic when I was anemic."

"Dennis," she said. "How is he?"

"He's well," I said politely. Then, more honestly, I said, "He's worried about his weight, and about getting older."

"Poor thing." She rose and took my bowl to refill it. "And Mary Ellis Root—how is she?"

She's horrid, I thought. But I said, "She's always the same. She doesn't change."

My mother brought me the bowl. "No," she said, her voice amused. "I don't suppose she does."

She folded her arms on the table and watched me eat. I felt her pleasure—probably every bit as much pleasure as I had, consuming the wonderful red soup.

"Did anyone teach you to cook?" she said.

"No." I reached for the tall blue glass of water she'd poured me. This taste, too, was a surprise, charged with minerals and an icy metallic aftertaste.

"The water comes from the mineral spring out back," she said, "After lunch I'll take you around."

"I can cook a little," I said, thinking of my sorry attempt at vegetarian lasagna. "And I can ride a bike, and swim."

"Can you row a boat?" she asked.

"No."

"Do you know how to grow an organic garden? Can you sew your own clothes? Can you drive a car?"

"No." I wanted to impress her, somehow. *I can turn invisible*, I thought. *I can hear thoughts.*

She cleared the table, saying over her shoulder, "I have my work cut out for me, I see."

A small cat with blue-gray fur and with pale green eyes strolled into the kitchen. It sniffed my leg, then rubbed its face against me.

"May I touch it?" I asked.

Mãe looked up from the sink. "Hello, Grace," she said to the cat. "Of course," she said to me. "Haven't you ever had a pet?"

"No."

"Well, here you'll have several."

Grace sauntered over and sniffed my hand. Then she turned her back on me. Clearly, I'd have to prove I was worthy.

The three of us, Grace trailing my mother and me, walked around the stable: a long blue building behind the house, each stall empty, smelling of sweet hay.

Mãe had four horses, grazing in a paddock. She called their names: Osceola, Abiaka, Billie, and Johnny Cypress. The horses came to her, and she introduced me to them.

"May I touch them?" I'd never been this close to the horses in Saratoga Springs.

"Of course."

She stroked Osceola's neck, and I petted Johnny Cypress. He was the smallest of the four, with a light gray coat and blue eyes. The others' coats ranged from pure white to ivory to cream.

I asked about their names, and she said they came from

leaders of the Seminole tribe. "I guess you haven't learned about them?" she said.

I shook my head.

"Native Americans who were never conquered. Osceola led them in battle against the United States. And you don't know much about horses?"

"I sometimes watched horses at the racetrack," I said. "We'd go early in the morning, when they were exercising."

"*We* meaning you and your father?"

"No. I had a friend. Her name was Kathleen. She was murdered."

I told her what I knew about Kathleen's death. She put her arms around me when I finished.

"The killer hasn't been caught?" she asked.

"Not so far as I know." For the first time in months, I wanted to call home.

"Raphael doesn't know you're here." She said it flatly, as if she knew it.

"I left a note." I didn't want to meet her eyes. "It was kind of vague, though. He'd left to go to some conference in Baltimore, and I felt—I wanted to find you."

"Baltimore? He left in January?"

I nodded.

"Some things don't change."

Osceola whinnied, and she said to him, "It's all right."

"Could I ride one of them, someday?"

"Of course." She took my hands in hers, and examined them. "Have you ever ridden?"

"No."

"All right then," she said, "we'll add riding to our list of things to learn."

Next she showed me the honeybee hives: stacks of wooden boxes like the ones Mr. Winters kept, near a grove of orange and lemon trees. "You can taste the citrus in the honey," she said.

"Does it taste different from lavender honey?" I was thinking of her cookbook, back in Saratoga.

She stopped walking. "Yes," she said, her voice soft. "Nothing compares to lavender honey, in my opinion. But I can't grow lavender here. I've tried. It always dies."

The path circled a garden patch, and she named the crops: peanuts, sweet potatoes, tomatoes, lettuce, gourds, squash, and beans of all sorts. A small blue-painted cottage bordered the garden. Mãe called it the guest house.

"We breed the horses, and that makes enough money to let us do the rescues," she said.

Rescues? I thought. I had more pressing questions. "*We* meaning you and—what was the name?"

"Dashay. She's at a horse auction today. She'll be back tomorrow."

"Are you and Dashay a couple?" I'd barely met my mother, yet I felt jealous. I wanted her undivided attention.

She laughed. "We're a couple of idiots. Dashay is my good friend. I met her when I was running away, like you. She helped me buy the land here, and we share the work and the profits."

I stared at my mother—sun glinting on her hair, topaz

eyes. "Are you in love with anyone?" I asked.

"I'm in love with the world," she said. "How about you, Ariella?"

"I'm not sure," I said.

May in Florida is a curious time. My mother called it the last-chance month; with June 1 came hot humid rainy days, she said, and the start of hurricane season.

That night the temperatures fell into the sixties, and we wore sweaters when we took a stroll after dinner, down to the river. A small wooden dock jutted into a harbor, and tied to it were three boats: a canoe, a motorboat, and a pedal boat. "Want to take her out?" Mãe said.

"Which one?"

"Let's start the easy way," she said.

I climbed awkwardly into the pedal boat, and she untied the lines and jumped in, so lightly that the boat barely moved. Then we pedaled off, down the river.

The full moon slipped in and out of clouds, and the night breeze was sweet, smelling of orange blossoms. "You live in a wonderful world," I said.

She laughed, and the sound of her laughter seemed to sparkle in the dark air. "I've built it carefully," she said. "I gave up my heart when I left Saratoga." Her face wasn't sad, merely thoughtful. "We have so much to tell each other," she said. "It can't all be told in one day."

The boat moved into open water, and ahead I saw the lights of the hotel where I'd spent the previous night, and the thin beam from the lighthouse on Monkey Island.

"Poor monkeys," I said. I told her about watching them from the hotel.

My mother's eyes flashed. "Do you know the story? The original monkeys were put on the island after they'd been used to develop a vaccine for polio. They were the survivors—the ones who weren't paralyzed or dead. So their reward was to become a tourist attraction."

We pedaled closer. Bob sat on a rock, staring at nothing. The other, smaller monkey hung from a tree branch and watched our approach. Mãe made a funny clicking sound with her tongue, and Bob stood up. He walked down to the rocks on the island's edge. The other monkey sprang out of his tree and loped after Bob.

What happened next is hard to describe. It's as if my mother and Bob had a conversation across the water, though no words were spoken. The other monkey kept out of it, and so did I.

"All right then," Mãe said after a few minutes had passed. She looked again at Bob. Then she steered the boat to the side of the island not visible from the resort. We hit bottom several yards from the shoreline. She waded ashore, moving so gracefully that she barely made a splash. I sat and watched, wanting to cheer, not making a sound.

When Mãe reached the shore, Bob was waiting. He wrapped his arms around her neck and his legs around her waist. The other monkey climbed onto her shoulders and clasped her neck. She waded back, more slowly now. The monkeys stared at me, their small eyes bright, curious. I wanted to greet them, but kept mum as they climbed into the boat. They sat on the floor, in the stern.

We left the harbor as quietly as before.

I was thrilled beyond words. Not only had I found my mother—I'd found a hero, and two monkeys as well.

Bob wasn't his real name, it turned out. He was Harris.

My mother and Harris sat in the living room later that night, working out the details. The other monkey, Joey, had a snack of apples and sunflower seeds, then went off to bed in the guest house.

Mãe and Harris communicated with gestures, eye movements, grunts, and nods. When they were done, they hugged each other, and Harris nodded at me as he left for the guest house.

"How did you learn to communicate with monkeys?" I asked.

"Oh, we've had monkeys here before." She stood up and stretched her arms. "Some were pets who'd been abandoned, and some came off Monkey Island. You realize that the hotel will replace Harris and Joey, don't you? They always do."

I hadn't thought of it. "Then we can rescue the new ones, too?"

"It depends." She rubbed her eyes. "Some like it on the island. Joey might have been perfectly happy there. But Harris hated it, and Joey didn't want to be left alone."

"Will you teach me how to talk to them?"

"Sure," she said. "It takes some time, but not as much as learning French or Spanish."

"I want Harris to be my friend," I said. I imagined

holding his hand, talking walks, maybe even trips in the pedal boat.

"He will be, for a while." Mãe looked hard at me. "You realize he can't stay here?"

"Why not?"

"It's not safe, for one thing. Someone might see them and then we'd have the hotel to deal with. You don't know yet how small this town is." She walked around the room, switching off lamps. "Even more important, Harris and Joey will be happier at a primate refuge. There's a sanctuary in Panama where we've sent monkeys before. They're rehabilitated and taught how to live in the wild again."

I thought this over. Sadly, it did make sense. "I really wanted him to be my pet."

"Someday, a monkey might turn up who wants to stay." My mother yawned. "But not Harris. He absolutely hates Florida."

How could anyone hate Florida? I wondered later. I lay in my soft white bed, watching the orange-blossom-scented breeze lift the white curtains, listening to the rhythmic song of tree frogs punctuated by the percussion of bamboo stalks clacking against each other. I felt as close to happy as I'd thought I'd ever be.

The next morning, after writing in my journal, I went out to the kitchen and no one was there. I sat down at the big oak table, not sure what I should do. A newspaper from Tampa lay at the table's head, and I read the front-page headlines upside down. Then I picked up the paper and skimmed it, story by story: Wars. Floods. Global warming.

Toward the bottom right side of an inside page, I read: "No Clues in Vampire Slayings." The story summarized the deaths of Robert Reedy of Asheville and one Andrew Parker of Savannah. Police asked the public to call with any information about the murders. Parker's family offered a reward for any tips. I carefully re-folded the paper, wondering how I would tell my mother I'd killed a man.

She came in a few minutes later, talking to a tall woman with the most interesting hair I'd ever seen: it had been rolled and twisted and pinned up into elaborate shapes like cabbage roses. Her eyes were enormous, caramel-colored.

"Dashay, this is Ariella," my mother said.

I said hello, feeling shy. I'd never known before how beautiful and animated women could be. No one like these women walked around in Saratoga Springs. I stared down at the table, listening to their voices.

Dashay talked about the horses she'd seen at the auction, about the people who were buying and selling. She hadn't been tempted to bid, but she'd met with three owners interested in breeding mares with Osceola.

Mãe asked detailed questions about the owners while she stood at the stove, cooking oatmeal. She set steaming bowls before us, and Dashay handed me a glass honey pot shaped like a hive. "Drizzle it on," she said.

We ate, and I savored each mouthful. The honey tasted of flowers and spring air, and the oatmeal's texture was creamy, soothing. Last night's dinner—grilled mahi-mahi with citrus sauce and puréed sweet potatoes—had been equally delicious. I didn't miss my tonic and protein bars at all, but I wondered when I'd need blood again.

My mother looked at me, questions in her eyes.

"So you were up early with the bees, huh," Dashay said. "Guess I'll do some gardening this afternoon, then take some honey down to the store."

Mãe was still watching me. "Two cartons of orange blossom are ready to go," she said. "Meanwhile, I'm going to give Ariella a riding lesson."

In short order I learned how to tighten a saddle, adjust the stirrups, mount and dismount, and hold the reins. I'd asked to ride Johnny Cypress. Mãe agreed.

"He's the gentlest of the bunch," she said. "I think it's because he's so grateful. His previous owner abused him. You should have seen him when we adopted him, poor baby."

We headed down a trail toward the river, the horses stepping briskly, enjoying the outing. I quickly got used to the rhythm and let myself relax in the saddle.

"You ride well," my mother said. It was the first time she'd praised me, and I grinned. "It's not always so gentle," she said. "Later we'll pick up the pace."

The dirt path led through mangroves, past small ponds and marsh grass, and then to the river, broad and blue, smelling of salt. Here we dismounted and sat on a large flat rock, shaded by mangroves. "We have picnics here," Mãe said.

For a while neither of us spoke. The wind played with our hair, and we watched the horses as they grazed. Osceola was a true beauty: tall and muscular and handsome in all respects. Johnny Cypress was small and jaunty, perfect for me.

"I want to ride him every day," I said, not realizing I'd spoken aloud until Mãe said, "Of course you will."

"Mãe, I need to tell you some things." Again, I hadn't planned to speak. Then the words all came in a rush. "I killed someone, I didn't mean to, you don't know who I am, it all happened so suddenly—" Clumsy words, but such a relief to say them.

She put up her hand, and the gesture made me stop talking and think of my father.

Her blue eyes were clear, untroubled. "Slow down and tell me."

I told her the story of Robert Reedy's untimely death in the woods outside Asheville. She interrupted only twice, to ask, "Did anyone see you get in his car?" (I didn't know) and "Did you leave behind any evidence?" (I hadn't, and I'd been wearing gloves.)

"Well, I wouldn't worry about it," she said, when I'd finished.

"But it's murder."

"More like self-defense," she said. "He would have raped you."

"Then why do I feel so bad?" I crossed my arms and gripped my shoulders. "Why do I think about it all the time?"

"Because you have a conscience," she said. "Something he probably lacked. Ariella, from all you've said I doubt that you were the first girl he took out there. Be glad you're the last."

I shook my head. "You're not even shocked that I'm—that I'm—"

She laughed. "You're so like your father," she said. "All this concern for things that really can't be helped. No, I'm not shocked. How could I be? I knew you were a vampire—although I didn't like to use the word—right from the beginning."

To be precise, she said, she knew from the first trimester that her pregnancy wasn't "normal."

"I felt terribly sick." She rubbed her forehead, then pulled her hand through her hair. "I threw up all the time, and I was mean to your father. I blamed him for everything. But in fact, getting pregnant was all my doing."

"It usually takes two." My voice came out sounding so prissy that she laughed again, and finally I smiled.

"In our case, I was the driving force," she said, her voice dry. "Hasn't he told you any of this?"

"Some," I said. "He said it was a difficult pregnancy. And he did say that you were the one who wanted me." I looked toward the river.

"That's not entirely true, either. Look at me. Are you sure you want to hear this?"

I wasn't sure, anymore. But I said, "I have to know. It feels as if everything depends on me knowing."

She nodded. She told me her story.

Imagine finding the love of your life, then losing him. Yes, people lose their loved ones all the time to war and disease, accidents and murder. But imagine watching your lover change before your eyes, devolve into some other being, and you're powerless to bring him back.

My mother told me about meeting Raphael, about their early months together, about packing for her trip to England as if it were a honeymoon. She described their reunion—the horror of seeing a man who wasn't Raphael inhabit his body, the futile desire to recover what he had been.

"He was brilliant," she said. "And funny. He could dance, and tell jokes, and of course he was beautiful—"

"He's still beautiful," I said.

"But he lacks something," my mother said. "Something that made him *my* Raphael."

She said that she'd hoped that with time and love, he would come back to himself. "The odd thing is, he imposed this new personality on himself," she said. "It didn't happen as a result of his so-called *affliction*. He felt guilty. He made himself into a sort of monk, so obsessed with doing the right thing that everything he did seemed stiff, programmed.

"You've known me exactly one day," she said to me. "But you've seen enough to know that I'm impulsive, and kind of silly at times."

"I like that," I said.

"So did your father, once," she said. "In any case, getting married was my idea. He didn't think it was ethical, a vampire marrying a human. I said, love isn't a matter of ethics!"

We didn't speak for a moment. The water nearby began to ripple, and as I watched, a gray-white mass rose to the surface and took shape. I put my hand on my mother's shoulder, mouthed the word *manatee*?

She nodded. The manatee turned its wrinkled face away and slowly sank again.

"Oh," I said. "To think such things really exist."

Mãe reached for me and hugged me hard.

Listening to my mother that day was something like hearing a horror story read aloud at a toddlers' picnic. Nothing in the place or the company was in keeping with the tale.

"I trapped him," she said. Nearby, butterflies perched on a flowering shrub. "He didn't want to have a child. I told him I was using two forms of birth control, so that he didn't need any. I lied to him."

For the first time, I felt I *was* hearing more than I wanted to know.

She seemed to sense my discomfort. "So when I learned I was pregnant, I felt triumphant—briefly," she said. "Then I was sick as a dog."

She learned she was pregnant in November—peak season for the Saratoga Springs doldrums. "The weather was dreadful, and I stayed inside," she said. "He hated himself for giving in to me, and his way of dealing with it was reverting to complete correctness. That is, he played the model husband—no, more like a nurse— looking after me, doing research about pregnancy and home deliveries, watching my diet, taking blood samples. He and Dennis were like two hens, clucking over me. They made me want to scream."

Two jays—males, their wings and tails a vivid royal blue—alit on the rocks near the river and looked at us. Suddenly, unexpectedly, I felt sympathy for my father. He'd tried to do what he thought was right, given the circumstances. My mother had been the greedy one.

She was watching me, and now she nodded. "He tried to do what was right. And he thought having a child was wrong. Well, Ariella, at least I won that one."

I took a deep breath. "Mother—Mãe, I want to know why you left us."

"That's simple," she said. "I wanted to be like you two. I was tired of being left out."

As her pregnancy proceeded, my mother had more indications that the child inside her—that I—was not a normal human. Extreme nausea and anemia of the kind she experienced were considered unusual, but not abnormal—that was the consensus of my father and Dennis and Root, who had recently joined them. ("I loathed that woman on first sight," Mãe said. "And she clearly resented me.")

Bad dreams weren't abnormal, either. "But my dreams were more than bad," she said. "I couldn't remember them, and that in itself was terrible, for someone who's always placed great store in dreams. I'd awaken with my mouth still open from screaming, the sheets wet, my sense of smell so extreme that I could taste the bleach in the pillowcases. I heard voices—not any I recognized, and certainly not yours or your father's—telling me I was damned. I wanted to answer back: 'Who damns me?' But my voice would dry up in my throat. I ran high fevers. I heard them say I was delirious."

A breeze swelled, running a line of wind shadows across

the water. The air ran right through me. I wondered if I should have been born.

"Ariella, I'm telling you this because I want you to understand why I left." She leaned toward me, only a small space remaining between us on the warm stone, and yet I didn't bend toward her.

"Tell me the rest," I said, my voice stiff.

"I asked him to make me an *other*. Like him. Like you," she said. "And he refused."

And she told me of their arguments, which I don't like to think about, much less write down here. Listening to parents fight—is there anything worse for a child, except hearing about it years later, knowing that you were the cause?

My father wasn't about to make anyone a vampire. My mother, sensing that I (in utero) already was one, wasn't about to be the only aging human in the family.

"Think of it," she said to me. "Growing old, getting ill. Losing strength and intelligence in the company of others who maintain theirs. The ultimate indignity."

I took a deep breath. "You both had too much pride."

In the end, or in the beginning, I was born. And my mother left.

My father examined me in the basement laboratory. What did he do besides count my toes? I wondered. Blood tests must have been run, but what else?

Upstairs, my mother slept. She remembered them covering her with a yellow cashmere blanket.

When she awoke, she was being lifted, still wrapped in

the blanket, into an automobile. She heard the engine running, and she smelled its exhaust. She caught a glimpse of Dennis's face as he shut the car door.

"Who was driving?" I couldn't be patient. "Was it my father?"

Mãe had been hunched forward, tracing patterns on the rock as she spoke. Now she straightened and looked at me. "Your father? Of course not. It was his best friend. A man called Malcolm."

My mother had known Malcolm for years, since she'd met my father in Savannah, and when he told her Raphael had asked him to take her for emergency medical treatment, she didn't question him. She felt weak and exhausted. She slept in the car.

When she awoke, she was in bed—not in a hospital, but in a house. "A rather grand house, somewhere in the Catskills," she said. "The room had long leaded casement windows. That's what I remember best: looking out the diamond-paned windows and seeing nothing but empty green fields and hills."

Malcolm brought her food, then sat by her bedside. "He told me that you'd been born with deformities," she said, her voice low. "He told me you weren't expected to live. He said Raphael was devastated, but that deep down, he blamed me. He hated me. Malcolm explained things calmly and rationally. He said I had some choices to make, the first of which was the obvious one: whether to go back and face the horror—*face the music*, is what he said—or whether to go on with my life and let Raphael go on with his. Your father, he said, much preferred the latter."

I stood up, shaking. "That's not true," I said. "That's not what my father told me."

Mãe looked up at me. She was crying. But her voice stayed clear and steady. "You can't know how I felt: sick inside, weak and stupid. He talked to me for hours about the ethics involved. How I hate that word! Ethics are nothing but excuses for behavior."

I disagreed, but this wasn't the time for that debate. "Why didn't you call my father?"

"He didn't want to talk to me. Malcolm told me the best thing for everyone would be for me to go away, start a new life, forget what he called *this misery* that I'd created."

Tears were streaking her face, and I wanted to comfort her, but something in me resisted.

"And he made me an offer. In exchange for leaving Raphael alone, he'd give me what I wanted."

"Which was?"

"To live forever. To be like you."

"So you left us, you abandoned us, for that?"

She looked so pathetic, and I wanted to console her as much as I wanted to strike her, or break something. I picked up a rock and threw it into the river, and then I remembered the manatee. I rushed to the edge of the water and peered down.

"It's all right." She'd come up behind me. "Look." She pointed downstream, at eddies that grew deeper, then parted as the manatee surfaced. We watched it for a while.

"I don't know how to feel," I said, my voice raspy.

She nodded. We went back to the rock and sat. The sun

was hot, and I moved into the shade cast by the tree. Somewhere a mockingbird sang a complicated song, then repeated it six times. High overhead, a bird with a vast wingspan
soared and circled.

"What's that?" I asked.

"A short-tailed hawk," she said. "Wouldn't it be great to
be able to fly?" Her voice was wistful.

"My father wished he could fly, too." I thought back to
the evening in the living room when I'd listened to his story.
"Knowing the truth doesn't set you free, does it?"

"I think that it does, in time." Her tears had stopped.

The sun had begun to move westward, and I noticed
that she cast no shadow. "So you're one of us?"

"If you mean what I think you mean, yes."

She told me Malcolm had kept his part of the bargain.
Afterward, he'd taken care of her for a month, until she
was stable enough to fend for herself. "It was the worst
month of my life." She said it without emotion. "Sometimes I thought I heard you crying, and my breasts ached.
I wanted to die."

"But you didn't come for me."

"I didn't come for you. Malcolm told me I mustn't—you
needed special care. And Raphael would hate the idea of
me being a vampire. Malcolm said I'd done enough damage, that I'd ruin Raphael if I interfered any further. He convinced me that he was right: Raphael and his research were
what mattered, in the end. It might have been different, if
we'd been happier together. Malcolm said that if you survived, which he doubted, he'd keep an eye on you, he'd act

as your invisible guardian. He wanted your father to focus on work, and he didn't trust Dennis to look after you. He thought Dennis would bungle things, somehow.

"So I agreed. But I never forgot about you. I had friends look in on you, from time to time, and they told me that you were all right, that you were growing stronger."

"We had very few visitors," I said. I was watching a bird with an impossibly two-dimensional head, an amber beak, and long legs that bent backward before angling forward as it waded nearby. It looked like a cartoon bird.

"These visitors were invisible." She said it matter-of-factly.

"Why didn't you come yourself?"

"It would have hurt too much." She stretched her hands toward me. I didn't move. "I tried to send you messages," she said. "I sent you dreams."

I remembered the crosswords, and the song. "'The Blue Beyond,'" I said.

"So it worked!" Her face lit up.

"The song came through," I said. "The crosswords were pretty garbled."

"But they brought you to me."

They hadn't, really. But to my mother, they were the invisible thread that had led me home. "Actually, it was the letter S that helped me find Homosassa Springs," I said. "My father and Sophie said you thought S was lucky."

"It is." She picked a leaf from a shrub and put it into her mouth. "The form of S symbolizes the waxing and waning of the moon. But I liked it long before I knew that. From the time I learned to write the alphabet, the shape and sound of S seemed special."

A snake swam by, and I stiffened.

"It's a bird," Mãe said. "Look."

Visible beneath the water's surface was the body of a bird—its long neck created the illusion of a snake. "It's called an anhinga. You weren't taught about birds?"

"Some. We focused more on insects, actually." I was thinking, hard, about all she'd said. "I think Malcolm is the *éminence grise* of this story."

"He treated me kindly, all in all."

"He stole you. He told you lies." More and more, I was convinced of it. "Didn't my father tell you how Malcolm treated him?"

"Malcolm was his friend," she said.

"He didn't tell you who made him a vampire?"

Her eyes were wary, now. "He never said. I assumed it was one of his professors."

Why would my father tell me, and not her? I wondered.

"How like him, to be so discreet." Her voice was bitter.

"You hear my thoughts?"

She nodded. "I don't listen all the time, I promise."

"Why can't I hear yours?"

"I'm in the habit of blocking them." Then she let her guard down, and I heard her think, *I love you. I've always loved you.*

I thought, *He loves you still. He never stopped.*

She shook her head. *He stopped the day I lied, the day I seduced him. When he looked at me after that, I saw shame in his eyes.*

"I've seen his eyes when he talks about you," I said. "He misses you. He's lonely."

"He prefers his loneliness," she said. "All in all, Malcolm was right. It was better this way."

I crossed my arms. "Let me tell you about Malcolm."

And so I told my mother about my father's "change of state" and all that followed. I told her everything he'd told me. After I'd finished talking, she didn't say a word.

We rode the horses back to the stable—walking first, then breaking into a trot, then a gallop. I hung on to the saddle, afraid I'd be thrown off, but I managed to hold my seat. My mother and Osceola flew ahead of me.

Back at the stables, we groomed and fed the horses. When Mãe wasn't looking, I gave Johnny a good-night kiss on his neck.

Finally she spoke. "I'm going out. Want to come?"

— Fourteen —

The parking lot was full, and my mother had to park the pickup on the street. We walked toward a long white building with a neon sign in a window reading FLO'S PLACE.

Inside, the tables all were occupied, and the bar had standing room only. The bartender called out, "Hey, Sara!" Mãe stopped here and there to say hello as we made our way toward a corner booth.

Dashay sat with a muscular man wearing a black cowboy hat. They were drinking something red. My mother slid into the booth, and I sat on the end.

Dashay said, "Ariella, this is Bennett. He's my boyfriend."

I shook his hand. He had a strong grip and a beautiful smile. "I like your hat," I said.

"Hear that? She likes the hat," he said. "Dashay's always telling me to take off the hat. Lose the hat, she says."

"Do you have a boyfriend?" Dashay asked me.

"Sort of," I said.

"What's he like?"

"He's quiet," I said. "He has long hair." I wondered if my mother had a boyfriend.

She looked at me and said, "No."

A server brought us two glasses of Picardo, and my mother raised her glass in a toast. "To justice," she said. Dashay and Bennett looked puzzled, but they drank.

I took a sip. Picardo was an acquired taste; this time I liked its smoky tang. When I looked around, I noticed that most of the others seemed to be drinking Picardo, too. Here and there I saw a beer or a glass of white wine, but the glasses of red liquid were twice as prevalent. "Why is almost everyone drinking the same thing?"

"Creatures of habit," Mãe said.

"What makes it so red?" I asked.

"Supposed to be a secret recipe," Bennett said.

"I read somewhere that the color comes from crushed insects." Dashay held her glass up, and rays from the setting sun outside gave the liquid a garnet glow.

"Very appetizing." My mother hadn't smiled once since our talk, and it made me realize how often she had, before. "Ariella, I need to talk to these friends. You're welcome to listen, but it will be the same things we've been talking about for hours. Or, you can play the jukebox." She dug into her pockets and pulled out a handful of change.

I didn't want to hear the stories again. In any case, I had my own thinking to do. I took the money and my drink, and

the middle of a long sentence, which ended with "—must be the Sanguinist influence."

I knew they'd been talking about my father; my mother let me hear her thoughts. "What's a Sanguinist?" I asked.

They looked at me.

"Well," Dashay said. "We need to talk about sects."

Bennett began to laugh.

"Hush!" she told him. "S-E-C-T-S is what I said." She turned her back on him. "I guess you weren't told about them? Some vampires are Colonists—they think humans should be penned up and bred for blood, like animals. Others are Reformers, and they're all about teaching humans how superior vampires are. There are some weird ones called Nebulists—extremists who want to wipe out the human race. Nice folks. Then there is what they call the Society of S. S stands for *Sanguinists*. They're environmentalists, conservationists—well, we are, too. After all, most of us think we're going to be around forever, so we have a real stake—stop laughing, Bennett. I mean it. We have a stake in preserving the earth.

"But the Sanguinists take it a step further. They practice abstinence, and they don't mingle much with mortals, although they think mortals should have, you know, democratic rights. The Sanguinists think biting people is immoral, and vamping humans is, too."

"Vamping?"

"Making mortals into vampires," Bennett translated. "That's Dashay's own word that she made up herself."

Dashay ignored us. "The Sanguinists, they're obsessed

with doing the right thing. They take life very, very seriously."

"We don't belong to any sect," Mãe said. She gave me an odd look. I was blocking my thoughts.

"We're crunchies," Bennett said. "You know, granola and organic gardening and all that. We don't mess with big ideas or obsess about ethics."

"We do what comes naturally," Dashay said. "Live and let live."

"Some sects assume that they need human blood every day to survive." My mother held up her glass. "But we get along nicely using supplements, so long as we pay attention to balancing our diet. Your father was a typical scientist— never much interested in food," she added. "He doesn't recognize the value of vegetables."

"We don't need blood?"

Dashay said, "We take the supplements. We don't need to bite people. Sure, we like it, but you can get the same rush from raw oysters or soybeans—they're full of zinc—or red wine or Picardo."

"Almost the same." Bennett sounded regretful. I wondered how he and Dashay had come to be vampires. Flo's Place must be full of strange stories.

"What about eating meat?" Asking questions gave me time to come to terms with the disconnected phone.

"Meat isn't necessary," my mother said. "We're pescetarians."

"Tastes gross." Bennett extended his fingers and wriggled them like worms. "But the Sangunists eat it. They think meat is necessary, that it kind of substitutes for blood."

"We have the supplements, and spring water." Dashay seemed eager to steer the conversation away from blood. "The river is fed by springs, did you know that, Ariella? And the water has the same minerals as salt water. Freshwater and saltwater fish both live in the river, and we eat them, too. The springs are one reason so many vampires settled here."

Mãe leaned close to my ear. "What's wrong?"

"I'll tell you later," I said.

The server brought us platters of raw oysters and a bottle of deep-red hot sauce. Despite the oysters' succulence, I ate little, without much appetite.

Later that night, I sat on the edge of the dock. Harris came out to join me, sitting about a foot to my right. The sun had set, but the sky remained pink. Nacreous clouds along the horizon glowed as if lit from within. They gradually faded, turned as blue as distant mountains; they made me think of Asheville, and I suppressed that thought, along with any thought of Saratoga Springs.

Harris and I dangled our feet in the cool water. An anhinga swam past me, still looking like a snake, and a mockingbird called from a tree nearby. I thought of a line from Thoreau's *Walden: The life in us is like the water in the river.*

All was calm—until I saw an ominous fin no more than two hundred yards away, skimming the river's surface. I grabbed Harris and pulled both of us backward. He leapt to his feet and disappeared into the trees.

I ran barefoot all the way back to the house and into the living room. "I saw a shark!"

My mother, Dashay, and Bennett, playing cards at the kitchen table, looked up. Mãe handed me a piece of paper and a pen. "Draw the dorsal fin."

I sketched it quickly.

"Looks like a dolphin to me," Dashay said. She took the pen and sketched in another fin, this one without the crescent-shaped backward curve. "That's what a shark looks like."

Wrong again, I thought. *Always wrong, and I used to always be right.* "I scared Harris," I said, my voice sounding as ashamed as I felt.

"I'll find him and explain," Dashay said. She went out.

Then Mãe pushed back her chair and left the room. She came back with two books: a field guide to Florida and a gardening handbook. "You'll learn, the same way I did," she said.

I took the books and sat in a chintz-covered chair in the corner. Grace the cat strolled past me as if I weren't worth noticing.

When Dashay returned, she said that Harris had settled down in the guest house for the night. "I explained to him what happened," she said. "He won't hold a grudge."

The card game resumed, but I could tell from their rush of idle talk that I'd interrupted a more important conversation. So I told them good-night and went to my room, carrying the books.

Later, as I lay in bed, Grace came in and sat at my feet. We watched an ochre moon climb the sky. Mãe knocked and opened the door. "Are you going to tell me what's bothering you?"

I kept my thoughts blocked, not sure what to say. "Tomorrow," I said.

When I awoke, sunlight glared in at me. I heard voices, and from the window I saw Mãe and Dashay outside the stables, talking to someone I didn't recognize. A Green Cross courier van was parked in the driveway.

I went downstairs as quietly as if they'd been in the living room. I took the cordless telephone from the kitchen and made my way back to my room again.

Michael answered on the third ring.

"Michael, it's me," I said.

After a pause, he said, "Thanks for calling. I'll let you know." And he hung up on me.

I held the dead phone. He'd sounded odd, formal and nervous. The click lingered in my ear, the sound of one more disconnection.

I was about to take the phone back to the kitchen when it rang. I answered at once.

"It's me, Ari." Michael still sounded nervous. "I couldn't talk."

"What's going on?"

"Agent Burton is here. He comes by every couple of months, checking in. I'm out in the garage now, on my mobile phone. I took your number off Caller ID."

So the McGarritts had finally updated their telephones. "Are you all right?"

"Yeah, fine. Where are you?"

"I'm with my mom," I said. "It's really nice here."

"Good, good. Don't tell me where you are. Burton keeps asking about you, and it's better if I don't know."

"He's asking about me?"

"Yeah. You know, since what happened to your dad and all—"

"What happened to my dad?"

The silence on the phone had its own tension.

"Michael?"

"You mean you don't know?"

"I haven't talked to him since I left. What's happened?"

Another silence, this one even more charged. Then a sentence, so rushed and garbled that it made no sense.

"I can't hear you," I said. "Say it again."

"He's dead." The words swam at me, mere patterns of sound. "Ari, your father is dead."

At some point my mother came in and took the phone from my hand. I was holding it without hearing, sitting on the floor. From a distance I heard her voice, talking to Michael, but the words didn't register. In my ears was white noise—the sound of all sound and no sound—and in my head was nothing.

The smell of incense woke me. I couldn't identify the scent—a blend of herbs, a few of which I recognized. Lavender was one, and rosemary another.

When I opened my eyes, I saw smoke; it wasn't from incense after all, but from a bundle of plants set on an iron brazier. Candles burned on nearly every surface of the room—maybe a hundred of them, white pillars with flickering flames. Yet the room was cool, the ceiling fan swirling lazily. I swore I heard the sound of women's voices chanting, but the room was empty.

I must have closed my eyes, because then Dashay was in the room. She wore a white dress and her hair was wrapped in a white scarf. She sat beside me and fed me clear soup with a mother-ofpearl spoon. I ate without tasting, not speaking between mouthfuls.

She smiled and went away. Grace climbed onto the bed, gave herself a bath, and licked my hand.

Sometime later I awoke again. The candles still burned. My mother sat at my bedside, reading. Her face in the candlelight reminded me of a picture that hung in the Mc-Garritts' living room titled *Our Lady of Sorrows*: a woman in profile, face serene yet dolorous, wearing a blue robe and hood. I slept again, and next time I wakened, sun dappled the periwinkle walls. In this manner I reentered the land of the living. Afterward they told me that I'd been "comatose" for nearly a week.

During that time, my mother and Dashay had been busy. Gradually, as I grew stronger, they told me what they'd been doing.

The vampire network, I learned, functions something like an underground railroad. When a vampire is in trouble, others offer transportation, food, and shelter. My mother's contacts also smuggle abused animals away from harm, and they barter goods and services. But most of all, they trade information.

Mãe's friends in Saratoga Springs told her that my father's

obituary had run in the local paper; they emailed her a copy. He'd died of heart failure. His body had been cremated, and the ashes buried in Green Ridge Cemetery. Her friends emailed a photograph of the grave. They took another of our house, a "for sale" sign prominent on the front lawn. Someone had chopped down the wisteria vine that traced one side of the house, making it look exposed, naked.

My mother didn't show me the photos all at once, to keep me from reacting too emotionally. But it was hard to keep my feelings in check, especially the first time I looked at the pictures. The image of the abandoned house shocked me as much as the one of the black marble gravestone. RAPHAEL MONTERO had been inscribed on it, along with a quotation: GAUDEAMUS IGITUR / IUVENES DUM SUMUS. There were no dates.

"What's the inscription mean?" Dashay asked.

"So let us rejoice / While we are young," Mãe said.

I hadn't known she read Latin. She turned to me. "He sometimes used that phrase as a toast."

The photograph had been taken close up, and visible in the foreground stood some sort of bottle.

"What's that?" I asked Mãe.

"Looks like the top of a liquor bottle," she said.

"Funny thing to put on a grave," Dashay said. "Maybe vandals left it."

I was lying in bed, propped up on pillows. Harris sat at the bed's other end, coloring in a coloring book. My mother had delayed the monkeys' transfer to the primate sanctuary, in hope of humoring me. That week, if I'd said I wanted an elephant, I believe she would have brought one in.

"Mãe," I said. "Could you email your friends and ask them to take some more photos? And ask them who signed his death certificate?"

My mother thought me stubborn, even delusional, but I sent a thought back to her, loud and clear: *I don't believe he is dead.*

You don't want to believe it, she thought.

If he were dead, I would have sensed it. I folded my arms.

That's a bit of a cliché, she thought. Then she blocked her thoughts and said, "Sorry."

"He was with me nearly every day for thirteen years," I said. "*You* weren't around."

She flinched. Then she turned and left the room.

While she was gone, Dashay told me her theory of my father's death: Malcolm had killed him. My mother had told her about him, and she considered him Evil Incarnate.

"The obit says heart failure," she said. "That could mean anything. I never heard of one of us having a heart failure, unless it was you know what." She made a fist with her left hand, thumb on top, and simulated a hammer with her right.

"Do people really use stakes in the heart?" My father hadn't been entirely clear on that point.

"It's been known to happen." Dashay didn't sound sure she should discuss this topic. "Sometimes, you know, people don't know any better. Ignorant folks get the idea in their heads that somebody's a vampire, and then they decide to get rid of the somebody." She frowned. "I don't like people

— SUSAN HUBBARD —

much. If I hadn't been one once myself, I wouldn't have any use for them at all."

She turned away from me, toward Harris. "Hey, that's pretty good," she told him.

Harris was coloring a seahorse purple, mostly inside the lines. The coloring book featured an array of sea creatures; he'd already finished the octopus and the starfish. I moved to look over his shoulder, inhaled his peppermint breath (he brushed his teeth twice a day). I didn't want him to leave, ever.

"Where's Joey?" I asked.

"Napping on the porch. As usual." Dashay didn't think much of Joey. "So, Ariella, you look more like yourself today. You must be feeling a lot better."

"I guess." I stared down at the photos again. "What do you suppose happened to our books and furniture and our other stuff?"

"Good question." She stood up, stretched her arms. "Don't know, but I'll ask."

It took a few days to get answers, during which time I grew bored with being ill. I began to walk around the house, then the yard. On the southern side of the house, my mother had planted deep blue hydrangeas and plumbago; they'd been green hedges and shrubs last I looked, but during my week away from the world they'd burst into bloom. I recognized them from photos in the book my mother had given me. The air smelled hypnotically sweet from night-blooming jasmine and the blossoms of orange and lemon trees. It was hard to stay depressed in Florida, I thought.

288

But later I ventured down a path I hadn't explored before, and I found a different sort of garden. Roses climbed a trellis edged by hollyhocks and snapdragons. Water trickled down the sides of a fountain shaped like an obelisk. Tall grasses bordered the patch. Everything in the garden was black—the flowers, the grasses, the fountain, the vines that climbed the fountain, even the fountain's water.

"Welcome to my garden of gloom." Dashay had come up behind me.

We sat on a black iron bench and listened to the fountain. I was reminded of a story I'd read by Hawthorne: "Rappaccini's Daughter," most of it set in a macabre garden of jewel-like, poisonous plants.

Yet I found this garden's darkness curiously comforting. "Why did you plant it?" I asked.

"I'd read about gothic gardens. Two or three hundred years ago, if you lost someone you loved, you planted a funeral garden, and when you sat in it, you did your mourning. You have to let yourself mourn, Ariella."

"Did someone you loved die?"

"I lost my parents and my first love, all in the same bad year." Her eyes were like amber, translucent yet clouded. "That happened back in Jamaica, a long time ago."

She looked from the fountain to me. "But you don't want to hear that story now. Afterward I saved my money and bought myself a one-way ticket to Miami. You don't ever want to go to that place. Gangs of *mean* vampires roam around Miami, biting people right and left, competing to grow their fang-gangs. And they're into that blood-doping thing—they steal blood from hospitals and blood banks and inject themselves. Vicious! I wasn't off the plane an hour when I got vamped.

"I didn't like that scene, so I headed north, looking for a place where folks would leave me be. That's how I found 'Sassa and met your mother." She smiled. "Sara's been my best friend ever since that first day we met at Flo's Place. We were both down on our luck, but we were feisty, and we trusted each other. We pooled what we had, and we built Blue Beyond. Hard work brings rewards, honey."

Dashay had survived more heartbreak than I'd encountered. Yet I felt a little jealous of her. I inhaled the spicy scents of the black snapdragons, wondering if I'd ever again have a best friend.

After I found the garden of gloom, I spent less time in bed. I joined Mãe and Dashay, and sometimes Bennett, for meals in the kitchen. I didn't talk much, but at least I was able to eat. Inside, I still felt numb.

One afternoon Dashay and I were having a snack—slices of honeycomb, cheese, and apples—when Mãe came in, papers in her hand. Her friends had sent new pictures of my father's grave. This time we could see the bottle clearly—a bottle of Picardo, half full, next to three long-stemmed red roses.

"Like Poe's grave," Mãe said. "You know, the cognac and the roses."

I didn't understand.

"Every year on January 19—Poe's birthday—someone

leaves a bottle of cognac and red roses on his grave in Balti-more," she said.

"I've heard about that," Dashay said. "Very mysterious."

My mother said, "Not really. Members of the Poe Soci-ety do it. They take turns. Raphael was a member and he did it himself, one year. He made me promise not to tell anyone. I guess keeping the secret doesn't matter, now."

"It's a sign," I said. "It means he's still alive. Father said that Poe was one of us."

They looked at me with pity, and I didn't want to see it. "What else did you find out?" I said. "Did Dennis sign the death certificate?"

"No," she said. "It was signed by Dr. Graham Wilson."

I'd let myself imagine a scenario in which Dennis signed it, helping my father stage his own death. Now my convic-tions began to waver.

"Ariella," she said. "I'm sorry to disappoint you."

"My father wasn't seeing Dr. Wilson." I crossed my arms. "My father never went to any doctor."

Mãe and Dashay exchanged glances. After a few sec-onds, Dashay said, "Find out about Dr. Wilson. It won't hurt to ask."

My mother shook her head, but she went back to her computer. Dashay handed me another slice of honeycomb. "How do you feel about taking the horses out?"

I knew she was trying to distract me, but what of it. I'd brood as we rode.

When we came back from our ride (Dashay on Abiaka, me on Johnny Cypress), we walked the horses around the paddock to cool them, then gave them grain and water.

Mãe sat on the front porch, waiting for us. I studied her face and tried to hear her thoughts, but nothing came through. She had a sheet of paper in her hand, which she gave me.

It was a copy of an email: "Sara, No problem at all. We checked with the real estate agent, and she said the house's contents are in storage. Apparently the will leaves everything to your daughter, and the executor is Dennis McGrath. Don't you know him? He's got an office at the college, if you want me to call him. There was some buzz when Ariella didn't show up for the funeral, but it's died down now. Sullivan handled the arrangements. Let me know if you need anything else. XO, Marian.

"P.S. Didn't you ever meet Graham Wilson? Nice guy. Good doctor. One of us."

I sent my mother a triumphant smile, and she sent me back a thought: *Maybe*.

We didn't agree on what to do next. I wanted to head for Saratoga Springs, talk to Dennis and Dr. Wilson. Mãe said that wasn't wise. Michael had told her about Agent Burton (they'd had quite a talk, she said), and we weren't going to take any chances.

"Then *you* should go," I said.

"Ariella, think for a minute. What purpose would that serve? If you're correct—if Raphael is still alive—he doesn't want the world to know that. After all, if he staged his death, he did it for a reason."

"Why would a vampire do such a thing?" Dashay shook her head.

"Because he wanted people to think he was mortal?" I said, thinking as I spoke. "Because somebody was going to expose him?"

"His motives don't concern us." Mãe sounded more and more authoritative, and part of me resented her taking charge. "If he's alive, he might have contacted us. But he hasn't."

"Why should he?" The email was a crumbled wad of paper in my hand, and I began to smooth it out. "*We* left *him*. We both did. And neither of us ever called and told him where we were."

"He could have found me, any time." Mãe crossed her arms— the same gesture I always made when I felt defensive. She heard me think that, and she set her arms emphatically at her sides. "I've always used my real name. It didn't take you long to track me down."

"Aunt Sophie called him after she saw you that last time. She told him you'd said you didn't want to be found."

"At the time, I didn't. I was honoring my bargain with Malcolm." She crossed her arms again. "What makes you think that Raphael wants to be found?"

"The bottle of Picardo," I said. "And the three roses. And the inscription: 'So let us rejoice / While we are young.' It was a kind of joke we had." I tried to sound persuasive, but I realized I had no proof that he was alive. All I had was a stubborn hunch.

— Fifteen —

My father had more than once expressed deep skepticism about attempts to distinguish creative thinking from analytical reasoning. Wasn't it obvious, he asked, that science and art demanded both? He liked to quote Einstein: *I have no special talents, I am only passionately curious.* His own mind was by nature so logical, yet so curious, that for him, the creative and the analytical were the same.

But I have a different sort of brain, one that proceeds from intuition and imagination as much as from logic. My discoveries often are unexpected, and they depend as much upon leaps as logic or patient plodding.

Once I decided to believe my father was alive, the problem was how to find him—because I'd also decided that whether he liked it or not, he would be found. I couldn't have told you why I was so determined. Perhaps it was pride on my part. I'd come too close to completing the puzzle to accept losing its first piece.

And so I plagued my mother with questions: Where had my father been happiest? Did he ever speak of living elsewhere? What things did he require, beyond the obvious?

She was working in the beehives, pulling out trays and checking them to see if the colonies were healthy. Unlike Mr. Winters, she didn't need a smoker to sedate the bees and keep them from stinging. All she had to do was talk to them. "Hello, my beauties. Did you smell the lemon blossoms this morning?"

In between comments to the bees, she answered my questions. He'd been happiest, in the old days, when he was in the American South. He liked warm weather and the slow drawl of Southern culture. He'd talked a few times about "retiring" in Florida or Georgia, by the ocean. As for things, he didn't demand much. He'd worn the same sorts of clothes and shoes since his Cambridge days; when they wore out, the London tailors and shoemakers made more. He had his books and journals, he developed his own blood supplements, and he had Mary Ellis Root to do his cooking.

"What happened to her?" I asked. "Is she still in Saratoga Springs?"

"Her name wasn't mentioned." Mãe beckoned to me. I stood close behind her and peered over her bent shoulder. "Good morning, Queen Mãeve," she said.

It took me a second to spot her. The queen's lower body was longer, more pointed, than those of the other bees. She moved from cell to cell of the honeycomb, laying tiny eggs the color of rice.

"How does he make the supplements?"

"You probably know as much as I do." She gazed at the queen with affection. "He extracts plasma from the blood of cadavers—"

"I didn't know that."

She looked up at me. "Why so alarmed? It's not as if he kills them. When I lived there, the blood came from Sullivan's funeral parlor. When they embalm a body, the blood is usually discarded, poured down the sinks. Your father paid Sullivan to deliver it to him. Recycling takes many forms."

"So he used human blood."

"And animal blood, too. He got deliveries twice a week, same as we do. You must have seen the Green Cross vans. They're the most reliable delivery service when it comes to transporting blood." She carefully slid the frame back into the hive. "He used the plasma to make the supplements— some in the form of tonics, some as freeze-dried particles. He kept what he needed and sold the rest to a company in Albany. I have some of the freeze-dried stuff in the kitchen; they market it as Sangfroid."

I'd seen the red and black canister in the kitchen. "Where do you buy Sangfroid?"

"Green Cross delivers it." My mother was staring intently into the next hive. "Come and look, Ariella. Have you ever seen a more beautiful bunch of bees?"

Hundreds of bees clustered on the glistening gold honeycomb, making tiny movements unintelligible to me. "So clever," she cooed to them.

"They're lovely," I said, feeling unexpectedly jealous. "When does the delivery van come next?"

* * *

My mother gave me a present: my own mobile phone. She said she had mixed feelings about the technology, but that since they used the home phone for business, I should have my own number.

At her suggestion, my first call went to Michael, to let him know I was all right. Obsessed with finding my father, I wanted to ask him about Dennis and Mary Ellis Root, but he'd never met them, and he had no reason to know if they were in town. I didn't have much else to say.

"I miss you," Michael said, his voice equivocal.

"I miss you, too." In a way I was telling the truth: I missed the boy he'd been before Kathleen's death. "Maybe you can come and visit us sometime."

"Maybe." But the way he spoke made it seem a remote prospect. "Ari, I need to ask you something. Kathleen said some things about you. She told me that I should be careful around you, that you weren't—" He stopped talking.

"She told you that I'm not normal?" I said. "Well, that's true."

"She said—stupid stuff. She was into that weird role-playing and witchcraft, and who knows what else. But she acted sometimes as if it were real. She said you were a vampire."

In my mind, the word glowed like embers.

"And I know that's ridiculous, but I still have to ask if you know anything about how she died. Do you know anything?"

"All I know is what I read, and what you told me," I said.

"I had nothing to do with her death, Michael. I wish I'd been there that night—sometimes I think I might have been able to save her. But I got sick, and you drove me home, and the next thing I knew, your father called mine to see if she was with me."

"That's what I thought," he said. "I'm sorry I brought it up."

"No apologies needed."

I asked him if there were any leads in the case. He said that the police were questioning stable hands.

Once I'd sorted through what I knew about my father, and what my mother had told me, some facts emerged as possible means of tracking him down. I wrote them in my journal.

First, every January my father went to Baltimore. Going to Baltimore next January might be of use. But January was months away, and I wasn't inclined to be patient.

Second, my father was devoted to his research. To conduct the business of Seradrone, and to stay alive, he needed a steady supply of blood. That meant inquiries should be made to the Green Cross service, and perhaps to funeral parlors. But where?

Third, he relied upon his helpers: Dennis McGrath and Mary Ellis Root. Find them, and a trail might lead to my father.

Fourth, contact his tailor.

Those were the immediately obvious avenues to finding him. Of course, he might have done something unexpected—run away to India, or begun a new life as a teacher or writer. But I didn't think so. As my mother had said, most vampires are creatures of habit.

That night after dinner, Mãe, Dashay, Harris, and I sat outside in the moon garden that lay on the house's northern side. (Joey had been sent to bed by Dashay; the moon excited him, and he made too much noise.) Mãe had planted an array of white flowers—angel's trumpets, moonflowers, flowering tobacco, and gardenias—in a circular plot, and we sat on two facing benches made of weathered teak, watching the flowers seem to glow as the sky darkened. A half moon hung low in the June sky, and the heavy perfume of the tobacco plants made me sleepy. Around us, mosquitoes droned, but never even brushed our skin. Their noise reminded me of high-pitched string instruments. I know it's not a pleasant sound for humans, who fear their bite.

I told the others about my plan to find my father. The Recovery Plan, I called it. They listened without commenting.

"I plan to begin making calls tomorrow," I said. "I feel well enough, and my head is clear again."

"That's good," Dashay said. Next to me, Harris made a sound of agreement.

Mãe said, "And what if you do find him, Ariella? What then?"

I didn't have an answer. Her face was half in shadow, and Dashay sat beyond her, nearly invisible. I tried to imagine my father sitting on the bench next to my mother, taking in the night air, admiring the lanternlike glow of the flowers, and I failed. I couldn't picture him with us.

The child in me wondered, *What if he doesn't like monkeys?*

Nobody spoke. Then the quiet was shattered by a sound: "Whawha-wha!"

I was the only one who jumped. Harris actually reached over and patted my hand.

The noise repeated, and this time it was answered by another sound: "Who-*whoo*."

The exchanges went on for nearly a minute. I couldn't tell where they were coming from. Then, they faded away, until all we heard was the drone of mosquitoes again.

"Owls?" I whispered, and the others nodded.

"Barred owls," Dashay said.

Suddenly I thought of my father's lullaby. Across from me, my mother's eyes flashed in the moonlight. She began to sing, to the melody he'd sung to me: *"Jacaré tutu / Jacaré mandu / tutu vai embora / Não leva méia filhinha / Murucututu."* Her voice was dark silver—as haunting as his, but sharper, sadder—and it shimmered in the moonlight. When she stopped, there was silence. Even the mosquitoes were quiet, for a moment.

Then I heard my voice. "What do the words mean?"

She said, "A parent is asking for her child's protection. She asks the alligator and the other beasts of the night to go away, to leave the child alone. Murucututu is the owl, the mother of sleep."

"How do you know it?"

"Your father," she said. "He sang it to you, before you were born."

* * *

Next morning I decided to press on, regardless of the consequences.

I began with Seradrone and Green Cross. Both had websites—dull, jargon-ridden websites, but at least they provided contact numbers.

Seradrone had a Saratoga Springs area code. But when I called, I reached the familiar recording: the number was no longer in service. Next I dialed Green Cross. I expect a terrorist calling the Pentagon might have got more answers.

I said, "I heard that Seradrone went out of business, and I wondered whether we'll still be able to get Sangfroid."

"Where did you hear that?" The voice on the other end was clipped, precise as a computer's speech simulator. I couldn't even tell the sex of the speaker.

"My mother told me," I said, keeping my voice young and innocent.

"What's her name?"

"Her name's Sara Stephenson." *Should I have said that?* I wondered.

"You may tell your mother that deliveries will continue as scheduled," the voice said, and the connection went dead.

Thanks so much, I thought. I went into the kitchen. Mãe was kneading bread dough at the table. The dough was a deep red color.

"Why are the Green Cross people so rude?" I asked her.

"Well, for starters, they're not *people*." She looked up at me, her hands still working the dough. "Want to have a try?"

301

"Not today." I didn't have much interest in cooking, anyway. In that, I guess, I took after my father. "Mãe, who makes Sangfroid? Didn't you say it comes from Albany?"

"Check the can."

I pulled down the black and red tin container from the pantry shelf. Its back panel read: "Made in USA. © LER Co., Albany, NY."

Back in Mãe's study, I used her computer to find a phone number for LER Co. An operator connected me to an extension for "consumer relations," whose voice mail took my request for a return call.

I went back to the kitchen. "Mãe, how do I dial London? I want to call my father's tailor."

She was washing her hands in the sink. The bread must be in the oven.

"Gieves & Hawkes," she said. "Number One Savile Row. I saw that label often enough." She reached for a towel, then turned to me. "Ariella, you're not going to call them?"

"Why not?"

"They won't tell you anything." She rubbed her hands dry. "British tailors are as secretive as the CIA. Probably more so."

"They can't be worse than Green Cross." I thought of telling her that I'd used her name, then thought I'd better not.

But she shook her head as if she already knew. "Green Cross won't give out information, even to other vampires," she said. "Medical couriers have to maintain confidentiality."

I was running out of ideas. "Maybe I'll call Dennis." But

I didn't look forward to talking with him—the man who'd helped Malcolm steal my mother.

My mother opened the oven door and looked in at her dark red loaves. "Can you smell the honey?"

"It smells pink," I said.

"To me it's the color of the poppies in the back garden." She closed the oven door.

Another call, another voice mail message. Dennis would be out of the office until August 15. I didn't leave a response, and I hung up feeling more relieved than disappointed.

But the Recovery Plan options were running out.

A few days later the Green Cross delivery van showed up. I met the driver with a smile and several questions. He said he didn't know anything about making Sangfroid, and he hinted strongly that if he did, he wouldn't tell a stranger.

I turned away. My mother came from the stables carrying two large baskets of Mayapple leaves and roots, which we'd harvested the previous day in the forest. Mayapple's other name is American Mandrake. American Indians used it as a medicine, and now it's being tested as a possible treatment for cancer. My mother traded it with Green Cross in exchange for blood supplements.

"We'll need two boxes of the Sangfroid," she said. "I trust the quality will be as high as the last batch."

The deliveryman loaded the baskets into the back of the van, then handed her two cartons marked LER CO. "No worries," he said. "Nothing's changed."

* * *

"I wonder where I'll live when I grow up," I said. "I mean, when I'm older."

My mother and I sat in the living room. A faint strain of music came from outside. Dashay and Bennett were out on the grass with a transistor radio, dancing.

Mãe looked stern. "You won't be older. You realize that, don't you?" Her voice sounded frustrated. "Didn't your father teach you anything?"

Of course he had. But I'd never thought through the implications: once you're an *other*, your biological clock is stopped. You don't age. You don't grow. Only your mind can grow.

"How old do I look?" I asked.

"Some days you look twenty." Her voice was dry. "Tonight you look twelve."

Somewhat insulted, I stood up and went to the window. Bennett and Dashay were in each other's arms, waltzing so gracefully that I shivered. I wondered if I'd ever be able to dance like that.

Why is it that the obvious answer to a problem often is the last one we consider?

Within one's field of consciousness, certain elements are the focus of attention, and certain others lie at the periphery. My attention tends to focus on what strikes me as unusual or problematic. Is it that way for you? Right now, I'm focusing on how to describe consciousness, and I'm paying little attention to the cat sitting at my feet, or the scent of the humid air around me.

You might say I'm unconscious of those familiar things. But they're part of my peripheral consciousness; the proof is, I can shift my focus to stroke the cat or mop my brow. Those things lie within my consciousness, even if I don't choose to pay attention to them.

Why didn't I notice the copies of *The Poe Journal* on my mother's coffee table? They were a familiar sight. My father had kept a similar stack on the table next to his chair in our living room. I suppose that if you'd asked me, when I was growing up, whether the average American family subscribed to *The Poe Journal* or *TV Guide*, I'd have guessed that they preferred Poe.

Having been out in the world, I now knew better.

I dialed the number on *The Poe Journal*'s masthead.

"My father is ill," I told the man who answered. And this voice decisively belonged to a male human. "He says he hasn't been getting his copy of the journal," I said. "I told him I'd call you."

"Let me see if I may help." The man's concern sounded genuine.

I gave him my father's name and address in Saratoga Springs.

In a few moments he came back on the line. "Ms. Montero?" he said.

"Ariella Montero," I said.

"Yes," he said. "Well, it appears that your father's subscription has been transferred. This is most awkward. Someone called back in February and asked for the subscription to be transferred."

"Oh," I said, thinking fast. "To my uncle?"

"That would be Mr. Pym?"

"What was the address?"

"6705 Midnight Pass Road," he said. "Is that correct?"

"Of course," I said. "He must have forgotten he'd made the change. So sorry to trouble you."

"I do hope that your father's health improves," the man said. "If he decides he'd like to receive the journal again, please let us know."

I thanked him and said goodbye. I never did find out the name of the man at *The Poe Journal*, but he gave me reassurance that good manners weren't entirely obsolete. I'm sorry that I had to lie to him.

— Sixteen —

O ne of the small ironies of my education took place the day my father lectured on John Dewey and the Pragmatists. Dewey, my father said, believed that learning came from action and inquiry. Knowledge grew from experience and events. Only years later did I see that all of my early learning had been passive, thanks to a life designed to be orderly, predictable, dull. Since I'd left Saratoga Springs, my learning had certainly been more active.

It took Mãe's computer approximately one minute to locate Midnight Pass in Siesta Key, part of Sarasota, Florida, and another minute for the online directory to inform me that there was no telephone listing on that street for any Pym. But the number might be unlisted, I thought, or listed in someone else's name.

Sarasota! My father was a creature of habit indeed—if Pym were in fact my father. One way or another, I was going to meet him and find out.

All I needed to figure out now was the best way to travel, and whether or not to tell Mãe I was going.

I'd come to appreciate the use of maps. Sarasota wasn't far, only about a hundred miles south of Homosassa. I could make it in a few hours.

Why, then, was I lying on the living room floor eating peanuts with my favorite monkey? I blamed the heat for my inertia. Walking outside felt like wading through a bowl of soup. The air smelled of overripe fruit ready to rot. It was too hot for any action, I told myself.

But I knew the true reason for my hesitation: the question my mother had asked. *What if you do find him, Ariella?*

And I remembered something he'd said, only months ago: *Life is all about people leaving.*

That night, as Mãe and I were washing dishes, I said, "I think I know where my father is."

Mãe let a plate slip from her hands into the sudsy water. She picked it up again, and began to wash it.

"I think he's in Sarasota." I rinsed the last glass and set it in the drying rack.

My mother said, "He always liked it there." Her voice was flat, emotionless. I couldn't make out her thoughts, only a buzz of confusion.

"Of course I'm not sure yet that the name I tracked down is him." I took the plate she handed me and rinsed it.

She was washing another plate. "Why don't you call him?" she said.

I explained my unsuccessful hunt to find any telephone

number for Mr. Pym.

"Pym," she said. She removed the sink stopper, and we watched the water spiral down the drain. "So what do you propose to do now, Ariella?"

I'd hoped that she'd tell me what to do. "I think I might go to Sarasota," I said. I hung up the linen dish towel. "I think I need to know if he's still alive, Mãe."

"In that case," she said, "I think I'd better go with you."

Sarasota is a strange mix of rich and poor, natural beauty and ostentation—a hard place to know, because every mile changes your impressions of it. On its outskirts we drove past the same strip malls and signs for gated communities that characterize nearly every Florida town. But the inner city comprised older, smaller buildings that seemed to come from another era.

As we stopped at a traffic light downtown, I saw two women, probably mother and daughter, wearing brightly pat-terned sundresses and dark glasses, reading a menu posted in a restaurant window. I envied them having nothing more pressing to decide than where to have lunch and where to go shopping.

Mãe said, "We could use some new clothes."

She swerved the truck out of traffic and angled it into a parking space. "Come on, Ariella. You don't want to meet your father looking crunchy."

I said, "Then you *do* think he's here."

"Who knows?" she said. "Anyway, it's good to be in Sara-sota again."

My mother proved to be a power shopper—in seconds she surveyed what was available and made her decisions, not bothering to try things on. I was slow. Except for thrifting with Jane, I hadn't done any shopping since roaming the Saratoga Springs mall with Kathleen.

The shops here were smaller, more specialized, expensive. It was fun to feel like a girl again.

I modeled dresses, and my mother nodded or shook her head. I liked a shirt patterned with hibiscus flowers, but she said, "Come on. You know how he is about patterns. That would freak him out." This might have gone on for hours, but we both grew hungry.

We decided to wear two of our purchases—a square-necked blue silk sheath for her, a smoke-colored halter dress for me—and we put the others in the truck, fed the parking meter, and headed for a café that advertised seafood.

My mother ordered Picardo on the rocks, and she tipped half of it into my glass of cola.

(Anyone concerned about vampires' relatively high rates of alcohol consumption may wish to read Dr. Graham Wilson's monograph "Metabolic Aspects of Alcohol in Clinical Nutrition Trials." Apparently, we have extraordinary livers.)

We ordered fish—blackened grouper for her and mahi-mahi for me. When the food came, she produced a small bottle from her handbag and shook it liberally over our food. It looked like red pepper flakes, but it tasted like Sangfroid.

"Freeze-dried," she said. "I carry condiments wherever I go."

* * *

On the drive to Midnight Pass, my mother pointed out landmarks familiar to her. "Over to the west are the Selby Botanical Gardens. That's where we were married."

"I know," I said. "I've got the pictures."

Mãe said, "I haven't seen those pictures in years."

I wondered what it would feel like to lose all one's possessions, even one's wedding album. *Should I give her the album? Or would it make her sad?*

We drove over a causeway. Sailboats dotted the bay, and I tried to picture my father living alongside a sandy white beach. My hopes began to fade as we drove down Midnight Pass Road, past row after row of high-rise buildings.

"This doesn't look like his scene," I said.

"His *scene*?" She was grinning. "What exactly would your father's scene look like?"

"More like the house in Saratoga Springs," I said. "Old and gray and gloomy."

"You won't find gloom here." My mother turned the car into a driveway. "And not much that's old. You said the number was 6705, right?"

The building loomed before us, thirteen stories made of pale pink stucco. Its name, engraved in a stone slab set into a circular patch of fountain grass, was Xanadu.

Mãe and I looked at each other. We both knew the Coleridge poem, and we mentally traded verses: *"In Xanadu did Kubla Khan / A stately pleasure-dome decree: / Where Alph, the sacred river, ran / Through caverns measureless to man / Down to a sunless sea."*

I didn't feel optimistic. The last place in the world I

would have expected to find my father was in a Florida condominium named Xanadu. The lush verses, supposedly written when Coleridge was in the throes of an opium-induced
dream, weren't to my father's taste.

But my mother was grinning. "Remember the line about
the 'woman wailing for her demon lover'?" she said. "Ariella, if he does live here, imagine how embarrassed he must
feel."

After we parked the truck, Mãe and I realized we had
no idea where my father might be. All we had was the street
number. We stared up at the anonymous doors and balconies above us. I hadn't anticipated this problem—I'd imagined him living in a house.

For a while we took turns in the mostly vacant parking
lot, asking strangers if they could help us find our friend Mr.
Pym. Strangers were few and far between. The third person
I asked looked at me with so much suspicion that I went
back to the truck.

"Where is everyone?" I asked Mãe.

"The snowbirds have flown north," she said. "It's a Florida phenomenon. Come May, many condos are deserted."

She was stretched back in the seat, listening to the radio.
Johnny Cash was singing a song called "Hurt," a cover of a
Nine Inch Nails song. By now I knew most of his music.
No matter what buttons you pressed on the jukebox at Flo's
Place, you got music by Cash or Nine Inch Nails.

"The Recovery Plan needs a new strategy," I told her.

"Hmm?" She sat up. Then she motioned for me to hand
her my mobile phone.

She punched some buttons, asked for the home office of Green Cross. Then she punched some more, and finally she must have reached a voice. "Where's our delivery?" she said, her voice alarmingly similar to Mary Ellis Root's. "I'm calling for Mr. Pym on Midnight Pass, Siesta Key, Florida." She winked at me.

"You did?" she said. "Where did you leave it?"

A few seconds later, she said, "Well, it's not here. Yes, you'd better do that. We'll be expecting you."

She ended the call and handed me the phone. "It's number 1235," she said. "And tomorrow, Mr. Pym or whoever lives there will be getting another delivery of who knows what."

While we waited for the elevator, my mother shifted her weight from foot to foot. She pushed her hair back from her forehead and made a funny noise (half cough, half imitation of the sound made by a surprised cat) in her throat. She hadn't been nervous around me before. She made me nervous. I lifted my hair from my neck and moved from side to side.

The elevator arrived empty. It had glass walls, and as it rose, the city of Sarasota emerged and shrank across the bay.

"We can go back down," I said. "We don't even have to leave the elevator."

"Yes, we do." She sounded as curt as when she'd done her Mary Ellis Root imitation.

The elevator doors opened, and we walked down an open

313

corridor—doors on the left, iron guardrails on the right. The wall had no windows. I could make out the roof of our truck far below, parked in a visitor's space.

The door of unit 1235 was painted white and had a peephole, like all the others.

My mother rang the bell. We waited. She rang it again.

Either no one was home, or the occupants of 1235 didn't want company.

"Now what?" Mãe said. I didn't have the gumption to bang on the door.

We retreated to the elevator. I felt deflated, but not surprised. How likely was it that we'd find him, based on hunches and lies?

As we rode down, we didn't look at each other. I watched the ground rising to meet us—and that's when I saw her: a short, obese woman, dressed in black. She walked slowly across the parking lot, carrying a paper bag in both hands. No one else on earth waddled as she did. The sun made her greasy hair glisten.

My mother saw her, too. She said, "When did I ever think I'd be glad to see Mary Ellis again." She didn't sound as surprised as I might have expected. "I must have conjured her when I imitated her voice."

"What will we do?" I asked.

Mãe pushed the button for the fourth floor. The elevator had just slid past the sixth. When the car stopped at four, I followed her out. We stood for a moment, facing a tattered notice for ballroom dancing classes taped to the elevator doors. Digital numbers above the doors marked the elevator's descent. It hit one, paused, and began to rise again.

She said, "This should be interesting."

What will Root do when she sees us? I wondered. I'd spent my childhood being taught the importance of compassion. But for her I felt nothing but contempt, and I knew it was mutual.

My jaw tightened, my back tensed. "Is she one of us?" I asked my mother.

"Who knows what she is." Mãe's lips pressed together tightly.

Then the elevator stopped at our floor. The doors slid open, and we stepped inside.

Mãe moved behind me to block any exit. She said, "Imagine meeting you here."

Root clutched her paper bag. She didn't look any older, only greasier. Did she ever wash that dress? But something about her had changed, I noticed at once: she'd trimmed back the three hairs that grew on her chin. They were less than an inch long now, mere bristles compared to their former state.

Neither my mother nor I knew what to say, so we said childish things, obvious things.

"Surprise!" I said.

"Look what the cat dragged in." Mãe folded her arms.

I ended with, "Small world, isn't it?"

Root's eyes moved from my mother's face to mine. Her pupils seemed dark and deep as wells. "Yes," she said, speaking directly to me. "It's a small, small world. We expected you yesterday."

* * *

When Root unlocked the door of 1235, a familiar metallic odor floated out to greet us. The smell of the night kitchen in Saratoga Springs, I thought. Whatever stuff she'd brewed in the basement there was being made here.

The condominium itself was modern and minimalist— white carpets and walls, black leather and chrome furniture. We passed the kitchen—and yes, a saucepot was simmering on an electric range— and went down a corridor lined with closed doors. It ended in a large room with an entire wall made of glass; outside it a balcony overlooked the bay. Facing the glass, three men sat on a sectional sofa.

The first to take notice of us was Dennis; as he turned toward us, the other two also turned. My father's eyes blazed at me, but turned surprised and soft when he looked at Mãe. If I'd been expected, she clearly hadn't been. I took a deep breath, watching him watch her.

The third man was someone I didn't know. He was tall and blond, wearing a rust-colored linen suit, and he smiled as if he enjoyed being himself. Next to me, my mother suddenly seemed taller, more rigid.

The stranger stood up. "We've met, but we were never formally introduced," he said to me. He walked over and stretched out his hand. "I'm Malcolm."

His smile and voice seemed artificial, designed to create a charismatic effect. I knew I'd seen him before, and a second later I remembered where—he was the man who'd sat at the Marshall House bar in Savannah, drinking Picardo.

I didn't take his hand.

He shrugged and withdrew it. He nodded at my mother, then turned to Root, taking the paper bag from her. I glimpsed the tops of two bottles of Picardo inside. He said, "If you'll get the ice, I'll mix the drinks."

Sometimes the ability to hear thoughts confuses, rather than clarifies. So many thoughts flew across that room, all of them charged with emotion. I looked at my father and thought, *I knew you weren't dead.*

None of us bothered to block our thinking—except Malcolm, and Dennis, who didn't know how. Malcolm sat down again, drink in hand, with an air of satisfaction that I found intolerable. I suspected he'd engineered this meeting, brought us all together for a reason only he knew.

My father's feelings were the most muted, yet the strongest. He looked exactly the same—dark hair falling back from his forehead, profile as severe and elegant as a Roman emperor's on an ancient coin. Any relief he felt at seeing me—and I did sense some—was buried beneath disappointment. The sight of me seemed to pain him.

About my mother, his feelings were raw, confused, as were hers about him. The only thoughts I could pick up were bursts of static, flying between them like sparks.

And Dennis? He was easiest to read of all. He felt guilty. He hadn't said hello, but he looked at Mãe and me with shame in his eyes. He sat at the end of the sofa, a bottle of beer in his hand, ill at ease.

Root handed me a glass of Picardo on ice. As I took it,

I saw something in her eyes that made no sense: respect. Root *respected* me?

The room, ice-cold from air-conditioning, suddenly felt suffocating. I backed away from Root and went outside, onto the balcony. The sun felt more intense, and the air more tropical, than in Homosassa. Far below, the water sparkled, and the sailboats skimmed along like toys. I took a deep breath.

"Did you know I saved your life once?" Malcolm's voice had a faintly nasal quality to it.

I didn't turn around.

"You were pretty young then. Much too young to be alone outside after dark. But the others were wrapped up in some experiment—one of Dennis's efforts, I'd bet, because it ended with an explosion. Wood and glass were flying, and there you were, watching. You could barely walk. I carried you to safety and brought you back when they'd put out the fire. Do you remember?"

I remembered the explosion, and the wool coat of the man who carried me away. And for the first time, I remembered why I'd wandered outside that night. From my window I'd seen fireflies in the garden, and I wanted to touch one.

"So that was you," I said.

He came closer, and I turned to look at him. I suppose he was handsome, with his smooth skin, wide eyes, and high forehead. But his smile seemed mocking, and in his eyes was clinical calculation. I moved away, next to the railing.

"I didn't expect you to thank me," he said. "Oh, it might

have been a nice gesture. But it's not important. Besides, you have too much to thank me for. I've made your family what it is."

"Leave her alone." My mother stood in the doorway.

He turned to her, looked her up and down. "A lovely dress, Sara," he said. "Have you missed me?"

"Leave us alone." She took a step toward us.

Then my father appeared. I'd thought his suit was black, but now I saw its silver pinstripe. "You're making so much *noise*," he said, although their voices in fact were low. "Malcolm, it's time for you to go."

"But we still have business—"

"Business will wait." Although his voice was pitched low, it resonated.

Malcolm looked at me. "We'll talk again."

My father took one step toward us. Malcolm left without saying more.

My father sat on the suede sofa, bent forward, elbows on knees, head in his hands. My mother and I sat at the other end, watching him.

Dennis and Root had left us to ourselves. Somewhere, the sun must be setting; our window faced east, but the light outside began to deepen, and a few crimson clouds scudded across the sky.

Nothing in the room was familiar. The place must have been rented already furnished. The walls were bare, but here and there I saw picture hooks.

When he finally sat up, my father's eyes were dark, and

I couldn't read his mood. "Well," he said. "It's all rather complicated, isn't it. Where to begin?"

I opened my mouth to say, *With your* death?

But Mãe spoke first. "Did Malcolm tell you about taking me away?"

His mouth twisted. He stared at her, hearing her thoughts.

I heard them, too. She told him about the night I was born, about Dennis helping her into Malcolm's car, about the house in the Catskills and all that followed.

He listened. When she stopped, he looked as if he wanted to put his head in his hands again. "It's worse than I'd thought." The words sounded even starker because his voice had no feeling in it.

"But it's better to know, isn't it?" Mãe leaned forward. The ceiling lights made her long hair glisten.

I haven't mentioned how exciting it was to see them in the same room, even if they weren't—how do I phrase this? They weren't *together*. Of course I'd entertained a soppy fantasy of them embracing, all the years of estrangement falling away. I hadn't believed it would actually happen, but I'd indulged myself in that fantasy many times.

Even if I couldn't read his eyes, I sensed that my father's feelings ran deep.

He looked from my mother to me. "I suppose," he said, "that we'd better go to dinner."

— Seventeen —

We sat outside at a restaurant called Ophelia's, down the road from Xanadu. We ate oysters and red snapper and drank red wine by candlelight. Sarasota Bay lapped a few feet away. We must have made a pretty picture, I thought: a well-dressed, good-looking American family.

Our server said as much. "Special occasion?" he'd asked, when my father ordered the wine. "What a lovely family."

If he'd known what we were thinking—or what we *were*—he would have dropped his tray. I felt happy that he didn't know, that someone thought we were ordinary.

My father let us know that he wasn't shocked by what he thought of as "the betrayal of my best friends," and he thought the word *friends* with dark irony. (When I hear thoughts, sarcasm and irony sound deep red or purple, depending on the degree. Is it the same for you?)

"I might have deduced it, from the way Dennis behaved,"

321

he said. "I suppose that I chose not to figure it out. It was more convenient for me not to know."

My mother twisted a napkin between her hands. She wanted him to forgive her for leaving, for becoming *other*. Even if her thoughts hadn't been loud, her feelings were plain on her face. The couple at the next table gave her a curious look as they left.

But my father instead turned to me. *What about these murders?* he thought.

Without saying a word, we discussed the death of Robert Reedy. *I killed him*, I thought. *But I didn't cut him up. And the other murders—I had nothing to do with them.*

The server asked if we wanted anything else. My father looked at Mãe and me. "Bring more oysters," he said. "And another bottle of mineral water."

By this time we were the only party left on the veranda. "It's safe for us to talk now," Mãe said. "I like to hear your voices."

"I've never seen you eat before," I said to my father, feeling shy. "You're not a vegetarian."

"No."

"Then why did you raise me as one?"

"I wanted to give you as much chance as possible to grow into a *normal human*." He spoke the words as if part of him were listening and disapproving of his phrasing. "I feared that meat might over-stimulate your appetite."

The candles flickered in the breeze from the bay. A crescent moon hung low in the sky. "A fine setting for a talk about blood and murder," my father said.

"How did you know about the murder?" I knew he wasn't likely to have read the newspapers.

"My *friend* Malcolm told me all about the deaths." My father ate an oyster with astonishing elegance. By contrast, Mãe and I slurped ours down.

"How did he know?" I didn't picture Malcolm as a newspaper reader, either.

"He knew because he was there." My father lifted another shell to his lips and deftly ingested its contents without pursing his lips. "He's been following you for years, Ari. You sensed his presence, remember?"

Mãe said, "Wait a minute. You knew he was stalking her, and you let it happen?"

"Hardly." He refilled our wine glasses. "Malcolm told me about it when he turned up last week to talk business."

"You're doing business with *him*?" Mãe shook her head.

"Wait, let's get back to the stalking," I said.

"Thank you, Ari. Yes, let's try to sort through this *mess* with a semblance of coherence."

I didn't like the tension between them. "When I sensed an *other* in the Sarasota house, that was Malcolm?"

"Most likely. But not necessarily. Vampires often look in on each other, you know. I don't happen to be that sort—"

My mother made a funny sound, as if she were suppressing laughter.

And then my father did something so unlike him, so unprecedented, that I nearly fell off my chair. He winked.

So this is how they were, I thought. He exaggerated his mannerisms to amuse my mother. She pretended to be irritated. They were almost *cute*—a word I'd never used even once before. It made me uncomfortable.

"Malcolm told me about the murders," my father said. His voice was deep and calm. "He said he saw you commit them, while he was invisible. He even commented on the delicate way you carved the bodies; he said he was reminded of *ikezukuri*, a technique used by Japanese sushi chefs he'd watched in Japan. A whole fish is carved live, reassembled on a plate, and consumed while its heart is still beating."

"But I didn't—"

"She couldn't—"

"Do you think I believed him?" He sipped his wine. "My daughter capable of such barbarism?"

My mother was shaking her head again. "I'm confused."

"Think it through, Sara." Their eyes met and held steady. "Malcolm has created a narrative in which he's the hero. For years he's been voluntarily acting as Ari's guardian angel, if you will, concerned only for her welfare. Now he comes to me with a proposal: he wants us to collaborate on developing a new oxygen delivery system. And by the way, he mentions that my daughter happens to be a serial killer, but that he certainly won't tell anyone else. It's a kind of blackmail, and he's awfully good at it."

"So you're playing along with him?"

"I'm not sure I'd phrase it that way. Yes, I'm going along with his scheme, for now. I want to know where it leads."

I pushed back my chair. "Father, who did kill those people? Do you think it was Malcolm?"

"I think it might well be Malcolm." He looked at the white tablecloth, smoothed out a wrinkle near his plate. "He's capable of killing without qualms. He has nothing but contempt for humans."

"Then he killed Kathleen." I said it softly, but inside I felt knives tearing at me. Mãe put her arms around me, and I leaned against her.

My father sat back and watched us. We didn't need to talk further.

Back at Xanadu (I enjoy using the name whenever possible), my father showed me the room where I'd be spending the night. He said my mother would be across the hall.

"We're going to talk a bit more," he said.

My parents went into the room that served as my father's study, and I walked out onto the balcony. Stars glittered in the night sky; I could see Polaris and Ursa Minor. Somewhere out there, I knew, were dark nebulae, dust clouds that absorb light and block our view of objects that lie beyond. I thought of asking for a telescope as a birthday gift.

A sound behind me made me whirl around. It wasn't Malcolm, as I'd expected. Dennis stood there, his eyes bleary, holding a bottle of beer. His shirt was only half tucked into his jeans. His face wasn't shaven, and he needed a haircut.

"So you found her," he said.

It took me a second to understand. "Yes, I found her," I said. "It wasn't hard."

He said, "Yeah?"

"One thing led to another," I said. "And there she was.

It wasn't hard. You and my father could have found her any time."

He came to stand next to me. We gazed down at the dark water and the lights of buildings on the other side of the bay.

"Ari, I need to ask you something," he said. "I need your help."

I waited. It was hard to remember how much I'd liked him, not so long ago.

"I want you to make me . . ." He hesitated. "Like you," he said.

With effort, I kept my voice low and steady. "What makes you think I'd do something like that?"

He coughed. "Don't pretend. I know you've done it. Malcolm told us about what you've done. Not just the ones you killed, but the kid in Asheville."

So Malcolm had been around when I was with Joshua, too. "I didn't make him a vampire," I said. "He was a donor. A most willing donor."

"Let *me* be your donor." He moved closer to me, lifted his hand as if he were going to touch my hair, then changed his mind. "Even if you haven't done it before, I can tell you how."

Of all the oddities of my life so far, this one took the cake (an expression Mrs. McG had used on more than one occasion). I stared at his affable middle-aged face, at the muscles in his neck. For a second, I considered biting him. Then a wave of revulsion hit me, so strong that I had to hold on to the balcony railing with both hands.

"You okay?" His voice sounded oddly distant.

I pushed back my hair and looked up—at the man who had once carried me on his shoulders, who'd taught me physics and the facts of life. "You know all about it, don't you?" My voice sounded hoarse. "You watched my father and Malcolm. So why don't you have Malcolm do it?"

Dennis didn't say anything, but his thoughts were easy to read. He'd asked Malcolm, more than once, and Malcolm refused.

"How could you have helped him take my mother away?"

"He made a good case for her leaving. She wasn't happy, Ari." But his thoughts went further. Malcolm had made a deal with him.

"So he led you on." I felt stronger now. "He made you a promise, and then he reneged."

Malcolm had used Dennis to get to my mother—then he'd refused to keep his part of the bargain. But he'd kept telling Dennis that he might change his mind if Dennis proved himself worthy. Dennis had kept on hoping. Now he was growing older and impatient.

At the time I didn't feel an ounce of sympathy for him. (Since then, I've reconsidered. Who wouldn't beg for eternal life? He was tired of being left out, just as my mother had been.)

"Why don't you ask Root?"

He shuddered. "I couldn't stand to have her touch me."

His eyes were dull, yet pleading. "You've had a lot to drink," I said, trying to find an excuse for his behavior.

"Ari," he said. "Please?"

"You." I couldn't think of a name bad enough to call him. *Traitor* came close. "I thought you were my friend," I said, and I left him and the balcony behind me.

When I awoke the next morning, I could sense tension before I left the bedroom. Root passed me in the hallway, headed in the opposite direction. She nodded. I couldn't get used to her acknowledging me. My reputation as a murderous vampire must have made quite a positive impression.

The others were in the living room, watching a long television screen built into a wall. My parents sat far apart on the sofa. Dennis stood to their left. He didn't look in my direction.

On the television screen, a map showed a swirling red and orange mass moving in the Gulf of Mexico. "A tropical storm?" I asked.

Mãe looked at me. "No, a hurricane. It's projected to make landfall a little too close to home."

The storm's ceaseless rotation was almost hypnotic.

"A hurricane is a beautiful thing, until you've been in one," she said.

She'd been on the phone with Dashay. Dashay and Bennett were closing up the house and getting ready to move the horses to a friend's farm, south of Orlando, out of the storm's projected path. "I need to get back, to help," she said.

This wasn't an acceptable part of my family reunion fantasy. *Don't go*, I thought, and she thought back, *I have to go.*

"I'll come with you," I said, but she shook her head.

"You're safer here. Sarasota will get some rain, but nothing like the winds headed for Homosassa and Cedar Key. You don't know how bad this can be, Ariella. The storm is already a Category Four."

The television image showed dotted lines emanating from the storm, projecting onto land. The announcer called the highlighted area "Hurricane Barry's cone of uncertainty." Homosassa lay close to its center. Mandatory evacuations had been ordered.

"There will be tornadoes." My father's voice made the prophecy sound poetic. "The North Atlantic Oscillation is in a strongly positive phase. Sara's right, Ari. You're safer here."

I shot a look of contempt at Dennis, but his eyes were on the television screen. My mother caught the look and sent me a question: *What's that?*

But she had enough on her mind. "Will you come back?" I asked.

She hugged me. "Of course I'll come back. I'm going to rent a second horse trailer, load it up, tow it down to Kissimmee. Then I'll drive here. The storm won't hit land for three days or so. I'll be back day after tomorrow. Meantime, start thinking about what you want for your birthday. Do you realize it's only a week away?"

"How about a tattoo?" I said.

The shock on my parents' faces pleased me. I said, "That was a joke. What I'd really like is to see a fireworks show." I thought of the night of my first kiss.

Clearly relieved, Mãe kissed me. "I think we can manage fireworks." She exchanged a veiled look with my father, then left.

One moment, my family was in the room. Then it was gone.

Dennis went off with Root toward the lab down the hall.

My father and I sat across from each other, and I let him know what Dennis had asked the night before.

My father's face changed—his eyes narrowed, his jaw tensed, and his body went rigid, as it had been on the night Michael picked me up to go to the dance. "You should have come and told me at once."

"I didn't want to interrupt you and Mãe."

He shook his head. "To think how I've trusted him," he said slowly. "He'll have to leave."

His voice was so cold that it scared me. "What about your research?"

At dinner the night before, he'd talked about their work in progress: developing polymer microcapsules to carry hemoglobin, a project he called "truly promising."

"I can't work with someone I don't trust," he said. "First that business with your mother, now you. He can go back to Saratoga, to his job at the college. He should feel right at home in that environment. Academics are more venomous than vampires ever could be."

I wondered if I'd ever go to college.

"I'll have to change my will," my father said. "Dennis is the executor, you know."

"How can you have a will if you're already dead?"

"Raphael Montero died," he said. "Arthur Gordon Pym lives."

While my father met Dennis in the lab, I tried not to listen. But the condominium walls were thin. I heard Dennis's voice from time to time, belligerent at first, then apologetic. Then it fell silent. I couldn't hear my father at all. Sometimes the softest sounds are the most powerful ones.

To pass the time, I opened the closet doors in my bedroom. One closet was empty. The other was packed with framed pictures and tall vases of artificial plants. I shut its door quickly.

When my father rejoined me, he looked as usual: face composed, eyes faraway, suit pressed, shirt crisp. Only the speed with which he moved suggested anything unusual. Root trailed behind him, a look of amazement on her face.

"We'll need to make our own preparations for the storm," he said. "Mary Ellis, will you ensure that we have adequate supplies of food and drink? Not to mention the supplements."

"I made a fresh batch this morning," she said. "And I can make more. Green Cross delivered serum this morning. Again. Some kind of mistake."

I could have explained, but I kept quiet.

"I'll get things ready before I go," Root was saying. "I'm spending the night with a friend in Bradenton."

Root has a friend? I thought.

"Ari, do you have all of the things you need?"

331

What things? I wondered. I ate and drank what he did, except for meat. Then I realized he must mean tampons. They were the only special need I had.

"I could use more," I said.

"You'll find a pharmacy in the shopping plaza around the corner," he said. "Better to go today than to wait." He handed me money and a key. "By the time you return, Dennis will be gone."

Good riddance, I thought. But a small part of me wondered if, in time, I'd come to miss him.

At the pharmacy I dawdled, browsing the magazine and makeup aisles. I didn't want to run into Dennis when I returned.

The line at the prescription counter was long; people were stocking up on drugs and bottled water. The pharmacist had a radio on, and the announcer said that Hurricane Barry was now "Category Five." That meant "winds greater than 155 mph, or a storm surge more than eighteen feet above normal." I didn't have enough experience of storms to know what *normal* was, but the worry in the customers' faces was daunting.

As I paid for my purchases, it struck me as funny, but not surprising, that my father, who knew so much about blood, couldn't bring himself to use the word *tampons*.

I headed home, up the side street. Xanadu looked different now. White metal hurricane shutters masked most of its windows. Our unit was one of the few whose eyes were still open.

I waited at the intersection for the "Walk" signal. As I crossed Midnight Pass Road, a man with a cane left the opposite curb. He was more obese than fat, and he wore a dark suit, dark glasses, and hat. As he came closer, his cane tapped ahead of his path, delineating his cone of uncertainty. Then he smiled at me, and I knew he wasn't blind at all.

Apprehension of evil begins at the base of your skull and travels quickly up and down the spine. I swayed with repulsion, but somehow kept moving. When I reached the other side, I broke into a run.

I caught my breath again in the elevator at Xanadu. Then I let myself in and put the pharmacy bag in my room. Voices came from the living room; I listened hard to see if one belonged to Dennis. Instead, I heard Malcolm's voice.

I like to think that vampires behave more rationally and ethically than humans, but, like all generalizations, this one is arguable. Yes, I eavesdropped. As I said before, the walls of the condominium were thin.

"I could have killed her," he was saying. "I could have killed both of them."

Then my father's voice, low, yet harsher than I'd ever heard it. "You're telling me that you spared them for altruistic reasons? I doubt that."

"I've never claimed to be an altruist."

I could imagine his grin.

"I spared them so that you'd see them for what they are, and come to your senses."

"And what are they?"

"An embarrassment. A constant reminder of your own weakness."

My face burned. I had to struggle not to burst into the room and—

And what? What could I do to someone like him?

"All the lies you told." My father's voice was even lower now. I had to strain to hear it. "How many times you said you were trying to help my family. Instead you tried to ruin it."

Malcolm laughed—an ugly sound with no amusement in it. "Listen to you. What do you know about *family*? You're like me, and you know it. Women have never been more than encumbrances to you. They've kept you from the important things—from your work."

"To the contrary." My father's words were clipped. "Ariella and her mother have given me more insights than you could possibly know about."

"But taking care of her, teaching her. All those hours, wasted. You know, it's thought in Cambridge that you've never fulfilled your early promise. But I've found the delivery system you need. We can make a substitute *better* than human blood. Think what that will mean for us. Think of the lives that will be saved."

"What do you care for saving lives? You've killed people for no reason. You even killed the neighbor's cat."

He killed Marmalade. I felt guilty for ever suspecting that my father did it.

"The cat got in my way. As for the people, each one died for a good reason. Do you know how many women Reedy raped? And that fellow in Savannah—he'd murdered three teenagers and buried them in his basement."

"What about the girl?" My father's voice was almost inaudible now. "What about Kathleen?"

"She was an annoyance."

I didn't think—I simply walked into the living room. "You killed her," I said.

Malcolm stood before the window, hands in his pockets, his linen suit outlined by gray sky. "She asked for it." He didn't seem surprised to see me. He'd probably known I was listening all along. "She asked me to bite her."

"You didn't have to! And you didn't have to kill her."

He took his left hand from his pocket and examined his fingernails. "She begged me to make her a vampire. You and your father are to blame for that. She wanted to be like you." Then he turned to my father. "And she wanted to *marry* you. Imagine, her a vampire! The very idea of it nauseates me. She was a *stupid girl*."

Kathleen wanted to marry my father? I shook my head, ready to defend her.

My father put up his hand, warning me not to respond. "We're wasting time here," he said to me. Then, to Malcolm: "You rant like any psychopath. Get out."

Malcolm's eyes were bloodshot, I saw now. His voice stayed deliberate, calm. "You're willing to sacrifice millions of lives because of a girl and a cat? What sort of ethics are those?"

"They're my ethics," my father said, "based on the virtues I hold dear."

I went to stand next to him. "That we hold dear," I said.

Malcolm's looked away from us, his mouth half open. As he left the room he looked up once more, at my father, and I couldn't believe what I saw in Malcolm's eyes. It was love.

— Eighteen —

One night in Saratoga Springs, when I was about to ride my bike home from the McGarritts' house, I overheard their next-door neighbors arguing. The father of the family bellowed, his wife pleaded, and their teenaged son shouted back.

"You never wanted me!" he said. "I wish I'd never been born."

I've felt that way, sometimes. Have you? All things considered, my birth set in motion events that might better have never happened. For every choice I've made, there are infinite other choices that might have been better ones. Sometimes I've envisioned those other choices as shadows of my actions, shadows that define me as much as what I did.

Bertrand Russell wrote, "All unhappiness depends upon some kind of disintegration or lack of integration." Failure of unity, he said, keeps a person from happiness. But once that person feels part of "the stream of life," feels herself integrated with a culture and its values, she becomes "a citizen of the world."

The day that my father had his confrontation with Malcolm was the first day I felt I might have a claim to such citizenship. My father and I were united, and we had Malcolm to thank.

My father and I dined on gazpacho and smoked salmon and salad in the living room, watching Hurricane Barry's approach on TV. The giant orange and red spiral tunneled up a cone of uncertainty again and again as the weather station replayed its hurricane maps. The storm was forecast to reach Sarasota's latitude later that night and make landfall north of Homosassa early the next day.

We didn't talk about Malcolm, although I tried. As we finished dinner, I said, "How could he do such things?"

My father said, "Malcolm never acquired the habit of virtue." His eyes let me know that the conversation was closed.

Mãe telephoned while my father was clearing our plates. She and the horses were safe in Kissimmee, along with Dashay, Bennett, Harris, Joey, and Grace the cat. My mother was watching the weather on television, too.

My father called from the kitchen, "Advise her not to travel until tomorrow."

I relayed the message.

"We'll see," she said. "Ask him how he feels about living with monkeys."

After I'd hung up, I watched the weather forecast again.

A Category Five was the highest on the Saffir-Simpson Hurricane Scale, and the litany of damage associated with it went far beyond wind and storm surges. The forecaster began to recite the list with inappropriate gusto. It began with "Complete roof failure on many residences and industrial buildings. Some complete building failures with small utility buildings blown over or away. All shrubs, trees, and signs blown down."

My father came back and switched off the television. "Enough melodrama for one day," he said.

I'd been about to tell him about the "blind" man at the intersection. I'd planned to say, *I may have met the devil today.* But he was right: we didn't need more melodrama that night.

For a few minutes we went onto the balcony, but it was too humid and windy to stay long. The bay water below raced toward the shoreline in whitecaps, and rain began to fall in tiny, stinging lines.

When we were inside again, my father locked the door. Then he pushed a wall button, and a metal hurricane shutter descended, inch by inch cutting off our view of the world. He'd already shuttered the other windows.

"I'll go to bed in a minute," I said. "But I want to know why Raphael Montero needed to die."

He frowned. "It's simple, really. I had no good reason to keep on as we had been. You and your mother had left. What did I want with a house in Saratoga Springs? And that fellow Burton kept coming around, asking questions. His pestering bored me."

"So how did you do it?"

He sat back on the sofa. "The entire business was easily managed. Dr. Wilson—you remember him, the fellow who treated your sunburn—is one of us, and he signed the death certificate. And old man Sullivan (another one of us) cremated an empty coffin and interred the ashes. Dennis"—he spoke the name with an expression of distaste—"arranged for the sale of the house, and the relocation of the laboratory here. All of your things, by the way, are in storage."

I took a deep breath. "It was a cruel trick to play. We saw photographs of your grave."

He seemed surprised. "Well, I *thought* that you would see them. I thought that the epitaph might amuse you, that it certainly would tell you that my death was a ruse."

"It did, I guess. In the end." I yawned. "Along with the Picardo and the roses."

He looked baffled.

I told him about the half-full bottle and the flowers left on his grave. "You didn't leave them, as a sign?"

"No," he said. "I wonder who did."

I had one more question. "May I tell Michael about Malcolm?"

"I don't think it's a good idea, Ari. Not now, at any rate. The McGarritts deserve to know who killed her, of course, but think of the repercussions for us. We'd have that man Burton after us again. Arthur Pym would have to disappear or die, and I've already died once this year."

I persisted. "When can we let them know?"

"When we've resettled," he said. "I doubt we'll stay here."

He frowned. "Xanadu. The place isn't to my liking, at all. Once we've found a new home, then you can tell Michael the truth. Let Agent Burton sit on Malcolm's back for a while."

Keeping secrets isn't hard for me. But I wanted to call Michael that night, tell him what I'd learned.

Instead I went to bed, but I didn't feel sleepy. Outside, the wind moved like an overpowered locomotive, making the building creak and sigh as it passed. My mind raced in spirals. I wondered when my mother would arrive. Would I end up living with her or with my father? Was it possible that I'd ever live with both of them? What might that life be like?

When it came, sleep was uneasy. I dreamed of shadows tall as Xanadu, of eclipsed suns, of incense, ice, and music. Then of real things, mementos of Saratoga Springs: the lithophane lamp in my old bedroom, the grandfather clock in the library, the shadowbox on the wall. But in my dream, the birds in the shadowbox were real. I heard their wings beat against the glass.

I awoke in a room full of smoke. The room had no windows, and when I opened the door, smoke swirled even thicker in the corridor. It had a strangely sweet smell. A wave of heat stung my face. The air-conditioning wasn't working, and the lights were out.

I called for my father. I could hear the pulse of flames, coming from the direction of the kitchen. I called him again, and then I began to cough.

In the bathroom I soaked a towel and wrapped it around

my head. I gulped down some water. The faucet sent out a stream at first, but tapered quickly, then stopped.

The bathroom had no windows, either. The whole central part of the condominium was windowless—a common design in waterfront condominiums, I've come to know since. A "direct water-view" is the selling point; aside from that, the units resemble kennels.

I took a deep breath and ran to my father's room. Its door was open, and the room, as far as I could see it through the smoke, was unoccupied.

Holding my breath, I ran to the living room, unlocked the balcony door. I yanked its handle, but it didn't budge. I pressed the button to open the hurricane shutters. Nothing happened.

Think, think slowly, I told myself. But my mind and my pulse were racing. My lungs burned, and I began to pant. On my hands and knees, I left the room and entered the study, and I tried to open the shutters there. Nothing.

We've lost electricity, I reasoned. *It's common in a storm, to lose electricity. To lose electricity is nothing unusual.*

I crawled to the end of the room farthest from the door, holding my breath, my mind singing its little song. *Nothing unusual. Nothing unusual. Nothing.*

"We're only born once."

Mãe says those were my first words in the hospital. And she says she replied, "Didn't he teach you about reincarnation?"

But I doubt that's what she really said. It wasn't a joking

matter, really. I'd spent most of a week receiving hyperbaric oxygen therapy (HBOT). The treatments were intermittent, and I was unconscious during the first two. I regained consciousness during the third treatment, waking up in what seemed to be a transparent cylindrical coffin.

My body was surrounded by 100 percent oxygen gas, dissolving in my blood and body tissues at concentrations much higher than normal—high enough to sustain life with no blood at all. I was told all of this during the third treatment by a nurse, who spoke slowly and clearly into a microphone connected to the HBOT chamber.

When I recovered the ability to think and speak, I thought, I'd ask a hundred questions about the treatment. I wondered if my father knew about it. Was it possible that we might not need blood if we had our own glass coffins at home? Then I wondered, where was home?

"Her eyes are open," I heard the nurse say. "She's trying to say something."

And then my mother's face appeared on the other side of the chamber.

Her blue eyes looked joyous and exhausted. "Don't try to speak now, darling," she said. "Just breathe."

What happened? I sent the thought to her. *Where's my father?*

There was a fire, she began.

I know that much! If she saw the words, they must be purple.

No need for sarcasm, she shot back. *I guess you must be feeling better.*

I opened my mouth, but she said, "Hush. Your father is alive."

In what we call "The Movie," Dr. Van Helsing makes a pronouncement found nowhere in Bram Stoker's novel: "The strength of the vampire is that people will not believe in him."

For many vampires, that statement is more than a favorite aphorism—it's a central tenet of the philosophy of the undead. Despite all evidence to the contrary, humans are more comfortable with the most convoluted theories that contradict our existence than with the simple fact that we share the planet with them. We're here, and we're not going away.

My father, recovering from third-degree burns, was given a tracheotomy and skin grafts he didn't need. The doctors couldn't accept what their eyes told them: despite being found unconscious and badly burned in a raging chemical fire, he'd suffered minimal damage to his lungs and skin, and he was healing rapidly. Yet they kept him under observation in the intensive care unit, and they didn't allow visitors.

I celebrated my birthday in the hospital. A candlelit Twinkie was delivered on a tray.

My gift was seeing my father for the first time since the fire. My mother wheeled me into his room, littered with monitoring devices connected to his body. The outline of his body beneath the sheets was slight for such a tall man. He was sleeping. I'd never before seen him asleep. His eyelashes, long and dark, lay against his cheek—like butterfly wings, I thought.

He opened his eyes. "*Butterfly* wings?" he said, his voice incredulous.

Mãe and I laughed, and he smiled—his real smile, not the scholarly one. "Happy birthday," he said to me. His voice sounded soft. "Your fireworks arrived a few days early."

I tried not to ask questions, but my brain generated them anyway.

"I don't know," he said, when I asked, *Who started the fire?*

"I don't know," he repeated, when I asked, *Who rescued us?*

"Well, I can answer that one," Mãe said. "I did. Along with the help of Siesta Key's finest fire squad."

Mãe had been driving down I-4 in what she called "hideous rain," when she picked up my first "distress signal."

"You couldn't breathe," she said. "It came through to me as clearly as if you hadn't been born yet." She turned to my father. "Remember that time when her heartbeat increased, and you thought she was in fetal distress? And I told you no, I'd *know* it if that happened."

"Isn't the idea of *knowing* such a thing a bit of a cliché?" My voice was as innocent as I could manage.

She rubbed her eyes. "You must be feeling better."

My father put his hand in the air—then looked at the intravenous needle taped to it. He thought about ripping it out, and my mother and I both said, "No!"

"All right," he said. "The needle stays. But only so long as Sara tells the story in a linear fashion, without a thousand digressions. Is that possible?"

She tried.

She'd arrived in Sarasota to find the traffic lights out, and only a few streetlights working. Her truck was the only vehicle on the road, and she blazed through intersections, feeling like an anarchist.

She apologized for the digressive simile. But she'd always wondered what it would feel like to be an anarchist.

When she arrived at Xanadu (my father shook his head at the name), flames coming from unit 1235 were visible from the street. The elevators weren't working, and in any case she knew the door to the condominium would be locked. She didn't have a key, or a mobile phone, but she remembered seeing a fire station at the intersection of Midnight Pass and Beach Road. So she drove there.

"They were sitting in the station watching the Weather Channel," she said. "They'd put out a fire about an hour previously—" She looked at my father. "All right, I won't tell you about that."

When the fire trucks arrived at Xanadu, she said, a ladder truck drove to the back of the building, and another crew went up the stairs, carrying extinguishers, a hose, and other equipment. They told her to stay behind, but she trailed after them.

"Ever the obedient one," my father said.

Then a nurse walked into the room, wearing a brightly patterned smock. My father shuddered at its design and closed his eyes.

"Time for visitors to leave." The nurse smiled at us, most insincerely.

My mother sighed, and abruptly hypnotized her.

"Only for a few minutes," she said. "Let me finish telling this. So, they were trying to get in through the metal shutters at the back, and the others used axes to break down the front door. I am very impressed with the Siesta Key firefighters, in particular the ones from Station 13. They pried off the shutters somehow and found Ari in the study, and carried her down in the basket thing. Or is it a bucket? What do you call it? Never mind.

"And you were the first one *we* found." She looked at my father as if she might cry. "You were in bad shape. Much worse than you-know-who, and much worse than Ari. You were black with soot, and oh, the burns on your back—"

"Who's you-know-who?" His shoulders moved off the pillows, as if he were trying to sit up.

I'd never known my father to interrupt anyone. He'd always said that, no matter how dire the situation, rudeness is inexcusable.

"Lie back." My mother stretched her hands as if to push him, and his shoulders fell back. "Malcolm," she said. "You-know-who is Malcolm. You're too weak to read my thoughts."

"He was there?" I asked.

"They found him in the entryway, not far from your father." Her eyes were on his face, not mine. "Didn't you know? Didn't anyone tell you?"

"How did he get in?" my father asked no one in particular.

"He must have made himself invisible," I said. "He might

347

have come in when I put out the trash. Then, when the fire got to him, he would have lost the concentration and become visible again. But Father might not have seen him in the smoke."

"I'd thought Raphael must have let him in." Mãe pushed her hair back, straightened her shirt.

"I saw no one." He lifted his hand again, looked at the IV with disgust. "I awoke with smoke in my room. I found the fire near the kitchen and tried to put it out, but it moved too quickly. The smoke was overwhelming."

"Ethyl ether," Mãe said. "That's how it started. The firemen found a canister in the kitchen. Whoever planned it did a thorough job. He even took the batteries out of the backup switch for the hurricane shutters."

"Malcolm started it," I said. "It makes sense."

My father said, "It could have been Dennis, I suppose. But I tend to agree with you—Malcolm's more likely. Why didn't he leave, after he set the fire?"

Mãe said, "I suspect he wanted to watch." Her voice was bitter.

"Where is he now?" I hoped that he was dead.

"Who knows?" Mãe's face looked far away. "They put him in an emergency van to take him to the hospital, but somehow or another they lost him. When they opened the doors, the van was empty."

"He escaped." My father sank into his pillows and closed his eyes.

"You need to rest." My mother woke up the nurse, and we said good-night.

Back in my room, I told her about the argument the day of the fire—and about the expression on Malcolm's face as he left.

She didn't show surprise. "Yes, he loves Raphael," she said. "I've known that for years."

And her face, and her voice when she said his name, told me that she loved my father, too.

— Nineteen —

On a sweltering afternoon about a month later, Harris and I were lounging at either end of a hammock on the front porch of a house owned by Mãe's friends in Kissimmee. The friends were in Orlando for the day, so we had the place to ourselves. An overhead fan kept the air circulating enough to keep us tolerably cool, and we drank lemonade in tall glasses through long, bendable straws.

I was writing in my journal. Harris was thumbing though an art book: *The World's Greatest Paintings*.

Hurricane Barry had not been kind to Homosassa Springs. Blue Beyond was no more. A storm surge from the river had destroyed most of the house, Mãe said, and the trees and gardens had been shredded by tornadoes. Luckily all of the animals had been evacuated safely—even the bees, whose hives had been moved off the property to higher ground and secured, before the storm. The statue of Epona also survived intact, and currently guarded the front door of the house where we were staying.

Mãe and Dashay sat up late, talking about whether the structure could be rebuilt. They'd been back to Homosassa twice, and each time they returned to Kissimmee with rescued items and more stories. Flo's Place and the Riverside Resort were ruins, missing roofs and walls, their windows smashed despite plywood nailed up to protect them. Monkey Island was nothing but a rock, its trees and rope bridges gone. Its lighthouse had been found floating in the river several miles away.

Today they'd left an hour before, to make another assessment of the damage and do some cleaning up. They'd invited me to come along. I declined. I didn't want to see the destruction.

My father was in Ireland. He'd sent me a postcard of an island in a lake; the message read "Peace comes dropping slow," a line from a Yeats poem, "The Lake Isle of Innisfree." After his too-lengthy convalescence in the hospital, he decided he'd had enough of Florida. Root went on a summer vacation, and my father flew to Shannon to explore, possibly to find a new home base. He'd invited me to come along. That offer, too, I declined. I needed time to sort things out.

For the first time in my life I wondered about my future life. Would I go to college? Get a job? It had been months since I'd spent time with teenagers. In becoming *other*, I'd lost my contemporaries, my friends.

Human friends, at any rate. At some point Harris nudged me and pointed at a painting in his book—John William Waterhouse's *The Lady of Shalott*. It could have been a portrait of my mother, I thought, and Harris thought so, too. Pleased that we agreed, he settled back into his end of the hammock again, and I returned to my brooding.

I wondered if I'd have a boyfriend. Michael and I had talked on the phone a few more times, but we found less and less to say. I couldn't tell him I knew who killed Kathleen, and that knowledge constrained my end of our conversations.

And I wondered if Malcolm was out there, somewhere. Would I spend my life being stalked by him?

Or would I spend it trying to reconcile my parents? I didn't know how things stood between them. My father had left for Ireland without confiding in me. When I asked my mother, her face was enigmatic. "The summer's not over yet," she said.

The front gate's buzzer rang, and I was glad to stop my thinking.

"Stay here," I told Harris. He'd been allowed to remain with us for the summer, as a gift to me. And in truth, he seemed to like Florida more now. Joey had been sent to the rehab center a few weeks ago, and early reports from Panama claimed his personality had blossomed.

I went down the driveway to the gate, not resentful at all about being disturbed, waving at the horses grazing in the paddock as I passed. Grace emerged from beneath a sweet olive shrub and followed me after a fashion, pausing frequently to sniff the ground or wash herself.

But my heart sank when I saw the man at the gate. Agent Burton stood in the road, talking into his mobile phone. His suit was too dark for a Florida summer, and his forehead glistened with perspiration. A white Ford Escort idled behind him.

In the space of ten yards, I formed a strategy.

He put the phone in his pocket. "Miss Montero!" His voice boomed. "Long time, no see."

I kept walking toward him. I opened the gate.

"Do you want to come up to the house?" I said. I made my voice young and perky. "My mother's not here, but she'll be back later. We're staying here with friends. We lost our house in the hurricane."

I should mention that I was wearing a two-piece bathing suit, because he noticed it. *Kid is growing up*, he thought.

He smiled. "I was visiting the area, you know, and I heard you were here—"

"Where'd you hear that?" But his thoughts told me: he'd traced one of my calls to Michael.

"Somebody told me. And, uh, we thought you might have some further insights into the death of your friend Kathleen. You left the Saratoga area very suddenly."

"I needed to visit my mom." I held the gate half open.

He was thinking it might be strategic if he came to the house, but it also might be risky. Better to do it with an adult present.

"Sure you don't want to come up? The house is cooler."

He wanted to. He didn't move. "No, this is okay. By the way, I was sorry to hear about your father's passing."

He wasn't sorry at all. "Thank you," I said. "But, you know, he isn't dead."

His thoughts began to swirl then, because all along he'd found my father's death hard to believe. *A man in his prime, dying so suddenly. But no indication of foul play.* "He isn't dead," he repeated. "You mean he's still alive?"

"*He lives, he wakes—'tis Death is dead, not he,*" I quoted. *Is she nuts?* he thought.

No, I wanted to tell him. *I'm fourteen.*

I recited a few more lines, making my eyes wide, using the full range of my voice:

> *Peace, peace! he is not dead, he doth not sleep—*
> *He hath awakened from the dream of life—*
> *'Tis we, who lost in stormy visions, keep*
> *With phantoms an unprofitable strife.*

Clearly Agent Burton didn't know Shelley's poem *Adonais*.

Poor kid, he thought. *She's gone over the edge. And no wonder, with all she's been through.*

I could have gone further. I could have recited the entire poem. Or, I could have told him, *By the way, my father is a vampire. So is my mother. So am I.* I could have told him who killed Kathleen.

I could have told him about the fire. The investigators weren't sure if Malcolm had set it, or if it was Dennis's form of revenge. Maybe Agent Burton could solve that one. Or maybe he could find out who left the roses on my father's grave.

I could have told him how things look, at fourteen, under an aspect of eternity.

Instead, I repeated, *"Peace, peace! he is not dead."*

I gave him a sad smile. In practicing the art of confusion, there is no better weapon than poetry.

"Yeah," he said. "Peace." He made the V-sign with his right hand, turned, walked back toward his white rental car. I heard him think, *This case will never close.*

And I turned, walked up the path back to the house, Grace following me. I'd go back to the hammock for a while, dream away the afternoon. For now, it was enough.

— Epilogue —

Long ago, when my father told me, "It's a pity that more vampires don't write the facts," I'd thought, *Well, I'm doing my part.*

But I decided to stop writing. I'd put down all the facts I had, and it was time for me to figure out what to do with them—to take two steps back and consider the puzzle as a whole picture, with light and dark and shadows. Later, I copied all the useful parts into this new notebook.

I'd like to think that someone will read my notes and find them useful—that *you* will read them. I dedicate this book to you—the child that I hope to have one day. Maybe you'll have an easier time growing up than I did. Maybe this book will help.

Maybe, someday, humans will read it, too. Once they take the first leap—believing that we exist—perhaps they'll begin to understand and tolerate us, even value us. I'm not naïve enough to imagine us living with them in complete harmony. And I know now that my life will never be *normal*.

But imagine what could happen if we all felt that we were citizens of the world, committed to a common good? Imagine forgetting ourselves, and forgetting that we're mortals and *others*, and instead focusing on bridging the schisms that keep us apart. I think I could do that, serving as a kind of translator between the two cultures.

In the last chapter of *Walden*, Thoreau wrote, *Every nail driven should be as another rivet in the machine of the universe, you carrying on the work.*

That's my plan, one way or another: to carry on the work.

Grace still is with me, but Harris is gone, off to the sanctuary in Panama to learn how to be wild again. Will there someday be a sanctuary for us?

— Acknowledgments —

I would like to send heartfelt thanks to the friends and acquaintances who gave me inspiration, information, and all manner of support as this book came into being. They include Ted Dennard of the Savannah Bee Co., Holley Bishop, Staci Bogdan, José Fernandez, Thomas Krise, Anna Lillios, Adam Perry, Kristie Smeltzer, and Sharon Wissert. Additional thanks to Clare Hubbard, Kate Hubbard, Mary Johnson, Tison Pugh, Pat Rushin, and, in particular, Robley Wilson, all of whom took time to read and comment on the manuscript. Special thanks to Steve Garfinkel, Marcy Posner, and Denise Roy for their extraordinary talents and true friendship.